"Everything you want is on the other side of fear."
~Jack Canfield

This book is a work of fiction. While references may be made to actual places or events, the names, character, incidents, and locations within are from the author's imagination and are not a resemblance to actual living or dead persons, businesses, or events. Any similarity is coincidental.

Printed in the United States of America

First Printing, 2019

Aggressive Publishing, Inc.

Distributed by Bublish, Inc.

ISBN: 978-0-9965195-3-3

PRIVATE AGENDAS

Katherine Smith Dedrick

CHAPTER

1

WILLOW KNEW HOW to make herself feel better. She needed only a needle and the liquid gold inside. It was her salvation, her savior. "It does a body good." She cracked up and rolled on the soiled sheets at that one. "Get it?" she said to no one. "You know, like milk does a body good?" She shrugged her shoulders at the lack of response, laughing so hard she almost fell off the bed.

Sometimes, she fleetingly remembered a different time, long ago, when someone had told her to stay away from drugs, that they could ruin her life. The image always presented vaguely as a boy and left her feeling oddly sad. *Who was that? Someone I had feelings for?* She hated when these thoughts and emotions danced around the fringes of her mind. They always left her with a raging headache.

She hurried to tie the tube around her arm. In a few minutes, she would have the cure. The memories and whatever or whoever that was in the fringes, would be silenced and she would find peace again. Jabbing the needle into her vein, she smiled as she felt the warmth spread. There was nothing to worry about now. As she began to doze off, she heard a loud rap on her door. Opening her eyes just a smidge, she saw Madame poke her head in.

Thank God, Madame thought. *At least this one still groomed herself. The ones from America are always the cleanest, but they're the hardest to break.* "Willow, you have a visitor. He's ordered the special. Make sure he's happy when he leaves."

Willow looked up briefly to see a male figure enter her room. She no longer cared what they looked like. She tried not to register reality or think during these times. Instead, she focused on the warmth of the liquid gold, knowing the visit would soon be over and she could once again slip into her private world.

CHAPTER

2

"**P**OOR BASTARDS. THEY'RE using them—the same way they used me. It's quite impressive, really." Victoria paced around the conference room, speaking with grudging admiration. "They're willing to sacrifice two of their best and brightest to convince the judge there's no systemic problem at the firm."

"Victoria, will you please sit down. You're making me nervous." Robert's eyes followed her as he sat at the expensive, hand-carved mahogany table, rapidly tapping his pen on his legal pad. "You should feel incredibly satisfied." He hated when his clients acted nuts. Calm and orderly, that's the way he'd practiced law for the past twenty years and it had worked out incredibly well.

"I like to move while I think. And, for the record, one thing I hate more than a man telling me to smile, is a man telling me how I should feel," Victoria snapped. "But since you opened that door, don't you men ever stop to think before you say that kind of crap? You have no idea how we feel, and maybe we don't want to smile."

"Don't pull that male-female BS with me, Victoria. You know that's not what I meant." Robert held up his hand to prevent her from interrupting. "Let me remind you that since last year, you and Kat have accomplished a great deal. You've opened your own firm; Kat's been placed in charge of her family's development projects; and together, you've successfully forced the insurance company to pay more than half its hurricane claims." Robert counted each accomplishment on his fingers for emphasis. "As if that wasn't enough, you've shone such a bright light on the company that the feds are investigating its former board. So, at the risk of having you jump down my throat again, you should be at least somewhat satisfied that you've moved the needle in a positive direction."

"Of course I am. But none of those things have moved my lawsuit any closer to resolution. It's been a whole year and we have no substantive evidence, no admissions, and no clear path forward."

"It's coming, Victoria. These cases take time. Just like dead fish eventually float to the surface, evidence of bad conduct always makes its way to the sunlight."

"Yes, well while that's a fabulous analogy and likely does the trick with your other clients, I'm not like your other clients."

Robert snorted as he got up to make a fresh pot of coffee at the fancy barista bar he'd installed last year to impress his high-end clients. "That's the understatement of the year."

"You know, I never realized what a wonderful sense of humor you have," Victoria said sarcastically, "but back to my point. I don't like where my case is headed. What happens if the judge believes Billy, Trever, and Adam when they argue that the only documents in their files having anything to do with discrimination and harassment concern the two sacrificial lambs they're offering up at her judicial alter?"

Robert shook his head. "I know this judge. She's smart. She's been around the block. She won't simply take their word.

She'll order them to produce relevant personnel files for review, and she'll allow us to depose witnesses. Trust me."

"Really?" Victoria asked as she changed her pacing stride and direction. "Billy, Trever, and Adam are incredibly powerful. The Troika carries a lot of weight in this city. On any given day, one of them is having his picture taken with the mayor or some other Chicago heavyweight. The judge is certainly aware of their clout. If we're not careful"—Victoria caught a glimpse of her frenzied expression in Robert's obscenely ornate wall mirror—"they might just convince her to limit our access to evidence. If that happens, our case will be in the shitter."

Victoria lingered at the mirror. When she'd first met Robert, he'd taken her and her mother, Sophia, on a tour of his office, and made a point to stop at this same mirror. He'd explained his belief that the eyes are windows to the soul and noted that he studied himself in this mirror before every court appearance to ensure he had the right look for each matter. At the time, Victoria had thought Robert was nuts with his gobbledygook about eyes, souls, and mirrors, but Sophia had been enthralled. In the end, Sophia's opinion and his sterling reputation had far outweighed his mirror fetish—as Victoria now called it when she wanted to yank his chain—and she'd hired him that day. Over the past year, he'd become not only a trusted advisor, but also one of her closest friends.

Looking at her reflection, Victoria thought that if her eyes were indeed the windows to her soul, then hers was probably manic. She took a deep breath to shift her energy. She'd read something about calming yourself by breathing in through the nose and out through the mouth, or was it the other way around? Whichever, it never worked for her. She sighed, scooted up onto the corner of the conference table, and leaned down toward Robert. "Here's the deal. I'm no longer interested in playing by the rules. You know how highly I think of you. You're one of the best employment lawyers in the country, but the Troika is pulling every string dangling from this judge's robe to try to unravel my case. We need to shake things up before one of those strings catches and she's reminded of—oh, I don't know—a large campaign contribution she got from their firm. We need to do something they're not expecting. They're no longer worried. It's been a year, we have little proof, and so far, Adam, Billy, and Trever have remained untarnished."

"What are you suggesting, Victoria? I'm not putting my law license on the line for a case—not even yours."

"Of course not, and I would never ask that of you. I am, however, suggesting we color right to the outside edge of that line."

"My question stands, Victoria. You're stalling." Robert was clearly annoyed with her critique of his litigation strategy. "You're not going to like it—at least, not at first—but hear me out. I've thought this through, and I think it will work. Don't be insulted…but…you're fired as…"

Robert shot up and glared at Victoria, his pale, Irish complexion now beet red. "You're joking," he growled menacingly. "Fired? Surely, you wouldn't fire the one guy in the city who helped you when you were booted from the only job you'd ever had. I stopped the Troika from publicly trashing you in the press and helped you start your law firm. Have you forgotten all this? Have you forgotten how you and your mother came to my office stressed out of your minds? I cleared my calendar to meet with you, dry your tears, and prevent you from jumping into the river. That's not someone anyone in their right mind would fire."

Victoria scooted off the table and walked calmly over to the coffee bar to refill her and Robert's cups. "You didn't let me finish. You're not fired—as in off the case," Victoria responded trying her best to ignore his drama while turning to replace the pot. "But—you're no longer my only counsel. I'm bringing Kat and also Jenny Acker onto the team. I want one of them at every deposition you take of these assholes."

Victoria heard a grunt and a thud and turned to see coffee splattered across Robert's white shirt and dripping from his right hand. The cup was lying on its side, trickling black liquid onto the formerly pristine carpet. She grabbed a cloth and pitcher of ice water from the coffee bar and wrapped a cool, wet cloth around his now red and swollen hand. "I knew you wouldn't be happy about this, but I didn't think you'd try to scald yourself to death. If you would calm down and just give me a minute, I'll explain. You're not off the case, Robert. You're just not lead counsel, at least not to the outside world."

"Victoria, I don't co-counsel with other lawyers, and I certainly won't work with two lawyers who have little, if any, litigation experience. Have you forgotten that neither of them sat for the Illinois Bar? They're not licensed to practice here. Besides, no judge in his or her right mind would allow a defendant's mother to be on the opposite side of her son's case."

"Oh, please, Robert. Their being admitted to practice law in Illinois is a minor detail. File a *pro hac vice* motion. You've filed dozens of them to handle matters for clients in other states. As for Jenny being related to Billy, so what? She never worked at Acker, Smith & McGowen, never represented his firm, and has no confidential information. There should be no problem. You must admit"—Victoria paused and flashed Robert a wicked smiled—"it would be unexpected and, at the very least, it should give Billy pause. The local press would have a field day, and the longer the case is in the press, the more difficult it will be for the boys to ignore us."

"What about their lack of litigation experience?" Robert snapped. "What are they going to do during the depositions? Shop online?"

Victoria became still. "Be very careful, my friend. You're about to cross a line. I'll assume that comment slipped out because you're upset and in some sort of shock after your unnecessary self-scalding. Did you forget Jenny is a former prosecutor? She had an impressive career until her ex-husband forced her to give it up. She went to trial in over one hundred criminal cases, and her conviction rate was one of the highest in Georgia."

"Victoria, seriously? Her ex-husband is the former chairman of the board of Highline Insurance, one of the guys you and Kat sicced the feds on! Jenny's presence will just muck this up. She also thought she had information that might help our case. Are you forgetting that little detail?"

Wanting to give each of them a chance to cool down, Victoria walked over to the window and looked down at the Chicago River. It was packed with sailboats waiting for one of the bridges to open so they could reach winter storage before the river froze. She watched in appreciation as the blinking and clanging railroad-like guardrails on either side of the bridge slowly lowered, the congested afternoon traffic came to a halt, and the bridge split in the center slowly lifting its massive arms into the air. Feeling a semblance of control return, she turned back toward Robert.

"If she had information and might be a witness, then I wouldn't be suggesting we bring her on as co-counsel. All she had was a vague recollection about Adam and some prostitution arrest he had more than ten years ago when they were all in law school together, and a comment she overheard him make about the firm hiring only female lawyers with certain personality traits. The prostitution bust isn't relevant, and even if it was, no judge would allow it in court this many years after the fact. The comment, without more, will get us nowhere. And the feds going after Jenny's ex-husband, Big Bill, doesn't matter one whit either."

"I couldn't disagree more," Robert replied, still nursing his scalded hand. "Jenny's the one who found his notes about stalling insurance payouts. She'll be called as a foundation witness in Kat's case."

"So what? That presents zero impediments to her working as my counsel." Robert opened his mouth to speak, but this time Victoria mimicked his earlier movement and put her hand in the air. "And since her divorce, she's focused her career on women's issues, with an emphasis on sexual harassment and gender discrimination. She also volunteers at a shelter helping abused women. She's ready for this."

"But—"

"Let me finish. This suit is bigger than just salvaging my reputation. It's about stopping the false narrative Acker, Smith & McGowen has been championing for years. The fact is they don't promote women. They have zero women partners, yet Billy gets award after award for his work with women in the law. It's absolute bullshit! I know. I was there. What the firm does do, however, is work the women to their respective bones for six or seven years, assigning them to mundane cases while giving the meatier ones to the men. Then, when it's time for partnership, the women are passed over and labeled unqualified because they haven't yet handled complex assignments, or they leave 'voluntarily,'" Victoria said, using air quotes, "or they're shoved out the door on some pretext." Pausing to read the text on her phone, Victoria gave a self-satisfied smile and continued. "So, why haven't any of these women filed complaints? Why would they just fade off into the sunset after years of hard work? Why wouldn't at least one of them have fought back?"

"You know why, Victoria. Hell, you almost took that same path! When we first met, your main concern was if you filed suit, you'd never be hired by another firm and your legal career would be over. So I understand how you feel about where we sit now with evidence, or the lack thereof...I really do, but let's be realistic. The Troika has built an internationally renowned, powerful law firm. They're going to fight hard and dirty to protect it, doing everything they can to shut down this idea of yours to bring Jenny and Kat on board."

Victoria walked confidently toward the conference room door. "That, my friend, is *exactly* the point." She opened the door, and as if on cue, in walked Jenny and Kat.

new me!" Jenny's excitement was infectious. She reminded Victoria of a puppy making everyone it met feel instantly better.

"Well, it certainly works for you." Victoria laughed, nodding toward the far side of the table. "Jenny, this is Robert, my lawyer and close friend. Robert, meet Jenny."

Robert walked around and extended his good hand. "Jenny, it's a pleasure to meet you. I followed your divorce closely, as did half of America. Congratulations on crossing the finish line."

"Robert, I'm so pleased to meet you. I've heard so many great things about you. I look forward to being part of your team."

"Yes, well, I've just been advised of Victoria's plan. I need to be straightforward with both of you," he said, nodding at Kat and Jenny. "I'm not on board. In fact, I'm actually quite opposed, for a number of reasons. First of all—"

Sensing Robert was about to launch into a tirade, Kat walked directly up to Robert and gave him one of her signature hugs. "Robert, you know I can't stand being ignored. It's good to see you again. I'm sure we'll get into all the details of V's plan soon enough. The good, the bad, and the ugly. For now, though, let's all get to know one another a bit more. I've taken the liberty of reserving a private room at that fabulous restaurant down the street. We'll be able to air all our opinions over dinner and a good bottle of wine or two. I'm in the mood for a big piece of meat. Shall we?" Kat asked as she crooked her arm through Robert's. "Tell me, what on earth did you do to your hand?"

Victoria felt a satisfying rush. If there was one thing she could count on, it was Kat's impact on men. Any time. An-

CHAPTER

3

"WHERE IS HE?" Victoria asked, leaning out the door and looking up and down the hallway.

"At the last minute, his father dragged him into a deal that needs to be wrapped up within the next forty-eight hours. He asked me to extend his apologies and said he'd catch up with us soon. And hello to you too!" Kat said, as she gave Victoria a hug and kiss on the cheek. Turning to the elegant woman behind her, Kat asked, "Victoria, you remember Jenny?"

Victoria was disappointed that Armond had not made the trip. She would have liked his input at their strategy sessions over the next few days, and if she was being totally honest, she wanted him there to back her ideas. Tilting her head and fixing a smile on her face, she shook Jenny's hand and said, "Of course. It's been a while, Jenny. You look fabulous. Something's different, but I can't put my finger on it."

"Victoria! It's so nice to see you again. It seems like forever since our last meeting. And yes, something is different. I colored and cut my hair, lost weight, and got a divorce! The Botox doesn't hurt either. All that adds up to a ywhere. Any man. She looked over at the appreciative look on Jenny's face. "You ain't seen nothing yet," Victoria said, ushering her out the door.

CHAPTER

4

THE WIND HOWLED and shook the windows while the train tracks sang in the distance, rocking under the weight of thousands of commuters being transported into the city from different Chicago suburbs. The gray, early-morning sky foretold another cold winter day. Gretchen looked out her kitchen window, sighed, and hung her head.

By thirty-six, she'd planned to be smack in the middle of a wildly successful law career, traveling the world defending executives against white-collar criminal charges brought by overzealous governments. At the very least, she should be a non-equity partner at a major silk-stocking firm by now. Instead, she was home, forced to communicate with only The Moms, as she called them, while they waited in gaggle formation, day after day, for their kids' music, ballet, or other inane class to end.

At first, Gretchen had been fascinated by them. They came perfectly coifed and beautifully dressed while she wore stretch pants and whatever top she found that was clean. Why dress up to sit on hard metal chairs, watching kids stomp around a dirty-looking tiled floor, waving their arms and pretending to be flowers? It was bad enough that

Gretchen refused to dress like them, but the real problems began the few times she had tried to discuss intellectually stimulating topics, like politics or the economy. At first, she hadn't understood it was intentional when The Moms physically shifted away from her. Finally, one of the women put her out of her misery, explaining they felt it best to steer clear of topics that might cause a rift in their group and hinder budding friendships among their children. Only vanilla topics were allowed: potty training, the best teachers for kindergarten, or the most sought-after pediatricians.

Gretchen refused to conform. Not because she didn't want to fit in, but she just wasn't made that way. Eventually, she became a sort of pariah. She was never invited to lunch after class or for nights out, when wine was guzzled by the bottle. She learned to bring something she could do by herself so she could coexist with The Moms, yet be spared the embarrassment of being shunned.

While she loved her husband and little girl, her current life was eating away at her soul. She was lonely, and she was wasting what her corporate law professor had told her was one of the best legal minds he had ever had the pleasure to teach. The monotony, combined with her inability to face her past, had become too much to bear. She was alone in a living hell, and there was no one to save her.

Pushing back off her kitchen counter, Gretchen walked into her husband's study and keyed in the numbers that unlocked the cabinet. When they'd first gotten married, she'd insisted he get rid of all of it. As a former marine, he argued that his guns were part of who he was, that it would emasculate him if he had to get rid of them, that it was his right to bear arms under the Second Amendment. It had been one of the few arguments she'd ever lost with him.

How ironic, Gretchen thought, as she grunted out loud and ugly laughed, *that my decision to let him win that argument will now work to my advantage.*

She had told herself it was boredom that drove her to spend hours on the Internet learning to load and fire the one weapon in his arsenal she thought she could handle. She assured herself she'd never use that knowledge, but today was different. Today, the gray sky and howling wind felt like they had etched themselves indelibly into her soul.

Reaching inside the cabinet, she picked up the gun and let the weight of it sink into her hands. She told herself a little hands-on practice loading the gun would better prepare her to protect herself and her daughter when her husband was traveling for business.

She opened the small box, took out a few bullets, held them, and began to load the gun. "Just for practice," she said out loud. Deep down, though, she knew. She was tired of the constant criticism in her head, the round and round about how her life should have been so different. As if it had a life of its own, the gun moved toward her head and tears gathered in her eyes. She no longer had the desire to resist. More than anything, she wanted to stop the pain.

"Momma! The movie stopped. Can you come watch with me this time?" Gretchen was startled. She looked into her daughter's clear blue eyes, which grew larger with understanding that something was wrong. Lowering the gun, Gretchen grabbed her daughter, wrapped her arms around the girl's tiny body, and began to cry hard, sobbing tears.

"Momma, don't cry. I'll fix it. Where do you hurt? Shh, shh. It'll be okay." Gretchen felt the soft, stroke, stroke, stroke of her daughter's small hands running down her hair.

It was then that she knew this was not her final chapter. She would fight back. Or, at least she would try. She would face what she had done and accept the consequences. Her husband might leave her, and she might lose custody of her daughter, but at least she'd have put up a fight. She would take one step at a time to find the confident, cocky woman she'd been only a few years before. She was ready to take back her life—for her daughter, for her husband, for herself.

CHAPTER

5

"I THINK YOU SHOULD consider a plea, William," Jeremy said, knocking the burnt ashes off the end of his cigar.

"Well, I just bet you do," Big Bill calmly responded in his heavy Southern accent, "but that's 'cause your ass ain't in the same sling mine's swinging in." He laughed as he poured himself another glass of his favorite fine Southern whiskey.

His client's big belly had grown even bigger over the past year, Jeremy noticed. It shook like one might imagine Santa's would if, of course, one was a child and believed in those things. Jeremy never had, thanks to having the fantasy kicked right out of him when he turned the tender age of seven. That was the last time Jeremy had seen his father outside of prison and the first time he thought about becoming a lawyer.

It was because of his reputation as a tough attorney and his personal bone to pick with the feds that high-profile criminal defendants hired his firm. Fortunately, Big Bill had the funds to pay his exorbitant fees or Jeremy would have kicked his narcissistic, fat ass to the curb months ago. Ignoring his client's sarcasm, Jeremy continued. "I hate to pile on,

William, but we recommend you settle the civil lawsuits, especially if you're thinking of pleading guilty to the Department of Justice's charges."

Scott expanded on his partner's advice. "William, they've got your handwritten notes setting out the scheme you intended to—and from the evidence they've gathered so far, did—launch onto unsuspecting policyholders. There's very little safe harbor for you."

"Well, now," Big Bill leaned back in his chair, lit one of his cigars, and let his gaze travel his Georgia plantation's conference room walls. Picture after picture showed him with presidents, prime ministers, and heads of state. He wanted to ensure no one, especially not this newest round of lawyers, doubted his clout. Clearing his throat, he scowled in disgust at the two sniveling men. "I pay you boys a fucking fortune, and you've got the balls to tell me all I get for a year's worth of legal bills is a recommendation to cave, settle, and plea? I could have done that a year ago and saved more than two million dollars in legal fees," he snarled as he smashed his fist into the table. "How 'bout taking a look at the fine lawyers who advised me and the board of Highline? Why don't we squeeze a few of their balls before we're so quick to grab mine? And, for fuck's sake, I was told you two were the toughest, ball-busting sons of bitches out there. Bring those balls back out into the sunshine, boys, and let's fight this bullshit." Big Bill's face turned red as his anger turned into a sickly laugh, followed quickly by uncontrollable coughing.

Jeremy jumped up, ran over, and began pounding on his client's back while Scott went to get water. Neither of them wanted to lose one of the biggest meal tickets to ever cross their legal threshold. They looked at each other over Big

Bill's head and shrugged, having done their ethical duty and advised him to settle and plea. They couldn't force him to do so. If he wanted to fight, it only served to help their bottom line.

Suddenly, Big Bill's hunk of a body heaved back, and the glass Scott had been holding flew across the room and shattered. Water splattered and ran down the wall onto the floor. "I'm just coughing, not having a heart attack, for Chrissake!" Big Bill choked out. "Now, listen. I know what's going through those pea-sized lawyer brains of yours: more money and less liability because you did your duty and told me I should cave. But either you devise a plan to get me out of this mess, or I will scream as loud and long as I can that neither of you advised me to settle and that you failed to tell me all the ramifications."

"That's ridiculous," Scott protested. "We'll put it in writing."

"Scotty, my boy," Big Bill began, "do you see all those fine presidents and important people lining my walls with their arms around me? I need only make a few phone calls and your careers will be in the toilet."

Stunned, Jeremy stood up defensively. "Are you threatening us?"

Big Bill got up and came around the table to lead them out of his office, slapping their backs on the way out the door and smiling. "That's it exactly. I can see we have a meeting of the minds. Now, gentlemen, I know you have a lot of work to do. Don't contact me again until you've come up with a real plan." Big Bill slammed the door, practically hitting the two lawyers on their way out.

CHAPTER

6

"ARMOND, WE'RE WAITING on you! We need the talent deals finalized and contracts signed so we can begin to market to investors. Filming begins in eighteen months, so you'll need to get the investors on board within the next six months to stay on schedule," Phillip said, looking at his son from behind his ornately carved gold-leaf desk.

"Yes, father dearest," Armond said. "I know what you need and when. If you recall, I grew up in this industry. And, what did you do to your office? It looks like a knockoff of the Versailles Palace. Could you have possibly stuffed it with any more gold antiques?" He took a seat in one of the gilded and intricately carved chairs surrounding, in his opinion, a ridiculously tacky desk.

"This was your mother's idea. I made the mistake of mentioning that many of the investors wanted more than to simply invest in a film for a solid return. They expressed an interest in having an experience—either by having a bit part or by being included in the making of the sausage. Next thing I know, she's decided we need to redecorate our home so we can invite potential investors to dinners and cocktail parties—the perfect way, according to her, to make them feel as if they're part of our movie-making family."

Armond laughed as he looked around the room. "Seems to me mother wanted to redecorate the Beverly Hills' house and used her idea as a ploy to get what she wanted. Sheer genius. I'll have to tell her so at dinner tonight."

Phillip ran his hand through his hair in exasperation, making Armond smile as he recognized the gesture as one of his own. "She also decided I needed an over-the-top home office so if someone decided to invest while enjoying our movie-making family atmosphere, we could have them sign the documents and complete the deal right then and there. Turns out, she was right."

"Well, better your office than mine," Armond said, enjoying that his mother, with whom he was close, had obviously out-maneuvered his father.

"Stop gloating. If I must be in here for these meetings, that means you must as well. So welcome to the club," Phillip came around the desk and patted his son on the shoulder. "Brandy?"

"I'll have whiskey neat, thanks." Armond stood to join his father by the newly designed bar. He noticed the elaborately chiseled wood that graced the back wall, and traveled across the top of an antique mirror and down the other side. "Where did you get that, and who in the world carved it? It's beautiful."

"It is, isn't it?" Phillip agreed. "No idea, I'm afraid. It's ancient and was excavated from some ruins in Thailand. Your mother insisted that since we've had an increasingly strong interest from Asian investors over the past two years that the office should house some of the region's relics to show our appreciation for their culture." Phillip sipped his brandy. "You, of all people, should know that once your mother has an idea in her head, she doesn't let it go. So," Phillip shrugged, "here we are."

Armond smiled and tasted his whiskey. "More likely they'll be insulted when they find out you stole one of their country's antiquities to hang above your overdone home bar."

The two men looked at each other and laughed when they heard the soft ringing of the dinner chimes float through the air. "Dinner is apparently served," Armond noted, shaking his head. "If you don't get mother under control soon, you'll have to show up for dinner every night in a tux."

"You talk to her, Armond. You two were always so close. She'll listen to you."

"Seems to me she's looking for something to do. Why don't you put her on the investment team? She loves to entertain. Give her a budget, a deadline, and an amount of money she needs to raise for the next film."

Phillip smiled at his son. "You know, Armond, I think that just might do the trick. Why don't you suggest it during dinner? If I bring it up, she'll think I'm trying to distract her."

"Well, you are," Armond said, raising his glass in salute to his father, "but I will. Now, let's go. I'm afraid of what tone those chimes will make if we don't show up on time."

CHAPTER

7

THE ROOM WAS filled to capacity. Twinkling lights gave it a romantic vibe, but the decorations reminded everyone it was a professional function. Scattered strategically throughout the ballroom were numerous legal artifacts, some of the more valuable being glass-encased white wigs once worn by English barristers, an original draft of the United States Constitution, and John Marshall's judicial robe. At each place setting was a gold-embossed copy of *Brown v. Board of Education*, the landmark Supreme Court unanimous decision that declared racial segregation in public schools unconstitutional.

Despite the legal and historical pomp, the purpose of the evening was to deepen camaraderie and have fun. But going hog-wild was frowned upon. Emails had been sent reminding associates and partners alike, that while this was a social evening, it remained a business function. Even so, it never failed. Trever smirked as he thought of past years. Inevitably, someone got shit-faced and did something scandalous. Last year, one of their newest partners decided to take a shortcut home and drove off the circular drive leading up to the club house of the private golf club. His path continued down a grassy hill, through manicured gardens, over the perfectly coifed eighteenth green, and into the adjacent lake. That little stunt cost the firm a pretty penny. And, there was always the reliable young, drunk associate, who would reach his hand down one of the partner's wives' dresses or grope an ass, leading to some sort of physical altercation.

Something always happens, Trever thought, as he smiled in appreciation and took a sip of his bourbon. Trever hated the mundane. Next year, perhaps he could convince Billy and Adam to place bets on what the social faux pas might be—a sort of roulette wheel of the top ten things that could happen—at $10,000 per chance. That would at least entice him to spend more than an hour at this function.

They were going to have to liven things up. The practice was becoming too routine. While most businessmen appreciated predictable because that's when deals get done and markets soar, Trever found it immensely boring. If things were running smoothly, he would purposely throw a grenade. It didn't matter what was at stake. He considered himself a connoisseur of people. He loved to track ahead of the curve and bet on what someone might do when presented with a particular set of facts. He'd create the mess and then clean it up in return for a portion of the profits.

Trever raised his glass in a silent salute to his granddaddy, Senator McGowen. The senator had taught him everything he knew about succeeding in business: how to read a room, manipulate the weak, and take advantage of a situation. He had represented the great state of Texas in Congress for the past thirty years and had sponsored a record-breaking number of bills, each of which purported to do good for the public. Take increasing Texas' oil production: more oil meant lower prices at the pump. But, almost every time the senator introduced a bill, there was a little something in it for his family. When Texas oil production increased, so, too, did the production on their family ranch, and, as a natural by-product, their family income.

"Well, Trever, from the look on your face, I have to believe you have a new deal in the offing." Adam clinked his glass with Trever's and smiled.

"Adam," Trever acknowledged. "Just a bit of reminiscing, and you're right. Despite all the turmoil of this past year, we're poised to have the best year in the firm's history. Our London office has handled some of the richest transactions we've ever been a part of, while the Bangkok office has been incredibly profitable, thanks to your hard work. And if your projections are accurate, it's slated to increase its revenue by almost 50 percent next year. That's record-breaking, Adam! You're to be congratulated."

Adam put his arm around Trever's shoulder and spoke in a low voice. "Our good fortune is getting noticed too. My cock-sucking brother called me last week to see if he could invest in our firm. I was elated to inform him it's unethical for nonlawyers to share in profits from the practice of law, but I told him I'd be happy to buy him out of the family business."

"I bet that was satisfying for you," Trever said, not wanting to delve too far into Adam's family drama. Trever believed family should stick together, no matter what, and Adam's long-standing feud with his family made him uncomfortable.

"I swear to God, Trever, I had such a hard-on after that call that I had to visit a special friend."

Trever's mouth and nose pinched to reveal his disdain over the turn of their conversation. "Adam, while I'm happy for your brother's apparent need to come begging to you after years of being a raging prick, neither Billy nor I want to see you in trouble again. Remember law school and the hassle we went through to get you out of that predicament?"

"When are you going to let that go? That was more than ten years ago, and there's nothing to that story."

"Adam, you were charged with prostitution."

"Yes, well. I was never convicted. You both seem to forget that. And, so what? How many other guys in law or grad school hire prostitutes? I was one in a million."

"Adam, neither Billy nor I are aware of anyone else hiring prostitutes. You, are our one and only," Trever said as he tipped his glass for a friendly toast.

"Well, whatever. Billy is far worse than I ever was. He screws just about every associate that walks through our doors. That's a problem waiting to happen. I think one of the only ones that got away was Victoria."

The smile on Trever's face quickly vanished. "Be very careful when you speak about her. We're in the middle of her lawsuit, and the legal community is watching. Our competition is hoping to bring us down over this. She's one of the few matters we haven't efficiently resolved—yet. Unfortunately, she's not going to give up as easily as the others."

Looking around to ensure no one was close enough to hear their conversation, Adam leaned in toward Trever. "She's a real problem. The good doctor's analysis on her was way off."

"Yes, I'm aware," Trever responded.

"Obviously, we're not going to respond to her lawyer's requests with the truth, and that bitch of a judge wouldn't dare defy us. It was our money that got her elected. Nonetheless, I don't like anyone poking around in our business. We need to end this."

"Adam, let's table this discussion," Trever spoke under his breath. "It's neither the time nor the place. Go occupy yourself with whatever slinky thing you've dragged in for the evening, and we'll talk in private when we're all present." Dismissing Adam, Trever turned to walk out onto the balcony to enjoy a Cuban cigar and the full moon reflecting on Lake Michigan.

CHAPTER

8

SERENA HAD ONE of the worst cases of jet lag she had ever experienced. As she struggled to open her hotel room door, she rapidly shook her head from side to side like a cartoon character, trying to shed the fog. "Finally," she muttered as the door opened. She walked in and plopped down on the bed, falling backward while fighting to stay awake and slither out of her clothes. *Maybe I'm getting sick,* she thought.

Over the past six years, Serena had traveled all over the world on business. She was one of the up-and-comers, or so she'd been told. A typical trip would take her to various cities in China or Thailand for a series of meetings and then back to Chicago. She was often away from home as long as a month at a time.

Pushing herself up with one hand, she moved her thick, shoulder-length, red hair off her face and tried to open her sleep encrusted eyes. *I must have fallen asleep with my contacts in. I never do that.* Forcing her eyes open a smidge, she noticed mascara smeared across the white bed spread. *Is that mine?* She heard knocking and looked around, disoriented. *Where the hell am I?*

"Ma'am, your dinner is here," she heard someone with an accent say. *Ah yes, Bangkok. I'm in Bangkok.* Serena couldn't recall having ordered food. But maybe she had. She felt so ill.

"Give me a minute," she croaked, snatching the hotel robe off the bathroom door. She caught a glimpse of herself in the mirror and noticed her nose was bleeding. Grabbing a tissue, Serena held onto the wall to steady herself as she shuffled toward the door. After a bit of fumbling, she unlocked it.

"I don't recall ordering—" The door opened suddenly, slamming her against the wall. As she fought to remain conscious, she saw the outline of two men. She felt herself slide to the floor and heard the smaller one speak in a familiar accent. She slurred, "Boston," then passed out.

Nudging her body with his custom boot, the smaller man turned to the larger. "You're an idiot. I told you none of them are to be damaged."

"Yes sir, but we were warned she would be a fighter. I thought it better if I controlled the initial meeting." Shaking his head in begrudging admiration, he continued, "She should have been out cold. I transferred more than enough product onto her skin when she checked in. This is exactly why I like the good old-fashioned ways: put it in their drink, sprinkle it on their food. Works like a charm."

Glaring at his companion, the smaller man growled, "If you ever discuss the details of your business in front of me again, I promise you'll end up worse than they do." Looking around the room, he nodded at her phone lying on the bed. "Get it, and have her moved to the usual location. No trace. And you'd better do something about that bump on her head. She'll be of little use looking like that."

CHAPTER

9

VICTORIA SMILED, LEANING back in her chair and watching two of her most trusted friends and Jenny, the newest member of their group, huddle near the head of the table. She hadn't been sure she could pull it off. After all, as lawyers, each comes complete with a ginormous ego. But watching them work together on her lawsuit was all she had hoped for.

"Robert, thank you for agreeing to try this," Victoria said as they began to wrap up.

"Well, the combination of too much wine last night plus you three does not a fair fight make." He smiled. "Truthfully, when you laid out your reasons, I realized the plan has some merit. I certainly can't dispute that we might have a better shot of getting other women to testify against the firm if there are female lawyers on the team. I'll try to get a hearing in the next two days to get the two of you admitted," Robert said, looking at Kat and Jenny while handing his assistant their revisions to the motion. "My bet is the Troika will argue both of you are too closely connected to Victoria, Billy or other matters their firm is involved in, and as such, she should deny our motion."

"I hope they do," Kat insisted. "Counsel doesn't have to be impartial to represent a client, and if they are stupid enough to put our connections to V and their firm at issue, we'll insist the judge hears all the juicy details," Kat smiled as she took a sip of coffee and spit it back into her cup. "God, that's awful!"

"That's because you poured that cup about four hours ago," Jenny pointed out.

Victoria flicked on the lights. The sun was setting and since it was creeping toward winter, little natural light was left by four thirty in the afternoon. "I agree. They won't want to bring details of the Highline Insurance fiasco into their hallowed Chicago courts, especially since they're doing their best to keep the firm from being added as a defendant in that case."

"I think Jenny is the one the court will have the most difficulty with," Robert said, swiveling in his chair to look at her. "Are you certain you're comfortable with this?"

"No, I'm not, but I want to work on this case. What happened to Victoria is unacceptable, and my son isn't named in the pleadings. Billy was Victoria's boss. It was some of the others that were the problem." Jenny was so glad to be practicing law again that she was willing to walk the fine line between allegiance to her son and commitment to her new friends. She saw the chance to get involved in what might be a precedent-setting gender discrimination lawsuit, and she couldn't wait to get into the courtroom again.

"Jenny," Victoria said, "I want to be perfectly clear. There's a good chance your son was involved. We just don't know yet."

"I can't see how that could be true," Jenny said. "He's received countless awards for being one of the foremost proponents of women in the law. I think someone at his firm is putting his good reputation at risk. But let's do a quick hypothetical. Let's say we find out he had something to do with having you fired. If that happens, I'll step out immediately."

Robert turned to Victoria. "What do you think? Are you certain it's worth it?"

Victoria answered, "Jenny, you understand part of the reason we're bringing you in is for shock value? We want to see if we can unnerve them enough to get a peek at what's behind the curtain and perhaps shake out some evidence about their hiring and treatment of women. If those reasons are offensive to you—and I understand if they are—then let's keep you working in the background and not have you make a formal appearance."

"I'm completely comfortable with this being a bit off the middle rail," Jenny responded, walking toward Victoria with her hand outstretched. "Deal?"

"Deal." Victoria smiled and shook her hand.

Turning at the knock on the door, Robert waved when he saw his assistant. "Come on in, Sandy."

"Sorry to interrupt, but I wanted to let you know before I left for the evening that the hearing is set for Wednesday. It's sixth on the nine o'clock call."

"Great, thank you."

"Also, I've made your dinner reservations, a private room with a view at NoMi. They'll provide any materials you need, and you'll have Internet access as well as printing capability. Is there anything else you need?"

Robert stood and grabbed the coat he had slung over the chair that morning, "No. Thanks for getting us set for this evening. Ladies, I'll see you in a few hours, and we'll run through the final details of our strategy."

"Listen," Victoria said after Robert left, "there's no reason both of you need to stay for the hearing on this motion. While I expect it to trigger some fireworks, Robert and I can handle anything that might come up."

"Are you kidding?" Kat responded as she pulled her hair up into a high pony tail, slid her heels back on, and packed her papers and laptop in her designer bag. "I fully expect those assholes to create major drama, and I want to be there so the judge can see who we are and so I can personally respond to any attempt they make to besmirch us. I'll fly out that afternoon."

"You can forget about me leaving too," Jenny added.

"You know you'll likely be the center of attention, right? Are you certain you're ready for this?" Victoria asked.

"I know what I'm doing and why I'm doing it. I understand the risks. Unless there's an objection now that the motion's filed, I'm going to call Billy to give him a heads-up," Jenny responded.

"No. No objection. I think that's the right thing to do, but what are you going to tell him when he asks why you're getting involved in the case?"

"I'm going to tell him what I told you. It's an opportunity for me to get back into litigation, and I want to get to the bottom of something that might ruin his and his firm's reputation."

"Okay then, it's settled. Anyway, it'll be good for you both to get a feel for this judge and the firm's defense team."

Victoria smiled at her friends. "Now, let's head back to my place. I want to change before dinner tonight."

* * *

Kat and Jenny insisted on staying in Victoria's tiny two-bedroom apartment—the same one she had rented since her first year of law school, and where both she and Kat had lived together during their last two years. Even though Victoria could afford to buy a larger place in the swanky part of the city, she had no desire to leave. She loved everyone who lived in the quaint, brick four flat. It was like a second family. She felt protected and safe.

* * *

The morning of the hearing, Victoria insisted they be ready to leave by no later than eight. While that was a full hour before the motion call began, Victoria knew Kat's predilection for being late and had no intention of adding to the stress of the morning.

"Ready? We need to leave now so we can be in the courtroom before the call begins," Victoria said. "This judge gets particularly pissed off when counsel arrive after she's on the bench."

"Ready," Jenny said, vibrating with excitement and boasting a smile that was out of line for a simple court appearance. "This'll be the first time I've stepped foot in court in more than thirty years, other than to agree to the divorce settlement."

Kat put her arm around Jenny and steered her out the door. "That's a long time."

"I used to be quite a prosecutor," Jenny responded. "We're happy to see the real Jenny find herself again, and we know you were good. We've seen your conviction record."

Jenny stopped in her tracks. "You spied on me?"

"I would call it performing the necessary due diligence before we let you get involved in one of our cases," Kat responded. "Oh, come on. You would have done the same."

"I guess you're right. I might have even had you investigated as well," Jenny said, turning her back to Kat and marching out the door. "I have a few things to tell you both about the firm defending Acker, Smith & McGowen."

"Well, tell us in the cab. We've got to move," Victoria said as she pushed her friends down the sidewalk and raised her hand to hail a cab. Usually they would have walked the eight blocks to the courthouse, but it was spitting thick, lotion-like rain that threatened to turn to snow. "Even though the boys didn't file a response to our motion, I doubt that's the end of it. I have a feeling they chose not to put anything in writing for a reason and they'll be in court to object. No matter what they or their lawyers say, I don't want either of you to react or say anything. You're to sit there and that's it. Capisce?"

"That's what I wanted to speak with you about," Jenny said, opening her notebook and fighting to keep the pages from blowing around as she read. "I got a call this morning from two of my former colleagues from the Georgia District Attorney's office. The three of us were extremely close. We handled our first felony trial together. It was a prostitution case, and you should have seen some of the evidence. There was this one picture of a guy's hand shoved—"

"Okay, okay, can we at least wait until we have a cocktail in front of us?" Kat interrupted. "Do you have something relevant about today's court hearing to tell us?"

"Oh, yes, sorry. I had asked if they had any information about the firm defending Acker, Smith & McGowen."

"Why would two former Georgia prosecutors have any information?" Victoria asked as she ducked into a cab and scooted across the seat to make room.

"Because they're not your average lawyers. They're now well-respected, highly-connected and working at the Department of Justice. In fact, one of them recently had his name floated as a possibility for the next Attorney General of the United States. Anyway, they called to tell me—off the record, of course—that the firm representing Acker, Smith & McGowen was investigated a few years ago. Apparently, an allegation surfaced that one of the firm's investigators used intimidation tactics to scare a plaintiff into dropping her discrimination lawsuit against a large corporation. No charges were brought as there was not enough evidence to support an indictment of the investigator or the firm."

"What happened to the plaintiff? Did she refile?" Kat asked.

"Apparently not. I'm told she was so traumatized by whatever happened that she abandoned her marriage and young son and disappeared."

"What do you mean disappeared?" Kat probed.

"Exactly that. By the time the FBI began investigating, she was gone."

"Those are some serious allegations. Why would two DOJ lawyers tell you this?" Kat added, surprised at Jenny's high ranking connections.

Jenny held up her finger to pause the conversation. When they arrived and stepped out of the cab, she turned and leaned toward Victoria and Kat. "Because they owed me."

"Um, okay. So what does it mean for my case?" Victoria repeated.

"It means the lawyers defending your former firm may have used some rather heavy-handed tactics to win cases. My friends are trying to identify which lawyers were the target of that federal investigation. That way, we'll know if the lawyers representing the firm in your case, Victoria, have any potential connection to that missing woman."

Victoria and Kat stared at Jenny, then looked at each other and burst out laughing. "Girl's got brains and balls!" Kat said as they turned to walk into the courthouse.

"Yes, ma'am," Jenny responded. "I believe I do."

CHAPTER
10

"WELL, WELL, WELL. What do we have here?" Trever leaned over and whispered to Adam, who was sitting next to him in the courtroom pew, waiting for the judge to start the call.

"And the fun begins." Adam nudged Billy, who was sitting to his right, and jerked his chin in the direction of the group that had entered the courtroom.

Billy smirked in disgust. "Oh, for Christ's sake. Well, this is going to get awkward."

"On the contrary, Billy," Adam said. "This gives you the perfect opportunity to let her know how this is going to end if she doesn't stay the hell away from our firm."

The three men looked up just as Jenny saw her son, smiled, and made a beeline directly toward them.

"Billy, darling, how are you?" she asked, leaning over to kiss his cheek, ignoring the other two. "I tried to connect with you to have dinner and chat about this motion, but your assistant said you were out until next week. Change of plans?"

"Mother, let's step outside," Billy said. Standing, he grabbed his mother firmly by her arm and steered her through the courtroom's double doors and into the hallway.

"Why are you, of all people, getting involved in this case? What in God's name are you thinking?" Billy spat as soon as they were out of earshot of the other lawyers and clients who were milling around while they waited for their cases to be called. He continued to walk her toward the glass walls of the thirty-one story courthouse that boasted some of the best views of the Chicago shoreline. Usually, Billy admired the view. Today was different.

"Billy, stop dragging me," Jenny said as she pushed his hand off her arm. "If you would have returned my calls, we could have discussed this before now. Listen"—Jenny softened her tone and smiled up at her son—"you have a reputation for being one of the staunchest supporters of women in the law. You must know that you and the firm you've worked so hard to build are being hurt by this lawsuit. Clearly, someone didn't have your best interest at heart when they fired Victoria. I think I can bridge the divide and do some good for both sides."

Sighing, Billy looked down at the ground, then directly into his mother's eyes with a steeled look he had learned from years of watching his father go from charming to bastard in the blink of an eye.

"Mother, let me be blunt. I am not going to allow you to get involved in this case. We're going to take very difficult positions against Victoria I doubt you'll like. I'm asking you now to walk back into that courtroom and withdraw your motion. If you refuse, I'm going to be forced to bring up some unpleasant matters."

A little alarm went off in Jenny's head. "What do you mean, 'unpleasant'? What are you talking about?"

"We don't have much time. The call begins in about five minutes. Let me just say that I would hate for your reentry into the legal profession to be tarnished."

"Tarnished? I had a sterling reputation, and I've lived my life admirably," Jenny responded.

"If you continue on this path, I will testify that during the divorce, you asked me to move large sums of money from your and Father's joint account into an untraceable offshore account. That will not only end your involvement in this case, but I'm quite sure the State of California will want to reconsider its moral character determination of one of its newest lawyers too. I wouldn't be surprised if your ability to practice law is suspended pending a full review, which as you know, can take months if not years."

Jenny stared at her son and felt a rush of heat run through her body. She was suddenly flooded with sweat. Tears swam in her eyes as she realized that her only child, one of the loves of her life, was not only capable of lying but was willing to ruin her reputation and potentially her return to the profession she loved.

Looking at his watch, Billy sneered, "Two minutes, Mother. What's it going to be?"

Jenny was surprised at how quickly her feelings changed from sadness to pure, red-fire anger. After all she'd put up with from his father, to now be treated like dirt by her son? She refused to let history repeat itself, but she had to be smart. This was her son's playground, not hers. Chicago judges were elected, and how much her son had personally helped elect this judge was unknown.

Guarding her feelings, she looked her son in the eyes. "I didn't realize how much this meant to you, Billy. Now that I do, I see that the best thing for me to do is withdraw my motion. I can't control Kat, of course."

Smiling and putting his arm around his mother's shoulder, Billy responded, "Of course not, and I don't expect that of you. This is the right decision. You'll see that in the end, Mother."

Oozing the confidence of a man who expects people to do his bidding, Billy turned and walked ahead of his mother into the courtroom, letting the door close in her face. Not more than a few seconds after Jenny returned, the door in the back wall opened with a whooshing sound and a swath of blond hair and black robe moved swiftly up onto the dais. "All rise. Court is now in session, the Honorable Margaret McLaughlin now presiding," the limping bailiff bellowed as everyone rose.

"Good God," Kat whispered to Victoria, nodding at the bailiff, "he's older than petrified wood." Victoria refused to look at her but sharply rapped Kat's ribs with her elbow.

Jenny scooted in next to her colleagues. For a moment, looking at the cherubic-like face of the diminutive, blond, bob-haired judge, Jenny played with the idea that she might be able to convince Her Honor that whatever her son might say about her wasn't true. But to what purpose?

Judge McLaughlin banged her gavel. "Please be seated. Bailiff, call the first case."

As the first group of lawyers approached the bench ready to argue their motion, the judge unexpectedly held up her hand. "Gentlemen, hold a moment, please." A huge smile spread across her face as she forced a few unruly blond curls into place behind one of her ears. "Billy, Adam, Trever, to what do I owe the honor of having the founding partners of Acker, Smith & McGowen in my courtroom? I didn't see anything substantive on the call this morning."

All three men rose in unison. Their perfectly coifed hair gleamed under the courtroom lights, while their custom suits showed just the right amount of sheen. "Your Honor, as always, it's a pleasure to see you," Billy said. "I believe the last time we were together was at the reception to celebrate your tenth year on the bench. May we approach?"

"Yes, of course." Turning to the sidelined lawyers, the judge said, "Gentlemen, the clerk will recall your case. Please step back." Then, turning to the court reporter, the judge ordered, "Off the record."

Smiling at the men now standing in front of her, Judge McLaughlin spoke in a low tone. "That was an amazing party. I appreciate your firm hosting the reception and all the work you and your staff did. Now, to what do I owe the pleasure?"

Victoria stared at Robert, wide-eyed to communicate how screwed she thought they were. Robert imperceptibly shook his head to let his client know she was wrong.

"Nothing of any real substance, Your Honor," Billy answered, glancing over his shoulder at his mother. "Just a request from plaintiff to add a slew of out-of-town lawyers to her case. We simply don't see the need for it."

The judge's eyes narrowed a bit. "Billy, the standard for whether I will or won't allow new lawyers on a case is not whether the opposing party sees a need for it. Did you file an opposition to their motion?"

"Your Honor, if I may?" Robert said as he approached the bench.

"Yes, of course. Robert, how are you?"

"I'm fine, Your Honor. Thank you. With all due respect, this is my case. I filed the motion, so if we're going to address it now, I'd like an opportunity to present our position."

"Please, proceed," she said, signaling her court reporter to go back on the record.

"The answer to your question is, no. They didn't file any opposition to our motion, and as you know, these motions are routinely granted. Moreover, defendants certainly don't have a say in the lawyers their opponents choose. Finally, I called their office"—Robert paused as he gave a sideways flick of his head at the Troika—"at least three times before the hearing today to find out if they had any objections, and I never received a return call. So I certainly object to any last-minute oral response."

Lifting her head to look out at the other lawyers waiting patiently for their own motions to be called, the judge rolled her eyes and sent them a conspiratorial wink as if to say, "Can you believe the shit I have to deal with every day?" Her theatrics were met with a smattering of laughter as the waiting lawyers tried to judge her temperament and gain her favor before it was their turn to step up. Billy, Adam, and Trever glanced at one another, signaling their mutual annoyance at being the butt of the judge's joke.

Leaning forward over the bench, the judge crooked her finger, motioning for all four men to move closer. "You know, boys," she said in a low, quiet tone, "I have neither the interest nor time to referee a fight between bullies pushing each other around on the playground. I'm not at all pleased by the childish behavior you've brought into my courtroom this morning." Turning to look directly at Billy, she warned, "Next time, Mr. Acker, if you want to object to a motion in my courtroom, you'll put it in writing. Understood?"

"Yes, Your Honor," Billy replied, his pale skin flushed red.

"This one time, I'll let you proceed orally. Now, step back." Picking up her gavel, the judge whacked it down hard, producing a sharp crack. "Five-minute recess," she called out, clearly pissed off, as she stood to walk back through the hidden door in the wall.

Robert turned and walked back into the huddle of Victoria, Kat, and Jenny. "Well, something's going on. They're clearly going to fight this, and unfortunately, the judge is going to let them."

Jenny touched him on the shoulder and said, "He threatened me. Take me off the motion. Get Kat in, but I'm out."

"What are you talking about, Jenny?" Victoria responded. "We talked about our strategy for hours this week. We knew they would argue against it. Why would you let him get to you?"

Tears sprang to Jenny's eyes. "I'm not strong enough yet. He said he'd ruin my career. He's going to tell the judge I asked him to hide funds from his father during the divorce proceedings. It's likely my bar admittance will be reconsidered if he makes those allegations."

"What? Why that son of a bitch," Kat muttered, looking over to see Billy smirking at her. "Let's get your divorce lawyer involved. She'll testify that nothing of the kind occurred."

"No, Kat. For what?" Victoria said, putting her arm gently around Jenny's shoulder. "All this nonsense will possibly hurt Jenny's career, deflect from my case, and waste time, which is what they want. Time is on their side. They're hoping witnesses move on and documents disappear. Jenny's right. She can't have her career interrupted at this point after all she's been through. She'll act as special counsel and help as we need. Does that work for you, Jenny?"

Pulling herself together, Jenny said, "I'm so sorry for all of this. I never expected my son would threaten me rather than let me on this case."

"Ladies, we don't have much time. The judge will be back on the bench any minute. Are we agreed?" Robert asked. Watching them all nod their heads, he turned and walked over to the boys.

"Okay, Billy. You win this one. We'll remove your mother from the motion, but know that I'm watching all of you so close your balls should feel the heat."

"We're shaking in our Italian-made boots. Now that you've finished your little speech, I want you to dismiss the whole motion. Kat has no business getting involved in this case. I'm sure she has more important matters to worry about, like whether her family can continue to get bank financing for all their little development deals. I'm sure she wouldn't want Trever's granddaddy to begin an investigation into their company."

Turning to see Kat watching their discussion, Robert signaled to her. Keeping one eye out for the judge, knowing they had precious little time, he spoke rapidly. "Kat, Billy here has just told me that if we don't dismiss the motion, Senator McGowen will investigate your family's business. I thought he should at least have the balls to threaten you directly."

"What?" Kat said, visibly stunned.

"Well, Miss Kat," Trever chimed in his exaggerated Texan drawl, "since you and I are from Texas, we both know how prickly our politicians can be if they think someone's cuckolded their state out of finances. I suspect there might be some problems my granddaddy can dig up about your daddy's construction company, perhaps about certain tax deductions he took or someone he paid off to get a permit. Seems someone's always doing something criminal in construction. Or, maybe your daddy got bored and took his mistress someplace special using some of his investors' funds. Who knows what might turn up?"

Robert put his hand on Kat's arm and tried to steer her away. "Let's take a minute to chat, Kat."

Shrugging Robert's hand off, Kat spat, "In less than five minutes, I'll be counsel in the case Victoria filed against you and your firm. And five minutes after that, I'll instruct my lawyers in Miami not only to go hard against the insurance company you set up to defraud millions of insureds, but I'll make sure they file discovery to elicit the advice it received from your firm. I'm convinced the board members didn't come up with delaying claim payments on their own. Why would they? They're all wealthy individuals and would have made significant profit if the company would have operated within normal standards. Someone enticed them, and I think I know just the firm that was behind that."

Trever challenged, "Good luck with that. No judge will ever let you get the privileged communications between the insurance company and its lawyers."

"Maybe not," Kat responded as the hidden door swung open and the bailiff announced the return of the judge, "but, may I suggest, gentlemen, that by screwing with me and mine, you've just upped the ante. Better clean house, boys, 'cause I'm coming for you hard."

* * *

"Well, that went well." Victoria sighed as they got into the elevator and headed down to the lobby. "Was it my imagination, or were they incredibly pissed at the judge?"

Kat burst out laughing. "Oh my God. I almost started laughing, listening to the dressing-down she gave them when they tried to keep me out of the case. One of my best days ever!"

"Yes, well, watch your back," Robert said. "I don't take their threats lightly and neither should you or your family. They're incredibly connected, especially Trever."

"I'm well-acquainted with the McGowen family and Trever's granddaddy. I've already texted my assistant to set a call with my father while I'm at the airport this afternoon. We have a few connections of our own and a number of strings we can pull. Rather stupid of Trever to threaten my family before he's fully thought through who we might know," Kat replied.

"Kat, I know how they think," Victoria added. "They're narcissists, but they don't make empty threats. Just look at what Billy was prepared to do to his mother. As disgusting as his threat was, I have no doubt he would have gone through with it."

Making a quick note on his pad, Robert said, "Their collective egos might also be their Achilles' heel. Let's work on that possible weakness. We need to connect before the end of next week to finalize our strategy going forward and to think through how we want to use Jenny, if at all," Robert said as he hailed a cab to take Kat and Jenny to the airport.

CHAPTER

11

VICTORIA WALKED INTO her apartment exhausted. She had spent the rest of that day returning client calls and working on a motion that had to be filed the next day. When her friends texted that they'd landed and were safe and sound in their respective home turfs, she was surprised at how late it was. Closing the door behind her, Victoria threw her bag on the floor, walked into her tiny kitchen, and uncorked a bottle of Italian red wine. Sniffing it appreciatively, she walked back into her living room and stretched out on the sofa. She had just turned on her television to watch some mindless nonsense when she heard her phone vibrate in her bag.

"Shit, shit, shit, shit. I'm so tired," Victoria said out loud. Trying to ignore her phone, she turned the TV volume up a little higher. Glancing daggers at her bag as the vibrating continued, she pushed herself off the sofa and dug to retrieve it. Looking at the caller ID, she smiled. "Armond. How are you? You're the only person besides my mother I would have answered the phone for tonight. How's la-la Land? Are you juicing and running shirtless on the beach?"

"Hello, my pet. How is that cold as a witch's tit Chicago treating you?" Armond answered, smiling as he looked out at the view of the city on one side and the Pacific on the other from his new penthouse on the outskirts of Los Angeles.

"How's the movie business? Are you settling into your role there?" Victoria asked as she took a sip of her wine.

"It's actually rather interesting. I've taken over the deal-making side of the business, which is why I called."

"Aww, that's so flattering. I thought perhaps you had called to see how I was or, oh, I don't know, maybe to talk to one of your best friends. Or, I know, how about to find out what happened in court since you bailed on our strategy meetings this week," Victoria responded sarcastically.

"Kitty has her claws out tonight, I see. Well, retract those things because I have a proposition for you that should make you very happy, with the caveat that I might change my mind if I'm forced to listen to more of your smart-ass comments," Armond teased.

"Of course, *mon capitaine*," Victoria answered, using one of the names she had called him when they'd worked together at the firm. It had always annoyed the crap out of him, which only made her use it more often. "I'm listening."

"I'm going to take a trip within the next month or two to Hong Kong and possibly Singapore. I thought I might be able to convince you to come along."

"Why in the world are you going to be traveling internationally? And, you do recall, don't you, that I'm just a hard-working girl from the South Side trying to make it in the big city? I have neither the money nor the time, although I would love to go." Victoria sighed, flopping back down onto the sofa.

"Well, while I'd like to empathize and say I know how it is, I can't. I grew up in the well-padded lap of luxury."

"God, you're an ass!" Victoria laughed and Armond smiled appreciatively at their banter as he ran his hand through his hair.

"I'm not asking you to go as a lark, Victoria. I'd like to have you on the trip in an official capacity, as Renoir Productions Company's outside counsel. I need your sixth sense to flush out potential investors. Of course, we'll pay your exorbitant fees and all expenses."

"What in the world are you talking about?" Victoria asked, stunned at his suggestion and sitting up again. "I'm not an investment banking lawyer, Armond. Why would you want me in your meetings? Not that I don't appreciate the thought."

"Contrary to what you think, you are a transaction lawyer. You're the one who got the insurance company up and running and registered in all fifty states, and you handled all of their contract matters. Most importantly, your intuition is the best I've seen. That's the part I really need."

Victoria got up to pour herself another glass of wine. "You mean like the way I trusted the Troika? Sniffed them out like a pig hunting truffles! That sixth sense? Please, the last thing you should do is consummate an international investment deal based on my advice," Victoria said, laughing.

After a brief pause, Armond said what was almost always on his mind. "I miss you."

"I know," Victoria answered. "I miss you too." A long silence passed as they enjoyed being connected, even if it was only through their phones.

Armond added, "It's not the same working on deals without the constant fear of you waking me up in the middle of the night to work through some random strategy that popped into your head."

Victoria was happy to continue down that line of conversation, as she wasn't used to the serious mood that had unexpectedly developed between them. "As I recall, you typically ran with one of those random ideas from my middle-of-the-night calls."

"Indeed. Nine times out of ten your midnight express ideas were good ones," Armond said, stepping outside on his balcony to watch the changing colors of the sky as the sun slid into the ocean. "So, tell me. How were the strategy sessions? Did everything go as planned in court?"

"The meetings were great, but as far as going as planned, not really. I have a feeling, though, that we'll look back at the outcome and realize the way it turned out was for the best. I'll tell you the details later, but the long and the short of it is Billy threatened his mother so we withdrew her name. She won't be involved, at least officially. The Troika threatened Kat, too, with an investigation initiated by Senator McGowen. You can imagine Kat's response to that. Wrong button to push. I thought she might grind her stiletto heels into their heads."

Laughing, Armond made a mental note to meet with Jenny, call Kat, and let his father know about the threat. His and Kat's parents were close, and his father would have some buttons of his own to push to help Kat's family if they needed it. "I'm quite sure, knowing Billy, Adam, and Trever as well as I do, that when they look at Kat, all they see is a tall, blond beauty they want to get into bed. I'm sure they don't believe she has a brain of any merit."

"Well, I don't intend to educate them that she'll be the one driving the Mack truck when it hits. Now, enough about that. On to important matters. When will I see you again?"

"That's the other reason I called, V. I have a few investor meetings out there in two weeks. I thought I'd stay through the weekend. That way, I can tell you more about what I have in mind for your job as counsel, and we can schedule the trip."

"Armond, did you even listen to me? I haven't come close to saying that I'm interested, and I'm not sure leaving the country is feasible right now. I have a number of cases that are heating up, and I really don't have anyone else who can handle them while I'm gone."

"I thought you'd say that, so I've worked through some ways we can deal with your concerns and satisfy my interests. Let's discuss it when I get there and then we'll see where we stand. Agreed?"

"Agreed," Victoria answered. "I can't wait to see you Armond. Say hi to your parents, and I'll tell my mom you'll be in town. She'll be thrilled."

"Tell Sophia I look forward to seeing her. Take care, V. See you soon."

As Victoria got up to head to bed, she smiled, thinking about the possibility of working with Armond again. She stopped at her laptop and did a quick search for the average hourly rate investor counsel charge their clients. Victoria starred dumfounded at the results. "Holy shit!" she said out loud, then laughed at the thought of what she would charge Renoir Productions for her time, a shit-ton for sure.

CHAPTER

12

BILLY WAS FEELING quite good as he strolled into his firm's Chicago headquarters. After the rather unsatisfactory court appearance, he had managed to enjoy a perfect weekend of mixing business with pleasure playing two rounds of golf at his very private, male-only-member club. Eleven of the beautifully choreographed eighteen holes ran along the lake while the rest meandered through protected prairie that backed up to historic mansions owned by foreign countries and reserved for their dignitaries.

During his first round on Saturday, Billy lucked onto a foursome with the consulate general of Japan. During the four hours they shared on the course, Billy turned on his rainmaker charm and got himself a coveted invite to Sunday dinner at the consulate's residence. That alone would have been enough, but as luck would have it, the host needed a personal favor Billy's firm could deliver. In return, Billy secured a commitment that the office Acker, Smith & McGowen planned to open in Tokyo would be met with favorable press and open arms by the Japanese government.

Billy even extracted a promise that his firm would be added to a short list of others bidding to represent Japan in its upcoming trade negotiations with the United States. The new American administration's penchant for picking trade fights with foreign governments had been a boon for the firm. If he could add Japan to the firm's growing list of government clients, their Tokyo office would be swamped with business as soon as it opened its doors. Billy made a mental note to put the wheels in motion to satisfy the promised favor as soon as he got to his office.

Nodding at the firm's security detail, Billy used the new biometric device that allowed him, Adam, and Trever access to a private elevator to their penthouse offices. As the doors opened, he smiled when he saw his new assistant. "Good morning, Sherrie. How was your weekend?" He stopped and leaned over her desk to get a better look at one of the hottest women he had ever hired.

"Good morning, Mr. Acker," Sherrie answered, trying to remain professional even though he consistently spoke to her breasts rather than her face. "How was your weekend?" she asked, surprised he was in such a good mood.

"Perfect, absolutely perfect," he answered as he rapped his knuckles on the waterfall marble countertop, winked, and walked down the hall toward his office.

"Mr. Smith, Mr. McGowen, and Jack are in your office. They've been waiting for about half an hour."

"Really?" Billy said, stopping mid-stride and turning back around. "What about?"

"They said they would fill you in when you arrived."

Billy hated surprises. His days were meticulously planned and his meetings well-orchestrated. Frowning in annoyance, he entered his office to find his three partners reading the paper and chatting amicably. Whatever it was, it couldn't be too bad. "Well gentlemen, to what do I owe the pleasure of your company this morning?" Billy asked.

"We've been waiting for you," Adam said. "Where the hell have you been?"

"Adam, please. Let's address the reason we're here, shall we?" Trever jumped in, nodding at Jack, the firm's senior litigation partner.

"Judging by the spring in your step, I take it you haven't seen this," Jack said as he handed the paper to Billy. Sprawled across the front page in big, bold print, the headline screamed, "Acker, Smith & McGowen Sued. Sex Discrimination Rampant?"

Billy's mouth dropped open. "What the hell? Why would this come out now? The lawsuit's been pending for a year. Who's the reporter on this story? We'll have him or her fired and then sue the paper for defamation," Billy sputtered.

"Well, that's a fine idea, Billy," Trever responded sarcastically, leaning on his Texas drawl to emphasize his point. "Let's do that. And since the paper's defense will be to prove that the story is true, they'll begin digging deep into our firm, and then what? Ah yes, then they'll get our statistics on female partners and maybe they'll dig up a few of the associates you took under your—what do you call it—wing."

"Trever, you can be such a son of a bitch," Billy responded, disgusted. "All anyone needs to do is to look online for the number of associates and partners at our firm and the number of women within those ranks. It's not a secret. If we don't respond with firepower and outrage, people will assume the allegations in Victoria's lawsuit are true. We need to do something, and quickly."

"I agree with Billy," Adam weighed in. "We can't sit quietly. Everyone will assume we have no defense. Jack, what do you think?"

Jack allowed a long pause to settle in among the tension. He'd been cleaning up behind these three ever since he joined the firm. "Billy, as head of the firm's diversity committee and a member of the National Bar Association's advocacy group on increasing female partners in firms, you'll issue a carefully worded statement about one of the recent awards you've received for your work in this area. You'll also highlight the new female partner the firm's welcomed. I'll follow up with a statement to the press about the unfortunate circumstances surrounding Victoria's firing and that we're saddened to see that rather than moving on with her career, she's chosen to take a path of destruction."

"What do you mean 'new female partner'? We have no plan to add a woman," Billy responded.

"You do now if you don't want this firm to become the poster child for gender discrimination by the end of this week." Jack paused. "Either give me the tools I need to get us out of this mess, or the three of you can get someone else to put his reputation on the line for the firm."

Adam shot out of his chair and sent it crashing to the floor. "Are you threatening us? There is no way we're going to add a partner to the firm just because—"

"Stop!" Trever demanded, glaring at Adam. "Sit down. This is not the time for your theatrics." Turning to look at Jack, he calmly confirmed, "We'll handle it, Jack. You'll get the name of our first female partner by the end of the day.

Now, will you excuse us while we work through a few matters?" Trever put his arm on Jack's shoulder and walked him out the door.

"For God's sake, Billy," Adam snarled angrily. "Look at the mess you created! Had we stuck with the plan and gotten rid of that bitch earlier, we wouldn't be in this situation."

"Shut the fuck up, Adam," Billy spat.

Trever stepped between Adam and Billy, sensing their ability to deal with one another as adults was nearing an end. "Boys, take a step back. I assume you don't want to be frontpage news two days in a row?"

Adam walked over to the sofa and sat down. "Trever, you haven't exactly helped. The paper included a section about Kat being added as counsel. They connected the dots. She's the general counsel of the company that sued Highline Insurance for not paying out on its hurricane claims, and it was our firm that got that insurance company up and running. Seems to me your threat to Kat only pissed her off. If she starts talking to the press, we'll have a shitstorm to deal with."

"Don't worry about Kat or her family. I'll handle them." Trever turned and walked to sit in the chair next to Adam. "Now, who's going to be our first female partner? I suggest we name the most malleable woman we've got, one who will be grateful and not demanding."

"We're not making this decision alone. That's why we pay the good doctor," Adam said, walking to Billy's phone and dialing his assistant. "Send Dr. Natarajan up immediately." Billy sat at his desk and glanced at his watch. He had about fifteen minutes before his first meeting. "Okay. We need our PR team on this right away. We can't let this sit unanswered. I'll have them do a splash piece about the number of women we bring into the firm compared to other firms of our size, mention my awards for diversity, and announce our first female partner. I like Jack's idea about appearing sympathetic toward Victoria and wishing her the best in future endeavors. We might also want to get the line in the water that she was responsible for getting Highline up and running and any problems it's experiencing now should be laid at her feet. Agreed?"

"Yes," Adam and Trever answered in unison.

"Next, I want Jack's team of investigators to find some disgruntled person from Victoria's past. She must have some dirt under her nails. If they can't find anything, they'll have to make it up." Billy stood. "We have a plan. I'll tell Jack to execute. I want us on the front page for all the good we've done, and I want Victoria's veneer to begin to fade."

"One more thing," Adam began. "We'll need to communicate with our clients, particularly the ones that have shareholders. They're likely to balk at being associated with a firm accused of gender discrimination. This could be a disaster!"

Trever stood and straightened his tie, catching his reflection in one of the windows. "As usual, Adam, your hysterics won't be of any help. The PR team will take care of that as well. Billy, is there anything else? I'm scheduled to leave for Washington, D.C."—Trever glanced at his watch—"now actually, with the senator, to get some of that lobbying business that's saturating the Capitol now that trade's up for grabs."

"There is one more thing. I'm concerned about security, Trever, especially since we're about to run an aggressive campaign against Victoria. I don't want anyone getting access to our core traits. What's the status with Dr. Natarajan?

I heard she was asking for more money to keep our system checked and balanced."

Trever was annoyed Billy would question him about security. His family's membership into one of the most exclusive clubs in Washington, the Senate, allowed Trever access to the best of the best, but in order to keep the peace and get to his grandfather's plane that had already been waiting for five minutes, he answered simply, "I've overseen security since we opened the firm. We have the finest systems and people at our beck and call. As for Dr. Natarajan, she's never faltered in handling our system or in the security we've asked her to maintain. I've already cut a new deal with her giving her a slight raise. Everything is fine. I'll see you boys when I get back. Let's not blow this out of proportion. Victoria is one little girl."

Hearing a knock, they turned to see the door open. "I was told you wanted to see me," Dr. Natarajan said as she walked over and sat next to Adam.

"We do. We have an important project for you, and we'll need your answer by no later than two this afternoon," Billy answered. "Trever, Adam, I've got this. As soon as the good doctor gives me her recommendation, I'll let you know. I'd like you both to be present for a celebratory ceremony for the lucky girl around five—photographers and champagne, that sort of thing. Trever, will you be back by then?"

"I will. It's a turnaround day trip. I should be back by four."

"Adam?" Billy questioned.

"I'll be here."

"Perfect. See you tonight."

Nodding their assent, the two men left Billy's office together.

CHAPTER

13

WILLOW WOKE TO horrific screaming. She hated being lucid enough to recognize someone's pain. She preferred the haze-like world she lived in twenty hours each day. If she had a choice, she'd stay oblivious the other four, but Madame insisted that her talent, as she referred to her girls, clear their minds for a few hours each day. Those hours, though, were for Madame's benefit, as they were used to follow her strict hygiene requirements because, as she often declared, "No one wants to pay for a dirty girl."

Willow had seen girls ripped from their rooms and thrown out into the street with nothing but the dirty sheet they'd been wrapped in if they refused her hygiene rituals. Once out of Madame's protection, the girls were left to die, snatched up by street pimps, or forced into sex shows and used until there was nothing left.

Putting a pillow over her head, Willow tried to drown out the heart-wrenching screams. Whoever this new one was, she was going to be labeled a resistor unless she calmed down, and things did not go easily for that group. One of the few girls Willow spoke to in the house had told her resistors were sold at auction to men who took pleasure in breaking women. Once sold, the girls were never heard from again.

Willow was becoming agitated. Opening her journal—the one thing she was allowed to have—she focused on finishing her latest poem. She couldn't remember where she had learned to write so well, but she must have been well-educated, or so Madame said. Madame enjoyed her poems and stories and would sometimes call for Willow to entertain her by reading her newest creation. That had saved her from some of the crasser, more violent customers.

"Willow, it's time," a deep male voice carried through her closed door.

"Coming." Willow threw her robe around her, grabbed the few toiletries she was allowed to keep in her room, and walked into the hallway to wait with the other girls in her group. It was the same routine every day.

"Good afternoon, Willow," the giant, as Willow thought of him, said in as soft a voice as he could muster. Standing at least six-and-a-half feet tall and weighing close to three hundred pounds, he seemed more monster than man.

"Good afternoon," Willow answered.

Speaking to the group, he rasped, "You know the rules. Keep your heads down. Do not look around. Don't ask any questions. Do your business in the showers and come out. You have thirty minutes."

He was their protector, or so they were told. Willow supposed that was why he tried to elicit some sort of a caring relationship with each of the girls. But she was cautious and, unlike some of the other girls, did not divulge any of the few thoughts or feelings she had left.

Once back in her room, Willow thought again of the boy. About eight, perhaps. "Who is he?" she said out loud.

Maybe he was just a character in one of her stories. He floated to the surface of her mind. Feeling his strong presence, she began to write. For the first time, she could remember. She saw what he looked like and wrote quickly before she received her dose of escape for the day and forgot once again.

CHAPTER

14

THE FLIGHT TOUCHED down at O'Hare with a loud boom as the wheels slammed onto the runway. "God-damn it!" Armond swore, not caring who heard him. Taking out his phone, he texted: *Just landed. Almost lost my life. Damn commercial pilots.*

Victoria read the text, laughed and responded: *No drama in you, my Hollywood friend. See you at my apartment.*

Getting up, she stretched and winced as she limp-walked out of her office. *Well, this is ridiculous*, she thought as she headed toward the coffee nook to microwave the last bit of coffee in her cup before she headed home.

"And we're walking like an old woman because…?" Mary asked when Victoria passed her desk.

"Because I've sat on my ass for the past five hours reading one of the depositions in the case for that new client. I actually feel worse than after I ran the half marathon last month."

Smiling at her boss, Mary asked, "Isn't Armond due in tonight?"

"Actually, he just landed."

"Good, I'm glad to hear it. I'm happy the two of you made up. I knew he couldn't have been involved in all that mess with our old firm."

Victoria cocked her head and looked at Mary, saying, "You always had complete faith in him. I would have happily run him down had I seen him in the street after I was escorted out by those goons. I have no idea why you felt so strongly he had nothing to do with it when my own eyes and ears saw and heard him letting me go from the firm."

"I understand why you would have felt like that. But remember, I'd worked at the firm with Armond from almost the day he began. You came along much later. I watched him develop. He was always pretentious and cocky, but underneath all the designer suits, pocket hankies, and fancy words, he was a really good guy."

"Hmm, I'm not sure I would have described him as 'a really good guy,'" Victoria air quoted Mary's phrase, "but far be it from me to argue with you. You're the best judge of character I've seen yet. I've got to get home because you know how pissy that really good guy can get if you keep him waiting."

Mary took the coffee cup out of her boss' hand. "Go. Have a great night, and please give him my best. Will I get to see him before he leaves?"

"Of course. We're meeting here tomorrow to discuss my case. But even if we weren't, I can't imagine Armond not stopping by to see you. You know he adores you." As the elevator dinged its arrival and the doors opened, Victoria turned and waved. "See you tomorrow!"

Walking the few short blocks to her apartment, Victoria threw her head back and slowed her gait so she could enjoy the lingering warmth of what had been a glorious Indian summer day. She was excited to see Armond. Even though they'd hit a rough patch last year, he remained one of her best friends and, it turned out, one of her most loyal defenders.

She smiled as she recalled their first meeting as mentor-mentee years ago. Armond had worn an impeccably tailored suit, complete with a nattily designed pocket square that matched his socks. At the time, Victoria thought he would be difficult to work for, and she was right. But buried beneath his haughty demeanor was a big heart, and their shared values of compassion for others had drawn them into a fast, enduring friendship. After Victoria was fired, Armond eventually quit and his father convinced him to return to LA to help run Renoir Productions.

Walking into her apartment, she made a beeline to her fridge, pulled out the bottle of champagne she'd bought for his visit, and quickly stuck it into the temperature-controlled wine rack he'd given her as a Christmas gift. She'd forgotten to do it before she'd left that morning and both Armond and Kat insisted—snobs that they were—that champagne, and anything else they drank, had to be the correct temperature. As far as Victoria was concerned, as long as it had a cork instead of a screw top, it was good enough. Rolling her eyes as she thought about her two best friends' proclivities for the finer things in life, the intercom buzzed. Pushing the button, she heard, "Let me in."

"Sir, yes sir," she responded, and within a few minutes, Armond was walking through her door.

"Well, my pet. It's good to see you. You look fabulous! And a chignon with your hair? Aren't we all grown up," Armond said, holding her at arm's length before drawing her into a hug.

God, he smells good, Victoria thought. *Why have I never realized that before?* "Well, my friend, I'm sure it's a hairstyle you haven't seen in a while, living amongst all those Holly-wood hotties with their long, fake extensions. Perhaps it's a bit too classy for you now."

Armond smiled, accepting the challenge. "My my my! Hasn't your tongue gotten sharper since you're now large and in charge of your own firm? Perhaps a bit too shrew-like, though. You might want to tone that down if you ever want to get a man in your life. Shrew is not the flavor of the month."

"Hmm, I think I'll pass on taking advice from someone who hasn't had a real relationship in—what is it—three years now."

"Touché," Armond said as they laughed. "It's good to see you, Victoria. Seriously, you have no idea the idiots I deal with all day."

She grabbed the champagne and handed it to Armond. "I bought your favorite and chilled it to your snotty perfection. I'll let you open it, as I'm sure there's some equally snotty way you want that done." Turning, Victoria pulled down her new crystal flutes. She'd be just fine drinking out of paper cups but Armond always insisted on proper glass-ware, pontificating that drinking should be an experience. She had learned early on not to fight him on the little things. Besides, she always learned something.

"Watch and learn, my South Side beauty," he said, adeptly popping the top with barely any effort yet still pro-ducing the celebratory noise. "Let's sit on your balcony before we head to dinner. I have a few things to discuss with you, and I'd like a moment to relax after that harrowing touchdown."

Settling into one of Victoria's balcony chairs, Armond nodded appreciatively at the changes she'd made to her deck. "I like the updates. It looks good."

Victoria looked around and nodded. "It turned out just as I pictured. The flooring is tile but has a wood look, and the flower boxes can stay out year-round. My mother and I always gardened together, and I've missed it."

Armond took Victoria's hand as they sat quietly enjoying each other's company, watching the hustle and bustle of her neighborhood streets as people headed home or out after work. While they had always been touchy-feely with each other, Victoria was surprised to feel a thread of...something. Unsettled, she pulled her hand out of his grasp and pretended to fix a strand of hair. "So, tell me what's new with your gold-encrusted Hollywood life?"

"Quite a bit, actually. Suddenly, being an investor in a Hollywood film and seeing your name on screen in the credits, has turned out to be quite the thing. We have more interest than we have films, here and in Asia. Obviously, we'd like to nail down as many investors as possible while interest is at its peak, but we need to find the ones that are financially solid, will abide by our contract terms, and understand their investment doesn't mean their mistress gets to star in the film. For foreign investors, we also need to ensure their money is from legitimate sources. The last thing we need is to be the target of a money laundering investigation."

"Armond, I'm happy to get more work, but I don't have experience in the financial arena. Wouldn't you be better off hiring someone who has done that?"

"I trust you and your instincts, and that quality is hard to find. Remember, you were the one who warned me something wasn't quite right when we were still at the firm. While I didn't doubt you, I didn't take you as seriously as I should have. That won't happen again. And, since I don't expect either of us to be experts in the investment banking arena, I've hired an outside firm and investigators to handle that part. What I need is someone to help me with the overall picture, look at all the data to determine the best investors for our films. My father's given us strict instructions not to allow any weirdos or crackpots, as he so elegantly put it. That's where you come into play."

"Armond, you've got a good sense of smell too. I doubt you'll really need me."

"You're also a contract geek. You know how I hate to read all those incredibly boring paragraphs. You love that stuff, and you're good at it. There. Now you have the whole truth and nothing but the truth," Armond said, raising his right hand.

"If I said yes, and emphasis on if, when would you want to leave and how long would I need to be away from the office?"

"I'd like to leave in ten days. We'll take Renoir Productions' private plane, so we can come and go as we please. The first round of meetings is in Hong Kong. Then, depending on how those go, we'll decide if we need to continue to Singapore. I'd prefer, since we'll be all the way on the other side of the world, to meet as many potential investors as we can. Then, when Renoir Productions is ready to green-light future films, we'll have a stable of pre-qualified investors to pitch."

"It sounds amazing, really. Other than Bermuda, I've never been out of the United States. But I've got a new firm to run and clients that need me," Victoria said as she walked over to grab the champagne from the ice bucket to refill their glasses. "I just don't see how I can make it work."

"I thought you might say that, and I have some ideas. If you can clear your court schedule, I don't think you'll have a problem. I've asked my staff to ensure we each have everything we need in our hotel rooms to keep our offices running. They've assured me there won't be a problem. And, with the hourly rate we're willing to pay you, frankly, I don't see how you can say no," Armond ended, handing Victoria a folded piece of paper. "Open it."

Victoria opened the paper and looked up at Armond with wide eyes and her mouth open.

"I thought that might impact your decision," he said, smiling.

Throwing the paper into the air, Victoria walked over to Armond and held out her hand to shake. Just before he took it, she pulled it back. "Not so fast. We still need to work out a few additional points."

"You're kidding me, aren't you, my pet?" Armond responded in the uppity tone she had heard him use when he was getting ready to put someone in their place.

"No, I'm not, and you can get rid of that tone. It doesn't work on me. I'll need a hefty retainer, and I want to be paid for my travel time. If you can agree to those terms, we have a deal." Victoria held her breath as she again held out her hand. After too long a pause, worried that perhaps she had pushed too far, she prompted, "Armond, what will it be?"

Armond looked into her eyes, grabbed her hand and pulled her into his lap. "We have a deal," he said, inhaling her distinctive scent as she instinctively clasped his shoulders for balance. For a moment, he admired the flecks of gold in her eyes, surprised he had never noticed before. Catching himself, he quickly shifted his weight forward to help her up and out of his lap. Grabbing his phone off the balcony railing, he began to flow through his emails. Without looking up, he ordered, a bit more gruffly than he intended, "Now, go do whatever it is you need to do to get ready so we can get out of this matchbox and celebrate!"

Victoria began running the numbers in her head as she walked back to her room to change. By her rough calculations, the amount she would earn over a three-month period working for Renoir Productions would almost equal the total revenue she had earned all of last year. It was obscene. "Armond," she said as she walked out of her room ready for dinner, "do you realize how much money your company will end up paying me for this work?"

"Indeed." Armond drawled haughtily as he attempted to recover his aloof demeanor. "If you're going to carry on like a street urchin laying eyes on a shiny penny for the first time, I might have to rethink my offer." Putting a bit of distance between himself and Victoria, he turned and took the empty bottle into the kitchen. Realizing he was being unnecessarily harsh, he explained, "Victoria, you do realize that I would have to pay even the most average of East Coast lawyers almost three times the hourly rate I've offered you? So really, you're a bargain. Now, I'm hungry and your apartment is quite stifling. Are we having dinner, or are you going to continue with your errant ramblings?"

Victoria almost laughed out loud. It felt like old times when she'd had to listen to Armond's cocky bullshit.

The more things change, the more they stay the same, she thought.

Standing in front of her hall mirror, she undid her chignon and easily twisted her long brown hair into a casual knot. Finishing, she turned to look at Armond.

"While I would typically take great delight in ripping you a new one for insulting my home and acting like a spoiled little rich boy, I'll let it go tonight. Hell, I'll go so far as to even let you pick the restaurant, even if it is one of those horrid sushi places you like. God knows why, though. I mean, if you take even five minutes to research, you'll find scientific documentation that sushi allows live worms to set up camp in your stomach. You don't want to hear what you have to do to get rid of them. Absolutely disgusting—"

Quirking one of his perfectly manicured eyebrows, Armond interrupted. "Is there any chance you could cease this tirade, delightful as it is, at least until we get in a cab?"

Victoria got a wicked gleam in her eyes. "Of course, Armond." She was always happy to oblige and play haughty to his spoiled brat routine. "Since I'm such a legal bargain for Renoir, the tab's on you tonight. I'll get the next one after I send you my first official, obscenely large bill for flying around Asia on a private jet." Turning, she headed out the door to enjoy a fabulous dinner with her newest client.

CHAPTER
15

"**L**ISTEN, I KNOW you wanted to have her on your team, but I think in the long run it will be for the best," Armond said, sipping his coffee. "Mary, thank you. It's perfect as always. If you ever decide to live in sunny California or if you tire of working for this ballbuster," he continued nodding at Victoria, "you'll always have a home at Renoir Productions."

"Oh, for heaven's sake. Are we finished with the love fest? We're all painfully aware that you're Mary's favorite and that she only gets flat whites for you. Now, can we continue our meeting?" Without waiting for an answer, Kat forged ahead on speakerphone from her Houston office. "Armond, can you explain why you think the information Jenny has is worthless? As I recall, she thought she had a smoking gun that would help V's case."

"A bit pissy today, aren't we, Kat?" Armond responded. "Let me guess, another riveting date with one of Houston's finest?"

"If I were you, I wouldn't start on dating unless you'd like a deep dive into your trysts with some of California's best bimbos," Kat lashed back. "You know, we get the tabloids out here in little ole Houston too."

"Touché. We'll call a truce for now. To answer your question, it turned out it was simply an overheard conversation about types of people Acker, Smith & McGowen prefers to hire. No real smoking gun, at least that I can discern. But then again, I'm not an employment lawyer. Robert, perhaps you've heard something that you can use?" Armond finished, looking at Robert.

Projecting Jenny's name followed by a list of words onto Victoria's conference room wall, Robert answered, "The fact that certain traits might be favored by the firm is not particularly unusual. We don't even know for sure if these are preferential traits, but assuming they are, some of them are not what you would expect a hard-charging international firm to want in its talent pool. The words Jenny remembered hearing— empathetic, emotional, pleaser, and giver— aren't usually associated with the kinds of lawyers most firms would want to hire. Maybe it was a list of what they didn't want in their rank and file."

Kat jumped back into the discussion. "We need to find out if this even exists."

"Even if we confirm the existence of some sort of a personality index, the firm can give us whatever explanation it wants for its purpose. It can be dismissed as anything from a list of traits it looks for in paralegals, to those it wants in its scholarship recipients," Robert responded.

"Armond, did Jenny have any more details about what she overheard?" Kat asked.

"She didn't," Armond answered. "She thought it might lead us to Adam. For some reason, she believes if there is any wrongdoing at the firm, Adam is behind it. She really has nothing more to offer."

"At this point, we'll need her to be on standby as a potential witness in case we discover corroborating evidence that then makes what she overheard relevant. Right now, though, we've got nothing of substance," Robert noted.

"I really think this is a dead end, but let's hang onto the thread just in case," Kat said.

"Agreed," Robert said.

Robert looked at Armond. "As much as I hate to do this, I need to ask you to leave so we can continue our discussions. Unlike Jenny, who may only be a foundation witness, you will be a substantive witness."

"Understood. I have appointments the rest of the day anyway. Apparently, there are a lot of—what do you call yourselves out here—ah yes, salt-of-the-earthers clamoring to invest in film." Armond shook Robert's hand, then nodded at Victoria. "I'd like to wrap up the engagement agreement between Renoir and your firm tonight, as well as the final trip details. My last meeting is tomorrow at noon, and I'm leaving as soon as it's done. I need to be back in LA for a dinner meeting. Will that timing work for you?"

"It's perfect. If we can meet around five tonight, that will give us enough time," Victoria answered.

"See you then. Robert, Mary, I'll see you the next time I'm in town. Kat," he said leaning toward the speaker, "let's connect this week."

As soon as she heard the door shut, Kat asked, "Okay, what the hell is going on: an engagement agreement, trips, planning meetings?"

Victoria smiled. "Renoir Productions is about to triple my annual revenue. I'll tell you about it later. Robert, where are we on tracking down potential witnesses? Did the firm answer our interrogatories about the identities and locations of the female attorneys who worked at the firm?"

Robert flashed the answers on the wall and told Kat to open the email he'd sent so she could follow along. "They did, and big surprise, they have no idea about the current location of the majority of those no longer at the firm. But, they did give us a list of names, so I've hired an investigator to track them down."

Looking at the screen, Victoria nodded. "I know a few of them. Hopefully I can add some meat to the bones about what they did at the firm and where they stood in line for partnership."

"V, some of these names look familiar. Didn't a few of them contact you after you were let go, interested in being involved in any litigation you might bring? What the hell happened to them?" Kat asked.

"Yeah, they did. Bizarrely, when I called them, those who hadn't disappeared told me they were no longer interested. I'm not wasting my time and energy on people who don't have the backbone to stand up for themselves."

"While I understand your frustration, Victoria," Robert began, "empathy is critical. Obviously, it would be better if we had witnesses willing to testify they worked fourteen-hour days for that golden partnership ring only to be tossed out at the last minute, but it's not unusual in this type of case for them to be all-in at the beginning and chicken out once they realize their names, stories, and testimonies will be bandied about publicly. Remember, some of them went on to work at other firms, and they don't want to muck up their careers by getting in the crosshairs of three of the most powerful lawyers in the country. We can't just toss them aside. We need to continue communicating with them, in hopes that one or more will change her mind and agree to testify."

"I get it but nothing will change unless women say enough is enough, support one another, and do something about it," Victoria responded, feeling suddenly overwhelmed and tired. She really didn't want to be the lone woman fighting the firm. She never asked for her personal business to be the fodder for the press and the courts. Yet, here she was, and she was determined to see it through. At times, she couldn't help but feel annoyed that others apparently expected her to fix the problem while they sat back and watched.

Sensing her best friend was feeling overwhelmed, Kat jumped in. "Why don't we see what we find out about these potential witnesses once the investigator finishes his report, and then reconvene? There's no point in going round and round about whether they will or won't testify when we haven't even found them yet. Besides, your situation is different. You have the Miami case against the insurance company and the misdeeds of its board, you were the one trying to point out to your firm the problems you saw with the claim handling, and Armond is completely on your side. You're probably one of the few women who has left the firm who actually has support from one of its male partners. All of that is good for your case, I'd think. Robert?"

"I agree. There are a number of facts in V's case that are different from the typical case. Let's see what the investigator turns up. Then, we'll make some decisions. In the meantime, I think we should continue working on our trial strategy."

"Great, count me in. V?" Kat asked.

"I think you and Robert should proceed without me at this point, as it looks like I'll be out of the country with Armond. Assuming she's not winging her way to the Pacific Coast to join Renoir Productions, Mary will set the next meeting for you two," Victoria added quickly before Kat could begin interrogation.

Mary laughed. "I'll let you know if I change my mind, but so far, I'm happy working for Ms. Ballbuster."

CHAPTER
16

"THEY'RE ON THE move to locate women who worked at the firm. They're quite serious about finding them, and they're paying me a hefty sum to do the job."

They stood huddled in the alley behind a nondescript bar in Chicago's Old Town neighborhood. It was a moonless, black night and a cold, soaking rain had begun to fall. While he didn't always like his clients, this one was different. There was a strong stench of rotten running through him. He couldn't quite put his finger on what it was, and truth be told, he didn't need to know, at least not yet. As long as the money continued to show up in his offshore account, he was happy to do his job. He had no qualms about getting paid by two masters. His own special brand of ethics allowed them to coexist. *No one gives a shit about ethics anymore,* he thought, *and by the time this ends, I'll be long gone.*

"Here's a list of some of the women and their current locations. The other women you won't be able to locate. Understood?"

"I have a reputation to uphold. I can't simply say I can't find these other women. I need to show what I did to track them."

"Here's a news flash. I don't give a rat's ass about your reputation, but go ahead and tell them whatever story you need to maintain control. I'm making your job easy by telling you the outcome you'll provide," his contact said, as he turned and walked away.

CHAPTER

17

EVER SINCE HER daughter saved her life, Gretchen had experienced nightmares. They'd come slowly at first, like fog floating gently into town. But they'd picked up steam, and the most recent ones had her moaning and crying so loudly her husband now routinely woke her to stop whatever terror she was dreaming.

She was getting so little sleep she had a hard time staying awake to care for her daughter. The other morning she'd almost fallen asleep at the wheel driving to one of her daughter's classes. It was only her daughter's squeal of delight at something she'd seen outside that snapped her awake. Gretchen realized she was becoming a danger to herself and her family and could no longer delay facing the consequences of her conduct.

Close to two hours after leaving home, Gretchen pulled off the highway and drove another three miles down a two-lane road, weaving through dense forests and bobbing over rolling hills. She made another turn and finally saw the sign announcing her destination was just two miles down the road. Turning onto the town's main street, she pulled into a parking spot for bank customers only. After a brief argument in her head, she walked in and handed her key to the lone banker sitting at his desk, playing with his phone. She signed in as requested and waited.

A few minutes later, Gretchen stood in the cold and eerily silent, private safety deposit box room and waited for the banker to leave and shut the door. She took out her key and looked at it. *Once I begin this journey,* she promised herself, *there will be no turning back.* She drew her shoulders back and with determination, opened the box. Two items lay inside. Gathering her resolve, she picked up the thumb drive and then the folded paper. Everything about that day more than two years ago came rushing back.

They had just returned from the beach after enjoying one of the last summer days before her daughter's first day of pre-school. When they'd walked through their front door, an envelope was lying on the floor, having obviously been slipped under. Gretchen had thought nothing of it as it was the way countless other work assignments had been delivered in the past, particularly if it was something important to one of the partners. She had tossed it on her desk and gone about the rest of her day.

Once her daughter was in bed and her husband was in the shower, she wandered into her office and picked up the envelope. Turning it over, she noticed it was marked confidential, and when she opened it, everything changed. Only two things were inside: the thumb drive and note. She had popped the thumb drive into her laptop and stared dumbfounded at the unfolding scene. Her first lucid thought was that someone was going to be mortified when they realized they'd mistakenly sent her a personal video. It was a sex party of some sort. Everyone had masks on and little else. Then a door in the back of the room opened and shock replaced curiosity. Someone who looked exactly like her entered and was the only unmasked person in the room. The camera zoomed in on her face, and a man off camera called her name. Over the next few minutes, her spitting image began performing a variety of sexual acts. She never watched the end.

Shaking her head in an effort to keep the past at bay, she forced herself to open the note and reread the words that had changed her life:

No one need know.

Gretchen suddenly felt dizzy and sweat broke out on her forehead. She grabbed the wastebasket under the table, fell to her knees and retched over and over until the retching turned to tears.

Sitting on the ground, she put her head in her hands and tried to catch her breath. Detesting herself for her weakness, she grabbed the counter and pulled herself up, shoving the items back into the box. After cleaning herself as best she could, she opened the door, signaled to the banker, and walked with him and waited while he used his key and then hers, to return the box to its crypt.

Gretchen walked out of the bank, got into her car, and sat and watched the people in the small town walk by, intent on their daily lives. While she was exhausted, she was surprised at how settled she felt. Recognizing she could not do it alone, Gretchen made the call she should have made years ago. She had failed today, but she would be damned if she would fail again.

CHAPTER
18

JENNY LOVED HER new home. It hugged a cliff in Corona Del Mar and seemed to hang over the ocean. While the structure itself was beautiful with west-facing glass walls, blanched wood floors, imported Italian marble, and fireplaces framed with hand-carved reclaimed wood, the feature that had sold her was its private access to Little Corona Beach. When the realtor had walked her down the long, flower-laden private stairs and opened the private access gate, she had been dumbfounded. *There really wasn't another word for it,* she thought, recalling the magic of that day. Spread out before her had been a small beach cove, hidden by rugged cliffs that cocooned it in privacy. Black rock formations jutted up along its coastline, holding miniature oceans complete with sea urchins, snails, crabs, and the occasional star fish—all caught and available to observe until the next tide changed the scene. There was also a swimming lane, built by Mother Nature, between a string of rocks that ran from the shoreline to where the cove opened to the deep ocean. She had envisioned herself swimming there every morning. That had been six months ago, and she'd never been happier.

She had a routine she only varied, reluctantly, when a storm was rushing in or the June gloom was too heavy. Every morning, she would pour coffee into her favorite cup and walk down to her ocean paradise. If the weather was warm and sunny, she'd swim laps. If it was too chilly, she'd sit on the beach, finish her coffee, walk back up, and use her lap pool. In the evening, she'd sit on her deck, drink a glass of wine, and simply inhale all California had to offer. She had decided that it was the sound of the waves she connected with. For her, they were invigorating in the morning and calming in the evening.

As she took her first sip of wine, she heard her phone. Frowning at the interruption of her private time, she reluctantly headed in to answer. When she read the caller ID, she scowled and demanded, "What could you and I possibly have to say to one another?"

"Hello, Mother," Billy said. "It sounds like you're still miffed about that little tête-à-tête in court a few weeks ago. It would appear you're going to overreact."

Hearing her only child sound so foreign and as if he couldn't care less about her filled her with sadness. It appeared that over the past year, she'd not only lost her husband, but her son too. Suddenly feeling exhausted and depressed, she asked again, "Billy, what could you and I have to discuss at this point in time?"

Sensing her disappointment in him, he became angry.

"Well, what did you think would happen?"

"Excuse me?" Jenny asked, not understanding his point.

"I know that tone of voice. How the hell did you think I'd turn out when you allowed Father to work me all day in the fields and then keep me locked up in meetings all night? If you didn't want me to turn out like him, perhaps you should have intervened," Billy finished, trying his best to make her feel sorry for him.

His little speech only fueled her. Standing up straight and turning to look out at the ocean, she responded in a steely voice, "How dare you blame me for your life of privilege. You grew up in the lap of luxury, with one of the largest tobacco plantations in the country as your home and inheritance, assuming your father doesn't lose it all paying his legal fees."

Billy had never heard his mother speak like this—ever. During his childhood, she was the obedient wife and loyal mother. She was always there for whatever his father or he needed or wanted. He wasn't quite sure how to handle this change, so he did what always worked with women. He turned on the charm.

"Mother, I apologize. We got off to a bad start, and it's my fault. I called to reconnect with you. I don't want anything to come between us. That's why I was so hurt when I found out you were trying to enter an appearance in Victoria's case."

Jenny could hardly believe what she was hearing. Apparently, her son thought her so stupid that all it took to get back into her good graces was a bit of charm. Shifting into trial lawyer mode and negating any personal feelings, she calmly responded, "I'm glad to hear that Billy. I must say I was quite stunned to hear you threaten me and with a lie about moving family money overseas. Why would you ever think to do that?"

"I was desperate."

"About what? You have a sterling reputation in the legal community and with women's groups. What are you worried about?" Jenny asked, genuinely surprised at her son's candor.

"I'm not worried about me or the firm, but having my own mother on the other side of a case against my firm? My partners wouldn't have understood, and frankly, they would have asserted immense pressure on me to handle you. If I'm being honest, I didn't understand it either. Really, after the divorce you and Father just went through, I felt having you work with people who are trying to hurt my reputation was the last thing I could handle. I've even contacted a therapist to help me handle all the family changes," Billy said, mustering the sad sack tone that had always worked with his mother.

"Billy, I've never known you to need a therapist. I'm sorry if the divorce and all of this is causing you that much stress. You should have come to me sooner. I'm always in your corner. That was one of the reasons I wanted to work on the case. I thought perhaps I could broker a resolution," Jenny said, balancing mixed feelings, not at all sure she could trust her son's sudden emotional barfing.

Feeling like he had his opening, Billy suggested, "Well, if you think you have a way to bring the parties together, I'm always open to that. As you know, there are rarely winners in litigation."

"I'm always here for you, Billy. I'll keep my eyes open and see what I can do. We'll talk again soon. Bye, and Billy, I love you."

"Yes, love you, too, Mother," Billy answered, out of duty and pleased with the way the call had gone.

CHAPTER
19

"**W**E NEED TO ensure our firm is never mentioned in the same sentence as that ruling," Adam nagged Billy for the third time since last week.

"Adam, your whining is getting old. There is no way we'll be associated with that decision. Except perhaps if you continue to talk about it in public," Billy spat as he waved his arm around, pointing out that he, Trever, and Adam were sitting in the business club at O'Hare waiting for their flight to Japan.

"Well, it's been headline news since the judge issued her opinion," Adam persisted. They each had private berths on the plane, so once they boarded, any further discussion would be difficult. "If the reports are correct, it's the first time a US court has allowed a child to be separated from his American parent to be raised in a foreign country."

"Adam, the consulate general is the one who got us an audience with the Japanese trade minister. You understand that, don't you?"

"Of course I understand, which is why I'm concerned some dogged reporter will be able to connect the dots be tween the judge, our firm, and our new engagement in Japan. What if the judge can't handle the pressure? She is, after all, a family law judge. I highly doubt she has any experience being in the limelight like she is now. What if she cracks?" Adam persisted.

Leaning forward with his cigar clenched to the side of his mouth, Trever intervened. "Adam, there is no reason Her Honor will crack, as you so elegantly put it. It would mean she would not only lose her seat on the bench, but she would also lose her law license and her pension."

Looking up at the server, Trever smiled. "Ah, thank you. Just in time." After handing a heavy crystal glass to each of his partners, he raised his. "This is some of the finest Texas bourbon ever made. To us, to our newest office in Japan, and to the opening of the firm's new trade department. I have a feeling we're going to continue to be in high demand by countries renegotiating their US deals."

Adam refused to be ignored. "I want certain assurances before we leave this topic."

Lowering his glass and looking directly at Adam, Trever asked, "What exactly do you want, Adam?"

"Is our usual backup in place for this judge?"

"Adam," Trever growled, "I love you like a brother. I really do. But you need to let it go. Believe me when I tell you there is an overabundance of information in the vault on her. If she ever thinks about opening her mouth, for even one second, she'll be crushed under a mound of shit. Are you going to trust I have this handled, as I've done for the past fifteen years, or do you want to know the details? Keep in mind that the burden on you and your potential liability, should any of this become public knowledge, only increases if I enlighten you."

"Trever, we each have our specialties and burdens. I just wanted to ensure you were taking it seriously."

"It's under control," Trever answered as he passed around their monthly profit and loss statements. "Adam, as much of a pain in the ass as you can be"—Trever paused to clink his glass with Billy over their shared opinion of Adam, just to yank his chain a bit more—"you're to be congratulated on the inroads you've made in Asia. The increase to our bottom line because of your new clients has already allowed us to surpass our projections for the year."

"Yes, well. Neither of you are a walk in the park," Adam answered, giving his pithiest response. He hated the way Billy and Trever always acted superior to him, especially since he had the highest IQ of all of them. He was currently off the charts on revenue produced this year, and if he maintained this pace, he was going to insist on having the final say in all firm decisions. Since their inception, that role had belonged to Billy, but Adam had been chomping at the bit to take control and in the time-honored way of law firms, whoever brought in the biggest book of business, ruled the roost. Adam expected to be leading the firm into the next decade, but now was not the time to discuss the changing of the guard. "Take a look at my forecast through the end of the year. I'm projecting another increase, and it's primarily due to my Asian connections. In fact," Adam continued, deciding now was as good a time as any to let them know, "I won't be flying back with you. I'm making a few stops to meet with new clients in Singapore and Thailand."

Billy and Trever couldn't quite figure out how Adam had gotten such a toehold in the Far East. Trever raised his glass once again. "Well, Adam, I'm impressed. When it comes to Asia and business, it seems you can find a whisper in a whirlwind."

"Yes, congratulations," Billy said. "By the way, we all need to get our final projections for the next year in by the beginning of November. The firm's annual meeting committee needs to compile them to let our attorneys know how many hours they'll need to work and bill next year. Adam, would you consider speaking to the associates at the annual meeting about how you've forged a new path into Asia over the past two years?"

Adam smirked. "No thanks. You know I hate speaking at those events. That's Trever's show."

"That's fine. I enjoy whipping our little widgets into billing frenzies," Trever responded, still sucking on his unlit cigar. "While we're on the subject, would you like me to make some of those stopovers with you? If some of those companies will hire our strategic consulting group to help grow their businesses, we can get two bangs for our buck."

"You can't seriously be continuing with your consulting business after the insurance company fiasco," Adam responded, shocked.

"Of course I am. It was a huge moneymaker. And, our strategic advice was taken totally out of context by a board that wanted more than a fair rate of return," Trever said with a straight face, looking directly at Adam, begging him to challenge his statement.

"Whatever you say, but I'll tell you one thing. You'd better hope that's the case 'cause I have no intention of going down with that ship."

Billy had watched enough of the accelerating schoolyard behavior between them. Picking up his bag, he stood up.

"Gentlemen, may I remind you that we are all in this together. There is no backing out now. Whatever one of us knows, so, too, do the other two. Now, I suggest we table this and get on our flight. It's time to make Japan our newest income stream."

CHAPTER

20

L OOKING AT HER reflection in the cracked mirror, she was shocked to see so many bones sticking out everywhere. She couldn't remember a time she had been so thin. *No, not thin*, she thought, *emaciated*. And her hair was…what? Disgusting was the only word that came to mind. She had been OCD about lice since she was about ten years old and began itching after wearing a wig for a school play. She still clearly recalled the night she'd been reading in bed and scratched her head, only to see a louse drop and scurry across the page. Even now, the thought made her want to vomit.

"Where the hell is everyone?" she groaned out loud, frantically scratching and shaking her head to see if anything would fall out. She could feel the panic building over the past—what—weeks, months? She had tried to maintain her composure, understanding that losing her sense of self would give whoever did this an advantage. "Someone must be looking for me. They must know I never showed up at the meeting." She'd heard somewhere that the best thing to do to keep your sanity in solitary confinement is talk out loud. She had no idea what that did, or if it even worked. But she sure as hell was going to try it. "Why hasn't anyone come to get me out of this hellhole?" *Surely, some of my clients have contacted the US office by now.* "Where are the Marines and the American Embassy?"

Without warning, tears began to slide down Serena's cheeks. Except for an aunt she saw every few years, she had no family. Her parents had died when she was in college and she'd been so busy traveling the world, she'd had little time for relationships. Her chances of being missed by anyone other than her peers or clients were slim. That's what scared her the most.

Hearing the door bolt click, she quickly wiped at her eyes and sat up as best she could. An expensively dressed and well-kept woman stepped inside. Her hair swung long and red, ending in soft curls around her waist. She had almond-shaped eyes that slanted distinctly up toward the outer corners of her face, but it was their color—a mosaic-like mix of sea green, emerald, and moss—that was most striking. Judging the woman to be in her early fifties, Serena was amazed she still had the presence of mind to wonder how much Botox had been pumped into that face. Feeling stronger at that thought, she stared straight back at the woman.

"Well, well. I see the reports are accurate. You still have your composure and spine, not always good things to hold on to in your new line of work," the woman said, holding her newest asset by her chin, turning her head from one side to the other. "Lovely features. I understand you're older than I prefer although you don't look it. What are you? Thirty-two? Four?"

"Listen. I don't know who you are or what this is about, but I'm an American citizen. You sound American. Please, help me. I'll reward you a hundred times over," Serena heard herself begging, and didn't care.

The woman was silent until she finished her 360 degree inspection. "Oh my. I'm afraid you've mistaken me for someone who gives a shit. And while I have a definite interest in my financial well-being, I make more than you could ever possibly pay me. Finally, to wrap up our little meeting, whatever my country of origin, my allegiance is to me, myself, and I." Dusting her hands together as if to knock off any filth she may have picked up while in the room, she paused and tilted her head. "Let's talk about what I'm interested in, shall we? I make money selling girls and sex. And you, my smelly thing, were given to me to use as I see fit. My my! You must have twisted someone the wrong way."

"You can't be serious. I'm a lawyer with a large international firm. I came here on business. There's been a mistake," Serena said with tears in her eyes, beginning to feel desperate.

"No, no mistake," the woman replied calmly. "We've been expecting you for some time. I think I'll put you in the general farm to start. Resisting only makes it worse. In fact, resisting often ends up forcing me to sell you to a rather violent but well-paying class of men. Up to you, of course. I'll give you forty-eight hours to consider how you'd like to begin your service with me." She turned and looked back at her new asset. "I suggest you pull yourself together. You're going to need all your strength. The sooner you accept your situation, the better off you'll be."

Hearing the door shut and the lock snap back into place, Serena rushed to the door, sobbing and pounding on it until her knuckles were bloodied. She banged her head against it over and over again until she felt herself fall listless to the floor and was rewarded with darkness.

CHAPTER
21

JACK PRIDED HIMSELF on his ability to see around corners. He had worked years to earn his reputation as hard-hitting, aggressive, and eerily clairvoyant. He was one of a handful of trial lawyers Fortune 500 companies turned to when their reputation or bottom line was threatened. While he handled a wide range of matters, his specialty was employment cases, particularly those involving discrimination; racial, disability, age or any other type a clever plaintiff's lawyer could conjure up. His favorite, however, involved gender.

Leaning back in his custom-made, caramel-colored leather chair, he gazed at the far wall of his office. Doing so always brought immense satisfaction. At least twenty different magazine covers and articles hung there, each framed with a plaque touting the name and date of the piece. He perused some of his favorites: "The Trial Lawyer's Lawyer," "The King of the Courtroom," "Do Female Jurors Stand a Chance?"

Jack pushed his chair back from his desk, walked over, and took one of the frames off the wall. He read out loud to hear the words and allow them to permeate his soul.

Plaintiffs' counsel admit to wondering whether they should ever have women on their juries if Jack O'Leary is at the defendant's table. After a jury returned a verdict against a female plaintiff, one of the jurors confessed, "With those dark brown eyes, coal-black hair curling just above his shirt collar, and easy charm, it's hard to resist whatever story he tells."

Placing the plaque lovingly back in its place, Jack opened his door and stuck his head out just far enough. "Molly, call a meeting for the associates assigned to the firm matter. Two o'clock this afternoon." Jack shut the door before he even heard an acknowledgement, knowing his word was her command.

* * *

Molly made certain all the associates were seated in the conference room. She knew her boss, and he had made it perfectly clear when she'd first started working for him that it was his time that mattered. She had kept him waiting on the phone once while trying to get his client on the line, but she never made that mistake again. Knocking and opening his door, Molly leaned in. "They're waiting for you in the war room. Would you like me in the meeting?"

"No, but get me out of there in sixty minutes. No more, no less," Jack ordered as he walked past.

Jack never carried notes or an electronic device. He believed it to be a sign of weakness. "If you're going to be a trial lawyer," he often pontificated when he lectured the firm's incoming class of wannabe litigators, "you can never depend on pen or paper. Everything you need must be in your head." Of course, what Jack never told the new associates was that he was one of the rare 2 percent of the population that had a photographic memory. That quality, of course, was particularly handy for cross-examining a witness or rehabilitating one of his own during trial.

Walking into the war room, he shut the door loudly. Without a welcome to his team, he barked, "Okay, where do we stand?"

The associates who chose to stick it out with Jack were stressed out of their minds. Half of them either drank heavily or were partial to prescription medication. Each of them hoped for litigation fame and fortune and so, dutifully followed in Jack's wake. While he didn't require his team to function without pad or pen, many tried with the hope of impressing him so he would choose them as second chair on one of his trials.

Samantha responded. "We've found that over the past five years, the firm has lost more than forty female lawyers."

Holding up his hand, Jack barked, "Speak deliberately. What the hell do you mean by lost? I doubt you mean we've misplaced them."

Samantha had been on Jack's team for three years now and while used to his bullshit, she had never gotten comfortable with it. "Right. No, of course not. At least forty female lawyers have left the firm. All but one of them—the plaintiff in the case, Victoria Rodessa—quit of their own accord."

Jack interrupted Samantha's dissertation. "What is the norm, for firms our size and the next size down, number of associates that leave? What number of them are women, and how do we compare?"

Jason stood. "That's my area." Clearing his throat, he began to tick off the information. "There are currently thirty US firms with more than five hundred attorneys. Of that thirty, we are the only firm that has experienced such a large attrition of female associates. The next closest firm has almost one thousand lawyers, and they've had sixty associates leave over the past five years, but only twenty were female. Our female attrition rate is almost double that of the firm that is the closest comparison. After that, the comparisons get even worse." Jason turned to the associates sitting beside him and passed out the chart he created. "If a picture is worth a thousand words, then this picture comparing our firm's stats to others is *War and Peace*," he finished. While Jason knew he was grandstanding, he had worked with Jack for more than seven years and figured it was now or never for partnership.

Jack examined the chart and furrowed his brow. Getting up, he went over to his favorite prop, the white board, and drew one simple symbol:

?

Tapping it with his black marker, he asked, "Why? What's the explanation we're going to give the jury? What's our theme?" Jack looked around at the lawyers at the table. Not one of them moved. "Well, well, isn't it exciting to be in this brain trust?" Without warning, the marker sailed across the room and slammed into the wall. With all eyes riveted on him, Jack continued in a menacingly calm voice, "Judging by your responses, your answer is you have no fucking idea. That's perfect! I couldn't agree more! We'll tell the jurors that we have absolutely no fucking idea why all these women left the firm. Then, with that solid and persuasive storyline, we'll finish with, 'Ladies and gentlemen of the jury, while we have absolutely no fucking idea why all these women on the cusp of promising careers left our firm, believe us when we tell you it's all their fault, not ours.' Or, maybe we go with the tried and true, 'They got pregnant, didn't want to work those hours, or wanted work-life balance. Believe us when we tell you there's nothing to see here. And with that riveting defense, we ask that you rule in favor of our firm and throw Ms. Rodessa's case out,'" Jack finished, almost breathless as he had run his sentences together.

There was complete silence in the room. The associates had seen these micro temper bursts build to crescendo many times. They always began the same way: unexpectedly. The game they all played now was to wait and see who would be the first to cave under the pressure of the utter silence that followed, and speak.

"Jack, we just got this information. We haven't yet developed our theme of the case," Samantha vomited out, then inwardly sighed, annoyed she'd been the first to break the silence. Unless someone else jumped in, she'd be Jack's target. One minute, Jack was a fantastic mentor and the litigation team had all their oars rowing in the same direction, and the next, he was an absolute nutcase, shoving them all overboard, leaving them pushing each other underwater in a race to reach the shore.

"Are you seriously telling me that for the twelve months this case has been pending that this is where we are?" Jack looked at Samantha with a calmness everyone in the room knew wasn't real.

"Jack, a good six months was spent waiting for you to green light our investigation because you thought you could get her to drop her claim," Jason burst out, surprising himself. *Shit*, he thought, realizing he had just placed the blame squarely on Jack, a definite no-no in any law firm world.

Tag, I'm it. Jason could feel his peers move ever-so-subtly away from him as he maintained eye contact with Jack.

"Ah, I see," Jack responded, nodding his head in acknowledgement as he held a viselike stare to Jason's eyes. The tension grew in the room in direct correlation to the length of the silence. Suddenly, a loud knock on the door sounded like a cannon shot. No one moved. The knock came again, and this time Molly peeked around the door. "Jack, your next meeting is waiting in your office."

My God, not again, she thought as she looked around the room. You could smell the fear. Molly had seen these cult-like scenes too many times over the years: utter silence in a room full of grown-ups, all waiting like trapped animals for one person to explode.

Jack ignored Molly, looked slowly around the room, and said, with an eerie calm, "I want our theme within forty-eight hours." Then, he shot out the door, leaving behind a room full of mentally rattled and stressed out lawyers.

CHAPTER

22

"MARY, WOULD YOU see if Jenny is available? Once you get her on the line, come into my office, and the three of us will review the calendar for the next three weeks."

"I thought you might want to have that call, so I checked yesterday. Anytime works for her," Mary responded, handing Victoria her morning cappuccino. "Apparently, Mona has her working on a few of her divorce cases, so she's spending the day going over those files and getting up to speed."

"God, this tastes good. Thanks, Mary. I have no idea how people start their day without coffee, or for that matter, end their day without wine. Always makes me suspicious," Victoria noted, taking a seat at her desk. "I'd rather get any scheduling problems out of the way first thing, then I can focus on my cases the rest of the day."

"I'll be back in as soon as I get her on the line." Mary poked her head into Victoria's office five minutes later. "Okay, she's on the line," she said, walking over to Victoria's desk and pushing the button on their new conference lines.

"Jenny, hi. I've got Victoria with me," Mary said.

"V! How are you? Are you ready for your big Asia tour with Hollywood?" Jenny exclaimed.

"Jenny, I swear you are the happiest person I know. Aren't you ever cranky?" Victoria answered, sitting back in her chair and sipping her coffee.

"Well, Victoria, let me see if I can paint a picture. It's seven in the morning in California, I'm holding a freshly brewed cup of coffee, my sliding glass doors are open, and I'm looking out past my deck to an unobstructed view of the ocean. The morning sun is just beginning to reflect off the water, and in about thirty minutes, I'll walk down my flower-lined stairs to a rarely-used and so, essentially private beach, where I will swim laps with the sea creatures. Does that answer your question?" Jenny finished with a laugh.

"Oh, for heaven's sake. Enough. I get it, and in the future I shall do my best to remember never to question your cheery disposition," Victoria responded sarcastically.

Mary tapped her watch. "Victoria, you've got a new client coming at ten thirty. Unless you're completely ready for that meeting, we should begin. We have quite a bit to go over."

"Mary's right. Okay, Jenny. Welcome aboard. I'm very happy you'll be working with my firm. Having you on an of counsel basis will be a huge help. I've drafted and set for hearings all the motions to have you added as counsel on my cases until you can be admitted to the Illinois bar. Since you've passed the California and Georgia bars, I doubt you'll have much trouble getting reciprocity in Illinois. Until then, though, I'm advising the judges you're in the process of filing your character and fitness paperwork, and I can't see any problem in getting those motions granted."

"It looks like, at least from the material I've reviewed, I'll be handling discovery matters on your cases, which is exactly what I'm doing for Mona. Must be contagious," Jenny said, smiling to herself. She was well aware most lawyers practicing civil law hated discovery because it often involved reviewing hundreds of thousands of mind-numbing documents to find one piece of relevant information.

"I can't think of anything I like doing less. I'm sure Mona feels the same, but I want you far more involved than that. While I'll be available and have electronic access to the files, I'll be in a different time zone and hard to reach. I'm hoping you can handle any client issues that arise if I can't be reached immediately."

It felt good to be needed and back in the game after all those years of being a wife to Big Bill. *Big indeed. Big body, little dick*, she smirked and laughed out loud.

"Umm, something funny over there in la-la land?"

"Victoria, yes. I'm sorry. I was just thinking about how amazing it feels to be in the thick of things again after being married to that jackass for so long," Jenny answered.

"No worries. I get it. It's a win-win for both of us."

"I know you're trying to get out of town, but I do have a few questions. If you have some time now, I'd like to go through them," Jenny said.

Victoria looked at Mary and waited for her say-so. "You have about an hour now and then your schedule clears again near the end of the day," Mary answered.

Victoria nodded. "Okay, let's get through as much as we can now. Mary will set another call for the end of the day if we need it. I also want to introduce you to three of our clients who need to have their hands held more than the others. Mary," Victoria said, looking up, "you know who they are. If you'll set those calls for tomorrow and then send the client background information to Jenny so she can review it before the calls, that would be great."

"Got it," Mary said.

"Jenny, the stage is yours," Victoria said, feeling a bit of her anxiety ease about leaving both the country and the day-to-day of her practice for a few weeks.

* * *

Three hours later, Victoria came up for air. She walked out of her building and down the street to grab another cappuccino and hopefully, if she could maintain some semblance of self-control, avoid the pastries and eat something healthy. Taking one of the open tables by the window, she sat down and flipped through her notes from the morning. Pressing her speed dial, she waited.

"Ms. Fontaine's office. How may I help?"

"Emma, this is Victoria. I thought this was Kat's private mobile, not that I'm not always happy to chat with you. She too fancy to pick up her own calls now?" Victoria asked.

"Ms. V! It is so nice to hear your voice. The press has been hounding her day and night about that lil ole lawsuit she filed against the insurance company. She's had calls from reporters from almost every state. Two days ago, she walked into the office, threw her phone on my desk, looked at me, and said, 'Handle it.' So, I am. Anyway, she's getting a new private number to give you, Armond, her family—all the people that matter."

Victoria had to laugh. Kat had hired a little Texas Southern belle to be her new assistant at Fontaine Development since Cassie had been promoted and was now her right hand. "Does that heavy Southern accent work on everyone?" Victoria asked.

"I believe it does, Ms. V. Yes, ma'am. I believe it does," Emma answered, enjoying their banter. "Hold on and I'll put you through to her office line."

"V! How the hell are you?" Kat let her excitement rush through the phone.

"I'm great, Kat. I just called to check in. You know I leave for Asia with Armond in two days. Remember I told you I was considering having Jenny babysit my clients and cases while I was gone?" Victoria asked, not bothering to wait for an answer. "Well, we just had a call to go over any questions or concerns she might have, and she was fabulous! Not only had she reviewed all the material, but in some cases, she even subtly suggested different investigative paths and legal theories I might want to pursue."

"I'm glad you hired her, V. I know she'll be a solid addition."

"Me too," Victoria agreed. "I can't think of anyone with her experience who would be willing to start at the bottom, so to speak, and accept the modest wage I can afford to pay right now."

"She's a millionaire ten times over, V. She doesn't need the money. What she needs is her self-esteem. And you and I, along with Mona, are just the ones to give that back to her." Kat paused. "I don't think I told you, but I flew Jenny out to Houston to take a look at my case against the insurance company and its board members. I wanted her knowledge, from a former prosecutor's perspective, on other strings we could pull. I figured with the kind of wealth the board members have, there's likely something in their past they'd want to hide—sex, money, or drugs."

"Wow. That's a cheery outlook. Couldn't they have earned their wealth through hard work and lucky breaks?"

Kat snorted, "Okay, V. Sure. I know you've led a rather sheltered life, but come on!"

"All right, my smart-assed friend. Continue, please," Victoria responded.

"Well, as I was saying before Pollyanna interrupted"— Kat laughed—"she actually did find quite a few strings we could pull. I'm paying these East Coast lawyers, supposedly the best in this area, a shit-ton and they never come up with any of these ideas."

"So, what'd you do?"

"Well, Jenny and I had a conference call with my apparently overpaid lawyers, and she nicely told them about all the holes for them to drill down. Of course, the head partner pushed back with some nonsense about why her ideas wouldn't work because of this or that bullshit."

"How did she handle that?" Victoria asked.

"Like a champ! She revved up that sweet Georgia accent of hers and took them through it, piece by piece, until the last one was like soft butter to her knife. By the end of the call, they were hightailing it to do her bidding. It was one of the sleekest maneuvers I've ever witnessed."

"I'm so glad to hear that!" Victoria happily responded.

"But wait. Here's the capper. As soon as we were off the call, she looked at me, batted her eyes, and said, 'You see, Ms. Kat. That is how we Southern women get things done.'"

Victoria and Kat burst out laughing, happy to have a new member in their group, one who could obviously teach them a thing or two.

"Aha! Is that why you hired Emma?"

"No. Emma came highly recommended and was already in the works."

"On a serious note," Victoria continued, "while we're quickly learning Jenny can handle herself, I'd appreciate it if you would call and check in on her and Mary while I'm gone. I know I'm being anal, but I'd feel better if I knew you were touching base with them. I'd also like to tell them they can call you if they need help and can't reach me. I assume that's okay with you?"

"Of course. In fact, I'm scheduled to be in Chicago next week to check on our developments. It would be great if I could work out of your office. I'd much prefer that to driving out to the corn fields and working out of a construction trailer."

"Perfect! Mary will be thrilled to have you. She's a big fan of yours, you know."

"Well, it's a two-way street. Ever since she gave you a heads-up before you were escorted out of the firm and didn't immediately cut off your electronic access, she's been one of my heroes."

"Plus, she left a high-paying job to follow me out the door and potentially off a cliff," Victoria added.

"The only one who thought you were anywhere near a cliff was you, but Mary does deserve credit for leaving a job that had a high-quality, industrial-grade cappuccino maker. What is that thing you have in your office?"

"Oh my God!" Victoria answered snidely. "You know I actually forgot how funny you are."

"No need to worry. I'm happy to remind you as often as necessary. Now, are you going to buy a decent cappuccino maker for your office, or shall I?"

"I'll have Mary coordinate with you, and you two can chose whatever fancy machine you feel you need. But no rearranging my office furniture. It's where it is for a reason," Victoria warned.

"Oh, yes, I'm sure there's a real feng shui reason for your amazing furniture arrangement choices. By the way, do you yet have even one picture of anything or anyone on your walls?"

"Ha ha. You know very well I don't. I'm practicing law, not running a design firm." Victoria hated decorating. Even her apartment was devoid of the knickknacks most people think necessary to make a house a home. For her, they were unnecessary clutter. "If you and Mary want to do my office, so to speak, have at it. You know what I like."

"Fine, but since you're headed to Asia, why don't you use some of the time on that long-ass plane ride to browse the Internet for some new furniture."

"That's not happening. The only things I'll be boning up on are the potential investors for Renoir Productions," Victoria answered.

"You know, it's interesting." Kat thought out loud. "We've been getting a number of hits from wealthy Asian investors' representatives wanting to buy our pricier condo units and penthouses."

"And?" Victoria asked, wondering if Kat had learned something that might help her and Armond in their upcoming meetings.

"We have quite a few under contract, and we're happy to do more. The deals are typically all cash, and the money's come through on time and without problems. As long as they'll agree to your terms and don't want their little girl or boy to star in the film, it might be a good source of funding for Armond's family."

"Great. If you don't mind, I'll let him know about your family's experience," Victoria responded.

"Don't mind at all. Give Armond a kiss for me when you see him, and make sure he shows you some of the sights while you're there. I've got to go. I have about fifteen minutes before I need to charm another banker into loaning us funds for a new project."

"Good luck with that, and thanks for watching over my firm. Call if you need me—anytime, day or night."

"Will do. Have fun!"

CHAPTER

23

A S USUAL, BILLY was early. He had developed that habit years ago, and it had served him well. During his late teens, his father had finally summoned him out of the back-breaking field work he'd been forced to do every summer since his ninth birthday and into the white-collar aspects of the family tobacco business. He remembered two things about his first day in the plantation office. The first was his mother dressing him in an incredibly uncomfortable custom suit, and the second was Big Bill's only instruction: arrive early.

As Billy grew into a young man, he began to understand the importance of his father's directive. Arriving early often resulted in access to information others didn't yet have, which was key to coming out ahead of the curve in business. Over the years, Billy had received information simply because he'd arrived early and was included in a pre-meeting discussion or more often than not, he'd simply overheard others talking.

Taking a seat at the darkened bar, Billy was surprised to see Adam in a back booth, involved in what appeared to be a serious conversation. When Adam noticed Billy, he motioned that he would join him soon but made no effort to bring his companion over for an introduction.

"So far, so good." Trever took a seat at the bar next to Billy and gave him a pat on the back. "Your little golf outing really paid off. I guess I'll have to stop bitching about the firm paying for your ridiculously expensive club fees."

"You should join me sometime, Trever. I think you'd learn to enjoy it."

"I prefer our family hunting trips. When the senator invites the lobbyists and their company representatives out to our family ranch, the amount of sucking up that goes on is more than a baby calf does to her mama's tit."

Billy winced. "Charming."

Looking around the bar, Trever nodded his head in Adam's direction. "Who's that?"

"No idea. Adam was already here with whoever that is when I arrived. I thought you might know."

"Judging from the amount of work Adam is bringing from Asia, I bet it's one of his contacts."

Glancing at his watch, Billy responded, "Well, whoever it is, we need to leave soon. I'm not about to be late to a dinner with the Japanese consulate and prime minister's representative. They'll be insulted if we're even a moment late or if all three of us are not at the dinner."

Standing, Trever signaled to Adam and nodded at his watch. Adam nodded in return. "He's ending the meeting. He'll be over in a minute. So, what's your estimate of billable business the firm will rake in, courtesy of the Japanese government, through the end of this year?"

Billy smiled, relaxing for the first time in days. "Since it's the end of October, there are only two billing months left, and December is always a crapshoot, with clients trying to delay payment until the new year. But since we're having our first billable meeting with the Japanese team tomorrow, I'm projecting an optimistic additional mil."

"That would mean your projections will increase to be around what—ten million— through the end of this year?" Trever asked.

"I think that's conservative. My gut tells me these boys want a significant increase in trade with the US. To do that, they'll need our Washington, D.C. office almost full time. Let's see what they say tonight. But all the indictors are there."

"Well, congratulations, Billy!" Adam walked up to the bar. "The meetings couldn't have gone better this afternoon. You've done an amazing job. Who would have thought a golf game could lead to this?"

"Adam, that's heavy praise from you. I don't think you've ever given me a compliment in all the years we've known each other." Nodding to the man leaving the bar, Billy asked, "Who's that guy?"

"One of the people I've developed a relationship with from Thailand happened to be here for business. We had a few loose ends to tie up before I head to Bangkok tomorrow night."

"What kind of business is he in?" Trever asked. "Exporting and importing, mostly one of a kind, rare pieces," Adam responded.

"I'd love to connect with him. The senator has quite a collection of rare antiques and is always looking to add more."

Cocking his head, Adam answered, "I'm not sure he deals in the type of merchandise that would interest your grandfather, but I'll keep you in mind."

CHAPTER
24

"ARE YOU READY for our adventure, my pet?" Armond asked, throwing his arm around Victoria's shoulder as they met in LAX after her flight from Chicago.

"Armond! You didn't need to pick me up, although I'm happy you did. I thought you were sending a car," Victoria said, surprised as she gave him a kiss on the cheek.

"It's no problem and it gives me a chance to catch you up on a few things before dinner tonight," he responded as he took her bags.

"You look—uh—well, I was going to say fabulous, though now that I look at you—hmm—you have a bit of the rode hard and put away wet look. Out late with some starlet making her debut in one of your father's productions, I presume?"

"V," Armond smirked, "I can't tell you how much your opinion about my looks means to me. I'm sure I'll soon begin turning to you for style advice. Let me see. What is your specialty?" Armond asked as he stood back and cocked his head to look her up and down. "Ah, yes, last year's fashion at bargain prices. I'm sure that works well in the incredibly cosmopolitan city of Chicago."

Victoria opened her mouth to let loose, but just as when he'd been her boss at Acker, Smith & McGowen, he held up a finger in his I'm about to pontificate fashion. "Actually, I'm glad you bought up the subject of style," Armond said, helping Victoria into the back of one of Renoir Productions' Bentley limos waiting by the curb.

Victoria politely took his outstretched hand and was quite proud of herself for not yanking his arm out of his socket. They had only been together a few minutes, and she could already feel herself getting annoyed. She was going to have to learn to control those feelings as they were not at all productive or rational. "What the hell are you talking about? Has the la-la land diet of green smoothies and quinoa turned you into a blithering idiot? I didn't say anything about style. And, stop looking me up and down like I'm some random possession you control."

Armond felt a hint of satisfaction, knowing he could still get under her skin so easily. *This is familiar territory*, he thought. He had always enjoyed their banter, and unlike whatever it was that had provoked his restless night, this he understood. With a self-satisfied smile, he responded, "I hate to burst your midwestern bubble, but you do work for me. Seems to me that gives me an excessive amount of control. In any event, this can't be how you treat your other clients."

Armond watched as Victoria's eyes turned from brown to a deep, inky black. *I can almost clock, to the second, the amount of time it takes me to piss her off,* he thought, trying not to show his amusement. He watched her take a few deep breaths in an effort to control her temper. "Now, open your suitcase," Armond demanded.

"Now? Here?" Victoria asked, no longer amused.

"Yes, now and here because I want to evaluate your choice of attire. We're going to be meeting with the Asian elite, and they'll be checking us out as much as we'll be checking them out. They have a nose for fashion and will expect you to be wearing the finest," Armond said matter-of-factly as he poked through Victoria's clothes. "The shoes will suffice but the clothes will not. You have no designer labels." Victoria felt herself go from zero to bitch instantly. "You really can't be as insensitive as you're pretending to be at this moment. You do recall I just started my own firm a year ago, don't you? And that I just started taking a salary? So, no, I won't buy new clothes, and if that's what you need—"

Armond again held up his finger to interrupt.

"We've yet to work on that temper, I see. Of course I don't expect you to pay for new clothes." He looked out the window and nodded as the driver pulled over. "Come on."

"What are we doing? I thought we were having dinner with your parents."

Armond took her by the hand and helped her out. "We are. There are just a few stops on the way."

Victoria looked around. People were everywhere, leisurely looking in windows and enjoying the afternoon sunshine. "Where are we?"

"This, my dear," Armond said as he waved his arm through the air like he owned it, "is Rodeo Drive." Grabbing her hand and pulling, Armond was met with stubborn rigidity, akin to what one might feel when a dog's found a good scent and refuses to budge.

"You know I can't afford these stores."

"And again, I don't expect you to. Renoir Productions is paying for your clothes. Listen, let's start over. I apologize.

I've been less than adroit. There might have been a better way to have begun this discussion besides rummaging through your suitcase and critiquing your style."

"Ya think?" Victoria responded, pissed.

"But the point is," Armond continued, ignoring her, "we'll be meeting with some of the wealthiest people in Asia, and as our counsel, you'll need to look the part. All you need to do is pick out what you like and the clothes will be tailored and ready by the time we leave tomorrow night."

"I'm not doing this," Victoria responded, sounding— even to herself—like a recalcitrant two-year old.

"V, who do you think pays for my tailored suits? Or my father's ridiculous collection of designer clothes? We're in the entertainment industry, *darling*." Armond emphasized the last word, Hollywood-style. "It's all a business expense." He waited while a flurry of emotions crossed Victoria's face, finally ending in what looked like joy.

"Really?"

"Really. So, release that last little bit of Catholic-girl guilt you're still holding on to and enjoy." Following Victoria's gaze, Armond knew he had her. "Well, I see from the look in your eyes and your laser-like focus on that dress in the window that your baser instincts have won. Good girl!"

"Well, I certainly can't be rude to my newest client." Victoria paused. "Seems I'm suddenly guilt-free. Oh, and by the way, I disagree with you on one point."

"What now?" Armond responded, quirking one eyebrow.

"While my shoes will 'suffice' as you say, they won't work for this trip. I'll need shoes as well," Victoria said, nodding at a shoe store kitty-corner from where they were standing.

"Don't get carried away, my pet," Armond warned.

"You don't want me to try to match my new clothes to my old shoes, do you?" Victoria said, batting her long eyelashes in a fake starlet kind of way. Without waiting for an answer, she pushed open the first boutique door of the afternoon and looked back over her shoulder at Armond. "Come along. You created this monster. We have a lot of shopping to do and precious little time to do it!"

The door shut quietly behind her, and she was enveloped in the boutique's loving arms, leaving Armond standing and staring at her from the Rodeo Drive sidewalk.

* * *

Four hours later, Victoria and Armond returned to their limo. "That was fun! I finally understand why some people like to shop. Makes a huge difference when you don't have to pay for it. What's next?" Victoria asked, exhilarated by the afternoon of pure outrageous spending.

"Dinner with my parents at eight. We'll be staying at their home tonight. They have plenty of room, and by the time we're through, it'll be easier than having to drop you off at a hotel and drive home. Dinner is formal. My parents are throwing a little soiree to introduce you to some of our VPs and a few of our starlets, as you like to call them, who are set to be in some of the films we'll be offering to investors."

"I assume I should be prepared for a night of giant knockers. Do I get hazard pay when one of them inevitably cracks me in the head?"

"Oh, ha ha, Victoria. I assume I can rely on you to keep your charming quips to yourself. And those knockers—by the way, yet another lovely midwestern turn of phrase you bring to the table—are heavily insured. They're considered valuable assets and ones our potential Asian investors will have a keen interest in while you're busy entertaining their wives," Armond answered.

"Did you say I'll be stuck entertaining their wives? Is that why you hired me?" Victoria turned to look at Armond. "Oh, for heaven's sake. Wipe that ridiculous look off your face. No, that is not why I hired you, but the reality is that while the women will have some influence, the men will handle the negotiations. We'll be on their turf, dealing with their customs. You realized that, didn't you?" Armond asked, a bit annoyed he hadn't thought enough about Victoria's lack of experience with other countries and cultures. The only country she had traveled to was Bermuda, and the only reason she had been there was for work. Other than men wearing shorts and knee socks as formal attire, Bermuda wasn't much of a culture shock.

"Of course. While I don't mind being off with the wives at certain times, I do expect to be in the room to help negotiate and close the deals."

"I wouldn't have it any other way." Armond nodded at his parents as the limo arrived at his family home. "Ah, well, I see you've managed to get the royal greeting."

"This is your home? You grew up here?" Victoria asked in awe, waving at his parents. She looked around quickly in an effort to get her bearings and while doing so, for the first time, noticed the long driveway lined with palm trees out the rear window, and then the sprawling outline of what could only be described as a mansion standing majestically against the darkening sky as the limo rolled gently to a stop. She thought she could make out what looked like avocados and lemons hanging from the trees that dotted what yard she could see in the darkening sky. Victoria tried to pull herself together before she spoke, but it was difficult. She had never seen, let alone expected to be, surrounded by such extravagance. She gave Armond a sideways glance. "Now I get it."

"Get what?" Armond asked, knowing by her look he was about to receive some form of shit.

"Why you turned out the way you did. Look at this place. There's no place for sidewalk chalk art, and I'll bet you never ran through a sprinkler or slid on a wet piece of plastic on a hot summer day either."

Luckily for Victoria, there was no time for Armond to respond as his father swung open the car door and pulled Victoria into a bear hug. "Victoria, darling. We are so happy to see you. It's been too long."

"It's good to see you, too, Phillip," Victoria said, genuinely happy. "And Angelika, it's wonderful to see you again. You look beautiful, as always."

"Thank you, darling. Aren't you nice to say so, but I have to give credit where credit is due, and that, my dear, goes to my plastic surgeon and whatever injectable of the day she decided to use. Now, let's get you inside and settled. I'm assuming our charming son told you about our dinner plans?"

"He did," Victoria acknowledged. "But until the rest of my clothes arrive tomorrow, all I have is a rather plain black cocktail dress. Will that work?"

Taking Victoria by the arm, Angelika led her into the house. "Darling, that is the perfect backdrop. I think my five-carat diamond drop earrings should do the trick, don't you?"

Laughing and looking back over her shoulder at Armond and his father, Victoria answered, "I'm definitely not in Kansas anymore."

CHAPTER
25

"OKAY, FOLKS. WHERE do we stand?" Jack walked around the conference room, scanning each associate's face. "Samantha, why don't you begin? Why have all these women left the firm?"

Picking up her notes to glance at them, her hands began to shake, and she dropped the paper like it was possessed. "We worked with the firm's HR people, asking that they turn over all the files they had on each of these women. We didn't want to take their word for why they left, so we drilled down into each file ourselves."

Jack nodded. "Good. Never rely on someone else's assessment of a document or witness. If you can get the source of the information, always review it or interview him or her yourself. What'd you find?"

Samantha was not at all comforted by Jack's compliment. Since she'd joined the firm, Jack had called her a selfish little bitch several times, and he'd said the same or worse to others. Holding her head up, prepared for the unknown, she responded, "The files are missing substantive documentation of the trajectory of their careers. It appears these women received their semi-annual and yearly reviews by entry of a few notes and a number that ranged from one to ten."

"What the hell do you mean they were reviewed by number?" Jack asked, his previously calm voice now sounding a bit more like a low growl.

"Let me show you." Samantha opened her laptop and tried to ignore Jack's tone. "I prepared this chart after looking through the only documents the firm retained on the women who've left over the past five years. I then compared their information to a random sampling of the same number of men who've been at the firm for identical time periods. You'll note the women have markedly lower numbers than the men, and strikingly, in my opinion, their reviews contain zero descriptors or narratives about their abilities, as compared to the men. This becomes particularly shocking when you look at this next chart. It lists the adjectives used to describe the men. Next to that is the list used to describe the women."

"The column has nothing in it," Jack stated the obvious. "Exactly. The difference between the men and women is stark. It will be hard for a jury to believe there wasn't a different standard by which the women were judged," Samantha finished.

The room remained silent, which was not part of the associates' plan. They had all agreed to pass the meeting quickly from one to the other as they had concluded Jack seemed to become volatile if there was a lull in the room. Samantha stared at Jason. If her eyes could shoot fire, Jason would have been a ball of ash. It was his turn.

"So," Jason began, apparently being jolted into consciousness by hostile mental waves from Samantha, "we went back to HR and asked for current contact information on the women, and the same for any men, who had left over the past five years. For the men, the firm has what appears to be complete forwarding addresses and current employment information. However, the firm has this same information for only about one in five of the women."

"Reason?" Jack spat.

"According to HR, the women don't want to provide their personal information after they leave the firm."

"Why?" Jack spat again

"We asked those same questions. HR says they don't know. They ask former associates if they will provide forwarding information and keep the firm updated on their future employment."

"Anything else?" Jack looked around the room.

"Yes. We contacted the women who provided forwarding information. All of them said they left for what they called 'a better opportunity,'" Jason explained, using air quotes. "They had nothing bad to say about the firm. However, it is noteworthy that this group of women left the firm within the first three years of their employment. In other words, they were all fairly new associates. It appears the women who left when they were more senior and getting closer to partnership provided little, if any, information."

"Point?"

"The point is that if Victoria and her attorney get this information, they'll certainly make a circumstantial case to the jury that things are just fine at the firm for women until they near partnership. At that point—"Jason shrugged his shoulders.

"At that point what? We tell all of these women they aren't partner material? We throw them off a bridge?" Jack stood and began to pace. "Okay, what else?"

"That's it," Jason answered.

"What do you mean, 'that's it'? What about Ms. Rodessa? What does her file tell us?"

Jason nodded. "Right. Her situation is unique. It's the only file we found where a woman was fired by the firm, and her firing is documented in some detail."

Jack walked over to the whiteboard, "Okay. We have only one female fired by the firm, and her file contains support for the decision. That's good. But, she disputes the firm's statement of events. No surprise there. The jury will expect her to disagree, but we'll have a number of very credible witnesses, including at least one of the firm's founders. Now, the negatives. First, Armond will support Victoria's story. Second, since she's alleging gender discrimination, the court will likely allow her lawyers to take a bit of a fishing expedition into the firm's handling of female lawyers and their paths to partnership. So, what do you recommend?"

Jason spoke up. "The information we discussed this morning will not go over well with a jury, so we need to do everything we can to keep this information from seeing the light of day."

Jack nodded. "I agree. What do you propose?"

"We'll object to opposing counsel's discovery request for additional information, arguing it violates the other women's privacy rights."

"And if we lose?" Jack asked.

"Then we'll have to produce it and come up with an explanation."

Jack looked around, then walked over and opened the door. "Thank you all for being a part of this brainstorming session. I know you have court deadlines in other cases. I'll see everyone this evening at five to go over tomorrow's calendar call. Jack, Samantha, you two stay since you're my first and second chairs for this trial."

As soon as everyone left the room, Jack shut the door and looked at his two senior associates. "Now, let's get real, shall we?"

CHAPTER
26

"I'M SURPRISED TO get your call. I thought you'd be winging your way to the Orient by now. When are you leaving?" Kat asked.

Victoria adjusted her phone so it cradled between her shoulder and head. "As soon as they finish working on my new clothes. I can't believe those words actually came out of my mouth."

"What are you talking about?"

"I'm on a private plane while two very talented seam-stresses"—Victoria smiled at the two women circling her on their knees—"finish tailoring a cocktail dress I bought yes-terday."

"You bought new clothes? I've been hounding you for over a year to get to a store. And a cocktail dress? Really? I couldn't even pry money out of your tight-fisted little grip to get you to buy new underwear so no one but me would ever have to live through the horrific experience of seeing you in that God-awful Catholic-girl underwear you insist on wear-ing." Victoria grabbed the phone. "Thank God. They're done.

And aren't you hilarious? I didn't buy the clothes. Ar-mond did.

Well, Renoir Productions did, not Armond. And, for the record, there's nothing wrong with my underwear. I simply don't choose to walk around with a thread of fabric up my ass like someone I know."

"If you say so," Kat responded. "In any event, I'm glad Armond had you pick out new clothes. The Asian elite are very judgmental on appearances. Where's Armond?"

"He went back into the terminal to make some calls before we leave and to give me privacy for this final fitting. He should be back any minute."

"Okay then, before he gets back, spill it. How's the plane?" Kat asked.

"Not to sound too pedestrian, but it's amazing!" Victoria whispered excitedly so the crew couldn't hear. "It's like nothing I've ever seen. I mean the private jet that took me back and forth to Bermuda when I worked at the firm was nice, of course, but it was nothing like this. There are two full bedrooms on board, and each has its own shower. As I speak, champagne—the good kind—is being opened, and they've put out cheese and nuts to hold us over until dinner."

"I swear you are the consummate creature of habit. If I never hear you order another cheese and nut board, it will be too soon. Don't you ever eat anything else? You do know, don't you, that cheese is not a staple in Asia? You'll have to learn to lean on something else, like chicken feet."

"Okay. Stop. I know you're just trying to make me nervous."

"I'm not. When I was in Singapore, one of the snack delicacies was fish eyes. They sit in a bowl in front of you and just kind of stare at you. Once in your mouth, they kind of pop and then slither down your throat. They're actually quite good."

Victoria grimaced. "If all I can eat is feet, eyes, and other oddities, I'll never survive the trip. Armond promised—"

"What did I promise?" Armond ducked his head as he came through the cabin door, looking perfectly cool and unfazed, even though it was blazingly hot on the tarmac.

"Give the phone to Armond," Kat ordered.

"Here," Victoria said, handing the phone to Armond, "it's Kat." Victoria gratefully accepted a glass of champagne and watched while Armond laughed at whatever nonsense Kat was spewing. Kat and Armond had become close friends years ago after meeting at Victoria's first Acker, Smith & McGowen summer cocktail party, where she and the other new associates had to introduce themselves to hundreds of attorneys. Victoria had taken Kat as her date. While a few hostile sparks had initially flown between them, once Kat and Armond realized they were really mirror images of one another, their mutual admiration club was launched. Now they were almost sickening to watch.

"Okay, that's enough," Victoria said as she grabbed the phone out of Armond's hand. "Good God. I can only stand the love fest between you two for so long," Victoria snarled, looking at Armond. "How's my firm? Is everything okay? I haven't gotten one call since I left."

Kat smiled at the anxious note in her best friend's voice. As VP of development at her family's company, she understood perfectly what goes through your head when you think you're being left out of decisions. "I worked out of your office all day. Mary told me Jenny handled a few calls from clients, as expected, and that things are just fine. You do know you've only been gone two days?"

"Yes, I know, but I haven't heard boo from Jenny. I thought she would at least call to update me on matters."

"Hmm. Well, did you ask her to do that?" Kat asked, knowing the answer.

"No."

"Then, why would Jenny call to bother you with the mundane? Seems to me she would assume she's doing you a favor by not calling without a reason."

"Okay, you can cram that psychology 101 crap where the sun don't shine," Victoria said, watching Armond signal to the pilots they were ready for takeoff.

"Hey—" Victoria yelped as Armond grabbed the phone out of her hand.

"Kat, my love, we're about to take off. I'm afraid I'll have to interrupt your tête-à-tête, as immensely intellectual as it sounded."

"Armond, take good care of her. You know as well as I do how naïve she is," Kat warned.

"Indeed. No worries, my queen. All will be well. I will guard her with my life," Armond said, ending the call.

"What the hell?" Victoria protested with a slight slur. "I wanted to say goodbye."

"V, my love. You are one of only a handful of people I know who can get tipsy from imbibing one glass of champers. You can call Kat when we arrive. Now, I suggest we sit for dinner. It's likely the last time you'll have access to food you can eat until our return. Fish head soup will be the order of the day," Armond said, riffing off the conversation Kat had told him she'd had with Victoria.

"Armond?"

"Yes, V?"

"Fuck off!" And with that, they had lift off.

* * *

A few hours later, Armond carried V into one of the plane's bedrooms. She'd fallen asleep almost mid-sentence as soon as she'd finished eating. It had been a tad annoying, as it had been his mid-sentence, but he couldn't blame her. She was still on Chicago time and had only about six hours of sleep the night before, and she had confessed to relatively little sleep the night before that, worrying about leaving her practice. He took off her shoes and pulled a blanket over her. Bending down, he kissed her forehead.

* * *

"What the hell?" Victoria moaned, the smell of coffee bringing her out of a deep sleep.

"Good morning, madam. Mr. Renoir asked that I wake you so you have time to shower and dress for the day. You have a meeting at ten, and we land at half past eight. Shall I lay out the clothes Mr. Renoir requested you wear?"

"Mr. Renoir requested I wear certain clothes?" Victoria felt her temper jump as she tried to get her bearings.

"Indeed. He suggested you allow him to guide you since you haven't been to Hong Kong before."

Victoria realized the truth in that statement and capitulated. "Fine. Thank you."

"You are welcome, madam. I will also help with your makeup."

"No. You won't help with my makeup. I am not a total bumbling idiot," Victoria snapped. "Of course not, madam."

Victoria watched in horror, and with a significant dose of guilt, as the young woman bowed her head and retreated to the corner. "Please don't pay attention to me. I apologize. Of course I want your help with my makeup. I really don't

133

wear more than lip gloss, eyeliner, and mascara, so if you have some magic you can work on me, I'm all yours."

A huge smile broke out on the young woman's face. "Of course, madam. I would be pleased to help."

"But on two conditions. First, you must call me Victoria, or V, as my friends do, and drop the madam. Second, while I'm in the shower, would you mind bringing me another cup of hot, black coffee and one of those amazing-looking scones I saw last night?" Victoria smiled.

"Yes mad—"—Victoria raised her eyebrow—"I mean, yes, Ms. V."

"We'll have to work on that until we get you to just V. But for now, I'll take it. By the way, what's your name?"

"I'm Chen."

"Chen. What a lovely name. How long have you worked for this airline?"

"Oh, I don't work for the airline. I work for Renoir Productions."

"Of course," Victoria said, beginning to understand the breadth of Armond's family company. "What is it you do for Renoir?"

"I'm an assistant to Armond. I provide advice on Asian customs and culture and translate when necessary," Chen answered. "The Renoirs are like my family. I am forever grateful and indebted to them," she said, a serious look running across her face for the briefest of moments.

"Where's your family, Chen?" Victoria asked, wondering why Chen felt such affinity to Armond's family.

"Ms. V"—Chen forced a smile and a cheery tone— "I do not wish to be rude, but we are running out of time. I will get your coffee and biscuit while you take your shower. Then we'll get you ready for the day. While we are doing your hair and makeup, I will discuss with you a few of the traditions you will be expected to follow." Chen bent her head slightly and left Victoria alone in her cabin.

"Well, great start, Victoria. You'll do a bang-up job with the people you're going to meet today. Not even off the plane and you've already insulted one of them not once, but twice," Victoria mumbled to herself as she stepped into the steaming shower.

* * *

"Good morning, V. You look fabulous." Armond smiled and nodded. "Chen, as always, you've worked miracles."

"Thank you, Armond, I think," Victoria answered. "Although somehow I feel like there was an implication in there that I'm in need of miracles. And, while Chen is amazing with a makeup brush, it's not like I'm totally inept at getting myself ready in the morning," Victoria raised her chin, challenging Armond to respond.

"I think there's a difference of opinion on that. Knowing how to paint between the lines to put on lip gloss is a far cry from understanding the subtlety and craftsmanship that someone truly talented with makeup can bring to the facial palate." Armond nodded at Chen.

"Facial palate? What the hell are you talking about?"

Ignoring Victoria, Armond looked over at Chen. "Did you have the opportunity to discuss the importance of women not using vulgarities?"

Not wanting to betray Victoria, Chen peeked at her and tried to stall for time. "I'm sorry, Armond, can you repeat the question?"

"Oh my God," Victoria jumped in. "Stop putting her on the spot. She explained it all very clearly while she painted my 'facial palate,'" Victoria said, using Armond's ridiculous phrase. "I understand but I am who I am, and it's hard to teach an old dog new tricks, particularly when it comes to the things that come out of my mouth."

"Perhaps the old dog would do good to remember the amount of money she is being paid to handle and learn a whole new legal service she can tout in the future. If she scares off the investors by being vulgar and crass, Renoir Productions will not take kindly to that."

Victoria considered responding with an even more vulgar comment but thought she may as well try to control herself sooner rather than later. "You're right. This is about business, not me. I will be the most submissive, quiet, and doting counsel you've ever worked with. You just watch and see." Victoria winked at Armond and pulled her seatbelt a bit tighter as the plane descended toward Hong Kong.

CHAPTER
27

ROBERT AND KAT had been at it for hours. Kat stood and pushed down on her lower back while she leaned forward to stretch her aching spine, then walked over to pick up another pile of documents. "How long have we been in this room?

Robert looked at his watch. "Over six hours. I don't know about you, but I'm starving and in serious need of caffeine. Let's take a walk, grab some food, and discuss where we are."

"Fine with me." Kat let the documents she had cradled in her arms hit the table with a loud thud. "This has completely refreshed my memory as to why I never wanted to litigate." She grabbed her coat and headed for the elevator. "Mary, we're taking a break. Do you want anything?"

"No thanks. I'm good, but I expect Victoria will be calling soon. Is there anything either of you want me to tell her?"

Kat pushed the elevator button and cocked her head. "Tell her Robert and I have been working our asses off on her lawsuit and that everything at the firm is fine. Tell her I expect to be treated to an amazing dinner and that I'm picking the restaurant. I want real food—not her healthy, rabbit-shit food."

"Wow! Glad I asked. Anything else?"

"Hmm. Well, knowing how anal she is, she'll probably want some details about her firm. In case she hasn't already called Jenny, let her know I spoke with her this morning and went through the to-do list, and just as we thought, Jenny has everything under control and is doing an impeccable job."

"Will do." Mary nodded, jotting down Kat's comments.

* * *

A few minutes later, Robert and Kat were enjoying the late afternoon sun-soaked streets of Chicago. The leaves had just started to turn color when Kat had landed a few days ago. Now, almost every tree displayed an all-out riot of color, and the air was deliciously warm, clean, and crisp—all at the same time. Smiling in appreciation, Kat raised her face to the sun to absorb its warmth. "Even though I love Houston, we have nothing like this. It brings back so many memories of returning for the start of each year of law school and living with V."

Robert smiled. "I knew you two were close, but I didn't realize how strong your bond was until we started working together on the case."

"V is one of the best benefits I got from law school. I consider her part of my family and a sister in the truest sense of the word." Shaking her head and laughing, Kat said, "I never could have predicted our first meeting would turn into such a great friendship. She was so naïve, and I had always made it a habit to stay away from people who were as Pollyanna as V."

"How did you meet?"

"We met on the first day of class. She sat next to me in criminal law and did her best to commit hari-kari by shooting her hand up in the air to answer a question from the most blood-thirsty professor ever to grace a law school's halls."

Robert smiled. "That sounds like her. Did you save her?"

Kat shook her head. "Nope. Tried. But she's persistent. V wants what V wants, and no one can stop her. Anyway, while everyone else was trying to appear smaller than they were to avoid being called on, her hand was going back and forth in the air. The whole exchange took no more than ten minutes, and by the end, he'd neatly ripped her a new one. It was horrific. Thinking back, I must have felt sorry for her because I can't come up with any other reason why I hung around and waited for her after class. After that, we were inseparable."

"She and her mother have a way about them, that's for sure," Robert responded. "I remember the first time we met. It was, I think, the day after Victoria was fired. Sophia decided Victoria needed to hire a lawyer to represent her against the firm. Apparently, Sophia chose me and one other firm. At our first meeting, Victoria barely spoke, but her mother was all over me. I considered turning down the case because I was worried about having to deal with an overbearing mother. As it turns out, Sophia treats me like family."

"Which would explain why we're obsessed with making sure we win this case against that shithole of a law firm," Kat offered.

Robert opened the restaurant door and nodded toward the patio. "Why don't you find a table outside? I'll grab us something to eat. What do you want?"

"I want a steak, now that I'm thinking about it. But for now, I'll take a glass of cab."

"You sure you don't want anything else? I don't want you keeling over in the middle of our conversation from all the hard work you're not used to doing." Robert ducked inside just as Kat tried to smack him with the lip gloss she was about to apply.

Finding the perfect spot in the sun, surrounded by trees that were rustling in the fall breeze, Kat pulled out the trial map they'd worked on all day. It still had too many holes. On the plaintiff's side, they had Victoria, Armond and Mary listed as witnesses. But Armond had a question mark after his name, as Robert predicted the firm would claim privilege and try to prevent him from testifying about certain conversations he had with his former partners before the firm fired V.

"What BS," Kat said out loud. She knew she needed to let her mind relax. She always had the best ideas when she relaxed and sat in silence. "Well, that's not happening now," Kat continued to talk out loud as she dug into her bag and pulled out the rest of her notes. "We need more evidence." Kat looked up as a shadow fell across the table.

"You do know everyone can see you talking to yourself from inside, right? I mean, it's not like you're invisible out here," Robert said, setting their wine on the table.

"You know, Robert, I had no idea you were such a co-median. However, as I'm sure you're aware by now"—Kat paused as she tapped her pen against her notes—"I don't give a damn what anyone else thinks." She took a sip of her wine. "Not bad. Now, I'll be able to think much clearer. As I was saying to myself, the trial map is too bare."

Robert shifted his chair closer to Kat to share her view of the map. "No question. We need to shore up our case with documents and witnesses. The documents we've received from the firm don't give us much. Victoria's employee file says she was headstrong, opinionated, and consistently chose not to follow instructions. We'll counter that with Armond's testimony. He at least should be able to give his opinion about the quality of her work, and it should carry more weight than anyone they put on the stand. After all, he was the partner the firm assigned to bring her along in the firm, and she worked almost exclusively for him."

"I thought you said the firm would try to prevent him from testifying?" Kat asked.

"They will, but they'll lose any attempt they may make to prevent his testimony about her capability as a lawyer. Anything else they want to keep out they'll have to prove was for the purpose of obtaining legal advice or in anticipation of litigation with Victoria and, therefore, privileged. I expect them to argue they were anticipating litigation for many months before she was fired, making all their conversations with Armond about Victoria privileged."

"I assume we're going to object."

"We are. Plus, Armond is on our side, so it's unlikely he'll agree with them when they argue what was discussed somehow fits into a privilege."

"That's all good news, but we need witnesses: corroboration. So far, we've got zip. What do we do about that?"

"Keep digging. We already have some facts that will help. Only one woman has been voted into partnership since the firm began, and that happened only recently. I actually like that fact. In addition, more than forty women have left the firm over the past five years. What we need is evidence and expert testimony to demonstrate this is not the norm and is way below what would be expected in a typical firm."

"Why would you like that they just named their first female partner? Doesn't that hurt our argument?"

"No. Are you kidding me? I'm weaving that right into the fabric. Lawsuit filed, lawsuit mentioned in the press, suddenly first female partner named. I wonder how long that was in the works. Ten to one if we depose her, she'll say she had no idea."

"Okay, but what about other witnesses. Seems to me we need them."

"We do."

"Well, are you going to pull them out of your ass?"

"You know," Robert began, noticing the sun was busy playing with the different shades of blond in Kat's hair, "you Houston women are so charming. Here, let me put it in terms you can understand. This isn't my first rodeo. Watch and learn." Robert tipped his glass to clink with Kat's.

"All right, cowboy. Where do we go from here?"

"The firm answered our interrogatories by giving us a list of former female associates and not much else. We have the investigator tracking them down. It also gave us a document dump of mostly irrelevant material. Not surprisingly, it did provide enough information to allow it to argue to a jury that except for Victoria, the other women all left voluntarily," Robert explained.

"We certainly can't take their word for it."

"We'll need to file a motion to compel asking the court to force the firm to respond to our document requests with complete personnel files. The firm has refused to provide this information claiming it would violate their former employees' right to privacy."

"Are they right on the privacy argument?" Kat asked.

"Unfortunately, they have an argument to make. Unless we can show a connection between why we need this information and V's case, we're going to have a hard time convincing the court."

Kat nodded, writing a note to herself. "Let's table that for a minute. What information do you need from my case?"

"Have your lawyers found anything to support Victoria's side, like someone's deviant agenda at work mucking up the claim handling process she had set in place at the insurance company?" Robert asked.

"Except for Big Bill's handwritten note and a few emails directing employees to focus on gathering claim information, rather than responding to policyholders, there's little tangible support for a plot to delay payments. In fact, the documents we've received seem to reflect the processes V says she put in place. However, I did receive a call from a lawyer who says she represents one of the insurance company's employees who claims to have critical information that will help our case. She's afraid to come forward, though, for fear of losing her job."

Robert stopped mid-wine sip and stared at Kat.

"What is it?" Kat asked.

Robert put his glass down. "I received a similar call about two weeks ago. I was contacted by someone who refused to identify herself. She wanted to know if I was the lawyer handling the discrimination suit against the Acker firm. When I answered that I was, the line went dead. It's been about two weeks since the call, and I haven't heard another word. I tried to reverse call and was told it was from out of the country, a dead end."

Kat frowned. "Hmm. It seems like things are starting to crawl out of the woodwork. Let's assume each of us has potential witnesses roaming around in the ether that might help our respective cases. For some reason, neither of them wants to step into the sunshine. Why? What's the common factor that might prevent them from coming forward?"

"Fear," Robert answered unequivocally.

"There could be other reasons, couldn't there?"

"Sure." Robert paused to finish his glass. "But there aren't. I've been trying cases for almost twenty years now, and every time a witness doesn't want to come forward, it's fear—particularly in gender discrimination cases."

"But fear of what?"

"Different things. Take the person who called me, and, for that matter, the person who called your lawyers. Maybe they're afraid of losing their jobs or maybe they lost their jobs and signed a confidentiality agreement, so they agreed not to discuss specifics but now they want to do the right thing and don't know where to begin."

"How do we get their information?" Kat asked.

"We'll have to offer them something better than whatever it is they're afraid of losing. We've got to make it worth their while to talk and testify."

"Um, I'm quite sure it's illegal to pay a witness to testify."

"Indeed, it is, Kat," Robert said as he stood and held out his hand. "Come, my Houston friend, let's get that heart-stopping steak you've been talking about. I'll fill you with more wine and explain it to you."

Kat looked up and smiled. With a pleasant buzz, she took his hand, and, much to her surprise, let him lead.

CHAPTER
28

S HE WAS FINALLY finished researching and vetting, having used all the investigatory skills she had developed while representing white-collar defendants. Before her life had come to a screeching halt, her peers had often commented on her uncanny ability to home in on people who were either bending the truth or had a private agenda. She had been so good at it that her colleagues used to bring her into meetings just to get her read on a person, and she rarely had been wrong.

Ironically, it never worked to her benefit. "Some great soothsayer I turned out to be. I wouldn't even recognize a jackass in my life if he wore a T-shirt that read 'I'm a jackass in your life.'" She snort-laughed at her own joke and slowed down to look for the address.

Pulling up to the house, she texted and waited. The door opened and out walked a tall, lanky boy who looked no more than twenty. Leaning down on the driver's side, he tapped lightly on her window. She froze, her heart beating so hard she had to clamp down on her chest to try to get it to regulate. He tapped again.

As she rolled down her window, he stuck his hand through. "Hi. I'm James. Are you Penny?"

"What? Penny? Yes, yes, I'm Penny."

"Okay," he nodded, peering into the car with a questioning look. "You're the one who hired me?"

"I am."

"Good. Well, we're getting somewhere. Why don't you come into the house and I'll take a look. You brought it, right?"

"I did."

James had recently opened his business to help pay his way through college. He was quickly learning there were a lot of weirdos he would have to work with, and "Penny" seemed to be one of them.

He tried again. "Would you like to come in? I can take a preliminary look and tell you what I think."

"Here. Sign this first," Penny ordered, shoving paper and pen out her window.

"What's this?"

"It's a nondisclosure and confidentiality agreement. It says that everything you see and all we discuss is confidential and cannot be discussed with anyone at any time. Any problem with that?"

"Nope. None." James took the pen and signed and dated the paper. "Okay, are you getting out, or shall I go back into the house and wait for you?"

"I'm getting out."

"Great."

While James was quite sure she was a nutcase, he somehow felt a little tinge of sorrow for her. She was waif-like and when she moved, her clothes looked like they were trying to dance off her frame. Her skin was pale, and her hair was unkempt. In fact, it looked as if it'd been cut with a butcher knife in a fit of rage. There were bits and pieces of different lengths, and each seemed to head in a different direction. But, she was smart. That much he knew, based on how thoroughly she had vetted him. Somehow, she knew her way around government and court websites, as she'd tracked back to junior high. He had easily followed her cyber steps.

He walked up the few concrete front steps and opened the door. "Come on in."

She paused and peeked inside. "Who else is here?"

"No one. I live with my parents, and they're both at work. They'll be home in about an hour."

"I'll be gone by then," she said.

"Okay. Let's get inside so I can look at what you've got." Looking around—and in every corner—Penny nervously followed James into the house. "How long have you been doing this?"

"Coming up on two years. I was doing it for free before I realized I have a skill people will pay for. I opened my business about six months ago. It helps pay for college."

James looked over at Penny fidgeting with her hands and looking around. *God*, he thought, *I hope she's not a crackhead.* "What about you?"

"What about me?"

"What's the story? What is it you want me to do?" James asked, seating himself at his desk and opening his laptop.

Penny felt her eyes fill with tears. Feeling disgusted with herself, and in an effort to prevent her emotions from controlling the situation, she blurted out, "Enough!"

Startled, James looked up from his laptop. "Look, if you have a problem that involves more than cyber issues, I can't help you."

"No. Please. I'm sorry. I'm nervous. I haven't trusted anyone with this—ever—not even my husband. So, this is—well—new ground for me."

"Listen, I know you don't know me, but you can trust me."

Penny burst out laughing. "Famous last words. But here's the deal. I'm tired of cowering and hiding and being ashamed—at least I'm trying to be." Reaching into her bag, she retrieved the thumb drive. "Here," she said. "It appears to be me in the video. It's mortifying. I was, and am, married. I have a young daughter. I don't recall any of it. I had a good job at the time. Please. I have nowhere else to turn."

James nodded and inserted the thumb drive. The screen came to life and there she was: fully exposed and compromised. He zoomed in on her face as she knelt to the floor on screen. "Do you really need to do that?" she asked.

"I do. Try to relax. You've made a decision to trust me, so let me do my job."

Penny watched as he switched angles, stopped, started, and reversed. A film came over the screen and seemed to somehow separate the video into frames. After about a half hour had passed, he stopped the video and leaned back in his chair.

"Well?" Penny asked.

"Well. That definitely appears to be you, but I can't make any determination yet. I'm working on a few programs that will let me back into the process that may have been used."

"What do you mean 'back into the process'?"

"The best way I can explain it is to think of it as rewinding a movie. That really doesn't do it justice, but I think it's as much as you need to understand for now. If I find out anything more, I'll give you a full explanation. Okay?"

"Fine," Penny said, feeling ashamed and unable to look him in the eyes.

"I'm sorry I can't tell you more right now. It will take a bit of time for me to work on it. Can I keep it for a few days?"

"No. I'm sorry, but no. I'll come back again. I should leave now since your parents will be here soon."

"Listen, my gut's telling me something's off. I just don't know what that is yet," James said as he handed the thumb drive back to Penny.

"Thank you." Penny left cash on his desk, turned, and quickly walked out of the house.

CHAPTER

29

"**H**EY, WAKE UP," Armond spoke softly, gently pushing Victoria's hair off her face. "We're here."

"Oh no. I'm sorry, Armond. I don't know what happened," Victoria said, sitting up straight.

"Nothing happened. You fell asleep on the ride from the airport."

"Oh my God, I was drooling," Victoria groaned, mortified. Handing her his handkerchief, Armond smiled. "There's nothing to be upset about, V. Jet lag always hits when you least expect it. One minute you feel great, and the next, you nod off. It's good you slept. Any last-minute questions before we head in?"

"Yes, where's the coffee? I need coffee before, during, and after the meeting."

"They'll have plenty of coffee. They'll be very attuned to our needs. Any questions about this group of potential investors?"

"No. I've read everything your team gave me, and I did a bit of research on my own before we left the States. I'm good."

"Good. Now, at the risk of getting on your wrong side—which is not hard to do, I might add—remember they will not expect you to take the lead, and if you do, they may become so uncomfortable they might end the meeting."

"We've been over this. I'm to be seen and not heard. If you and your company want to pay me a shit-ton of money for sitting there and looking pretty, well, then have at it."

"Hmm. That comment makes me more, rather than less, uncomfortable. It's nothing personal. It's the culture."

Victoria paused to freshen her lip gloss. "Armond, would you like to know what I think about that?"

Armond accepted the now-used handkerchief from Victoria, stuck it in his man purse, and pulled out a perfectly-folded clean replacement. "No. But unfortunately I believe that was a rhetorical question."

"I think 'it's nothing personal' is one the most passive-aggressive phrases ever uttered," Victoria answered determined he would hear her out. "Of course it's personal. In fact, whenever someone wants to make sure you know they're giving you a personal dig, they say that." Victoria put her lip gloss away, took one last look in her mirror, and smiled at Armond. "And as far as you being uncomfortable, well,"—Victoria shrugged her designer-clad shoulders—"you'll just have to deal with it and wonder when I might snap like a twig. Okay, I'm ready. Let's get this party started, shall we?"

Sighing, Armond followed Victoria out of the car.

CHAPTER

30

B IG BILL STOMPED around his mansion like the proverbial bull in a china shop. Except for the staff, he was alone. He still had a hard time believing Jenny had gone through with the divorce. He had always been able to control her. Damned if he could figure out what burr had gotten under her saddle.

While he didn't miss her, he did miss the consistency and stability of marriage. Since he ran the plantation business from home, he had naturally depended on Jenny to have things arranged and in order. She had been particularly good at ensuring his meetings were adequately staffed and business lunches and dinners were properly prepared and served on time. She had been relentless about learning little details about his investors and then using the information in just the right way so each of them felt special. During their marriage, they had effortlessly—or so it had appeared to Big Bill—hosted black-tie affairs for senators, governors, and even two vice presidents at their home.

Since the divorce, nothing was the same. So far, he'd gone through two highly recommended managers, who couldn't handle shit as far as he was concerned. Shaking his head in disgust at his current state of affairs, he called over his shoulder as he headed out the door, "Jeremiah, call the boys and let 'em know I'm heading over to shoot." Normally, he would have driven, but today he was jacked up and felt like walking.

"Yes, sir." Glancing at the time, Jeremiah gave a gentle reminder. "Your lawyers are scheduled to be here within the hour."

"Tell them to kiss my ass. For the amount I pay them, they can wait. If one of those assholes has anything to say about that—and I mean even one fucking little peep—tell him he's fired."

Jeremiah nodded. He'd been employed by Big Bill for twenty years and was extremely well-paid. He intended to stay another twenty, so he had no qualms about delivering Big Bill's message, word-for-word.

As Big Bill walked toward his skeet deck, he was disturbed to realize he was still thinking about the divorce. "What more could she have wanted?" he said, surprising himself with that comment. He had given her a mansion, wealth, and a place in society. She certainly never would have gotten any of those things as a low-salaried prosecutor, running around the courthouse dealing with the slime of the earth. The fact that he screwed women on the side should have come as no surprise. That it had apparently been the straw that broke Jenny's back was baffling. His friends all had mistresses and they kept them within a thirty-minute drive of Atlanta so they could see them as often as they chose, while he'd been considerate enough to house his in Bermuda. *Well, no good deed goes unpunished*, he thought as he stepped onto his deck, pulled his cap down low on his forehead, and pushed his sunglasses closer to his face to block the sun's glare so he could have clear shots. "Morning, Sam. You ready for me?"

"Yes, sir. Got your favorite right here," Sam answered.

Big Bill picked up his favorite gun. *That's another thing Jenny fucked up for me*, he thought as he nestled the barrel into his shoulder. "Pull!" he yelled, and a clay disc soared through the air for a few seconds until he brought it down.

"Nice shot, sir."

"Thank you. This is just what the doctor ordered. Pull!" Jenny and his mistress had somehow connected and the next thing he knew, Wilhemena was represented by Jenny's lawyer and asking for a pile of cash and the Bermudian house. When he objected, all the lawyers did their bullshit powwow thing and he was told if he didn't acquiesce, Wilhemena would go public with the fact that he had started banging her when she was seventeen.

"It's not like she wasn't asking for it," Big Bill said to no one. "Pull!"

God, that felt good, he thought. Loading his gun, he suddenly realized what he needed to do. He needed his life back, the way it had been. He'd get married again, find another mistress, and go back to the way things had been when life was good. "Sam, you know there ain't nothing like a little shootin' to solve life's problems," Big Bill slapped him on the back and handed him his gun.

"Yes, sir."

Feeling at peace, he turned and walked back toward his house, ready to deal with his lawyers and start the next phase of his life.

* * *

Big Bill walked into his board room, glanced at Jeremiah, and smiled when he saw his almost imperceptible negative nod. "Well, gentlemen, I understand you were both good boys and waited patiently. I appreciate that. Cigar?" Big Bill opened his humidor and offered the lawyers their choice of some of the finest cigars available on American soil.

"We're more than happy to wait," Jeremy responded as he stood and shook his client's hand. *It's your money, after all*, he thought to himself, *and we're charging you for every minute.* "We have some significant matters to discuss."

"I hope you've got some better ideas than the ones you had last time we met. What's the total amount I've paid you?"

The lawyers were not surprised by his opening salvo, as this was the way Big Bill began every one of their meetings. "At the end of last month, the total attorneys' fees for all of the matters we're handling for you was close to three million," Scott answered.

Big Bill nodded his head, leaned back into his leather chair at the head of the table, and gazed at the ceiling while he enjoyed the first few puffs of his cigar. "That's a crapload of money, wouldn't you agree, boys? For that much money, I should have bought and paid for at least one judge's summer home on some damn shoreline by now, and all this nonsense should be at an end. Why am I still talking to you boys and paying your bills?"

"Bill, your comments suggesting we should pay off a judge are untenable. We have never, and will never, agree to do that. Let me be clear. If you ever suggest this again, or if we find out that you've engaged anyone else to pursue such a course of conduct, we'll immediately file a motion to withdraw and report the judge and any lawyers you involve."

In a sudden fit of laughter, Big Bill used his immense size to propel himself out of his chair. He continued laughing as he walked over to the sideboard and poured a shot of whiskey into a cut crystal glass with his plantation's initials chiseled into its side. He then walked over and slapped Jeremy on the back. "For Christ's sake. You're such a pussy," he said, sitting the whiskey bottle and two more glasses on the table. "Pour yourself a drink and get off your high horse. I'm not suggesting you bribe a judge."

"Great. Then there's no problem. Now, shall we move on to the reason for our visit?"

"You boys have thirty minutes."

"We've got good news. The Bermudian authorities have decided they're not going to prosecute. Your former mistress has refused to testify. There's little point in proceeding without her testimony, and they don't want the bad publicity the case would bring to their little tourist island. That means the statutory rape charge is resolved, so to speak."

"Well, boys"—Bill paused while he puffed on his cigar, which now appeared sopping wet from his constant sucking—"here's what I think. Neither of you did jack shit to get rid of that trumped-up rape charge except dot some *i*'s and cross some *t*'s, while I had to give away a significant amount of money and my Bermudian home. I could have done that on my own and without paying you out the ass."

While both lawyers were used to Big Bill treating them like dog shit, his lack of appreciation and constant insults were still soul-crushing at times.

"Bill, whether you like to admit it or not, you were staring down the barrel of serious criminal charges that carried significant jail time. We're the ones who worked on Wilhemena's lawyer to convince her not to pursue her preferred course of action. As you know, Mona has quite the reputation for getting her clients in front of TV cameras so they can air all the dirty laundry they have against the defendant to the whole nation. It would have been quite the coup for Mona to have announced on TV that she not only expects to get significant compensation for her client but that she is also cooperating with prosecutors to take you off the street so you can't molest other teenage girls."

Big Bill grew still. Using his cigar as an extension of his finger, he leaned across the table and pointed it at Jeremy. Little bits of spittle flew out of his mouth as he snarled, "Don't ever say that to me again. If you do, I'll make sure you never work in this town or anywhere within a thousand miles of here."

"Bill, I understand how you feel, but Wilhemena's lawyer was gunning for full prosecution and monetary compensation. Based on the evidence they have, there's no reason she couldn't have gotten her wish. I want you to understand how serious this was. We had to convince Mona that if she pushed for prosecution, we wouldn't be able to get any money or the home for her client—that the only way we could get you to contribute to Wilhemena's future was if she gave you room to breathe—outside of jail. Once she understood we would drag out any civil litigation and you would refuse any compensation if you were thrown in jail, she finally relented."

"Let's get one thing clear between us. Wilhemena wanted what I was giving. She knew exactly what she was doing. I don't care how old she was."

Neither lawyer responded to his crass comment. The matter was legally closed, and it wasn't their job to instill moral character into their clients. If Big Bill wanted to believe there was nothing wrong with his conduct, then so be it.

As the silence set in, Big Bill suddenly felt uncharacteristically tired. He needed to get all these matters behind him and move forward with the next phase of his life.

I need a personal lawyer, he thought. *One who is loyal to me and won't pontificate about what I can and can't do. My next mistress will sign an airtight agreement that spells out the terms of our relationship. That way I'll never have this disruption again. Lawyer first, new mistress, second.*

Thinking about his plans, Big Bill felt the pressure that had been building inside him lessen. Feeling better now that he had decided his new course of action, he ordered, "Let's move on. My next meeting starts in five minutes. What's the status of the insurance lawsuit?"

"The plaintiff, Fontaine Development, is claiming you and others on the board ordered the slow pay of insurance claims to increase company profits and thus, the value to the board."

"Yes. I'm aware. Have you dug into Trever's involvement in this matter?"

"Bill, if we go down that avenue, it might put your son's partner and their firm at risk."

"Hmm. Let me see," Big Bill said as he held his hands in the air, palms up, and acted as if he was weighing different amounts in each hand. "Either my fortune, heritage, and reputation are ruined or my son's firm or his partner goes down." Suddenly, he used the full force of his arm and swung it down so hard on the table the whiskey glasses jumped and almost fell on their sides.

"Jesus. What the hell are you doing?" Scott asked, grabbing his glass.

"We've had this conversation before. Apparently, neither of you understood I was serious. I ran the board. I did not come up with any schemes to harm anyone. I am not an expert in insurance. I run a tobacco plantation and simply had the idea to bring together a number of wealthy people to provide the initial capital to create an insurance company. That does not make me anything other than an investor."

Taking a document out of his satchel, Jeremy asked, "Then why do we have one of the only smoking guns I've ever seen in all my years of litigation? This is your handwriting, and right here, in black and white, you wrote, 'delay claim payments and increase ROI.' How do you explain that?"

"You explain it! You're my fucking lawyers. But apparently that doesn't get me very much since I need to come up with all the theories. How about telling the jury I was writing down what someone else was saying? And that someone—Trever McGowen, one of the founding partners at Acker, Smith & McGowen—was the one who was giving us business advice. By the way, my son was running the legal end of things, getting the company off the ground and approved by state regulators. He was not involved in the consulting side. That was all Trever, so I want the focus totally on him, not my son. Got that?"

"No one is going to believe that."

"Why not? I'm not in the consulting business, but Trever is. And, by the way, it's your goddamn job to make sure everyone believes whatever the fuck our theory is. That's why I'm paying you the big bucks, right? Now get your asses out of here, and go get the evidence we need to pressure Trever into settling, with his or the firm's money, and make this all go away."

As the two lawyers headed out the door, Big Bill shook his head in disgust. *Goddamn lawyers today have no sense of how to get things done. They're all so afraid to play hard ball it's as if the only qualification you have to have nowadays to practice law is the loss of your balls.* Snorting out loud in agreement with himself, Big Bill signaled Jeremiah.

"Sir?"

"Jeremiah, I'd like you to find out all you can about Trever McGowen and his grandfather. Use whatever means necessary. Understood?"

"Completely."

"Then, begin a search for my first in-house counsel. I want someone who will think outside the box, not some mealy-mouthed, run-of-the-mill, spineless lawyer—someone who understands how to get things done, will cover my ass, and won't bother me with the details. Understood?

"Yes, sir. I'll get on that right away."

"Oh, and one more thing, Jeremiah."

"Sir?"

"He must be loyal to me. Understood?"

"Completely."

"Good man," Big Bill said, slapping Jeremiah on the back a few times as he walked out the door to his next meeting.

CHAPTER
31

"WELL, THAT WAS interesting," Victoria said as she kicked her shoes off and threw her coat and purse on the table. Stopping in her tracks, she turned to look at Armond. "Wow. This room is stunning. Is this yours?"

"No. It's yours. Mine is next door."

"Well, thank your father and mother for me, will you? This is amazing. It's bigger than my apartment."

Preening a bit, Armond said, "Almost anything is bigger than your apartment."

"Ah, there he is, that snotty Beverly Hills boy I love to hate. I wondered where he was today," she said, walking into the bedroom to change into something comfortable. "Hey," she yelled, "my clothes are hung and put away. So is my makeup."

Rolling his eyes, Armond said, "Really, Victoria. You're going to have to stop acting like a country bumpkin. Our staff handles all of this. Everyone except the pilots has more than one job when we travel. It's likely Chen was the one who unpacked your clothes. Be sure to thank her." He winked and walked out of her bedroom. "I don't know about you," he called, "but I'd like a drink and dinner. I'm famished. I'd rather not go out, if that's okay with you?"

"Bless you! There is no way I want to sit at dinner and have to act all speak only when spoken to."

Picking up the menu, Armond asked, "Shall I order?"

"Yes, I'm starved, and I'll have some—"

"Let me guess," Armond interrupted, "red wine, full-bodied and smooth, no tannin aftertaste. You're such a mercurial creature when it comes to food and drink, it's hard to keep pace."

Walking out of the bedroom in her favorite ripped jeans and cotton tee, Victoria messed Armond's hair as she walked by. "Ha ha, very funny. I'm a woman who knows what she likes. One of my many assets, as far as I'm concerned."

"Yes, so you've insisted in the past. And, don't screw with my hair. You know it annoys me."

Victoria walked up behind him as he was opening a bottle of wine and smooshed both her hands into and all through his hair. Turning quickly, Armond grabbed both her wrists, flipped her around, and pushed her back against the bar. "You have such an odd sense of humor. It's going to get you into trouble one of these days," he said as she leaned her head back laughing.

"Armond, you're so easy to rile. It's hard to pass up the opportunity," Victoria said.

Catching her scent and feeling her body between him and the bar, Armond couldn't help but push slightly forward. Victoria was suddenly still, alert that something had shifted. He tugged gently on her hair, her face turning up toward his, and bent down. There was a moment's hesitation. Then, he kissed her.

Pushing him gently away, Victoria was mortified. "Armond. What just happened?"

He smiled, watching panic run across her face. "I believe that's called a kiss."

"I know what it's called, you dolt. But why?"

"Because I wanted it, and so did you."

"Don't tell me what I want. I don't know why all the men in my life continue to believe I need to be told what I want or how to feel. First Robert and now you."

Armond turned to pour a smidgeon of wine into her glass. "Here, taste this, and tell me if it meets with your very untrained, yet finicky approval."

"Don't try to change the subject," Victoria said as she took the glass and sipped. "Yes, it's perfect. Thanks. This is terrible. We work together. I'm your company's lawyer. Shall I resign? What will we tell your father?"

"What the hell are you talking about? It was a kiss. You do know you can't make babies by kissing, no matter what Sister what's-her-name told you? And why in God's name would we not work together anymore or, even more concerning, tell my father?"

"Because you've ruined everything," Victoria almost wailed.

"You know, I believe you might be even more dramatic than some of Renoir Productions' self-absorbed stars. Now," Armond said as he handed her an overly large pour of wine, "sit down, drink your wine, and decide what you want to eat. Nothing's changed. We'll eat and discuss business as usual."

"Fine. I'm fine with that as long as you can handle it."

Armond raised his trademark eyebrow. "Yes, Victoria, I think I can manage."

* * *

After a few hours of eating and reviewing the investor files, Armond stood, stretched, and looked at his watch. "I don't know about you, but I've had it."

"Well, suck it up, *mon capitaine*. We need to finish this last one. Our meetings are first thing in the morning."

"Fine," Armond said, returning to the sofa and opening the last folder.

Victoria looked over at him. "You know, it's close to seven in the morning, Pacific time. Technically, we've been up all night. I think it's safe for you to take off your tie. I doubt any investor is going to come busting through the door at this hour."

"I can see from your very trendy attire that you have no qualms about dressing down. I, on the other hand, prefer to do business in business attire. It keeps me focused."

Victoria shook her head at his stubbornness as she flipped through the last of her papers. "Well, well, well. Look at this. It seems we have a real live female as an investor candidate. It can't be true. A woman who walks, talks, has a brain, and her own money? Seriously, I thought you said I had to be seen and not heard, yet here she is," Victoria finished as she set her file down and walked over to the table to sip the last of her peppermint tea.

"Look at her name." Armond tapped his pen against his folder and waited for Victoria to retrieve and flip open hers.

"And?" Victoria asked.

"She's American. Her bio says she was born in the United States and brought to Asia at a very young age. She's apparently lived in several countries and, it seems, made a fortune in the auction business. She owns some of the most well-respected auction houses in Asia."

"She certainly seems to have a healthy bank account. Your accountants concluded that her business is solid. I do have one question, though."

"What is it?" Armond asked, skeptical at the tone in Victoria's voice.

"Since she's American, can I speak at this meeting, or do I still need to sit in the corner like the good little girl that I've been?" Victoria asked sarcastically.

"I'm not sure yet," Armond answered, surprising Victoria.

"She's American and a woman in business to boot! What could possibly be your reservation?"

"She was born in America, but she's lived in this part of the world most of her life. Let's not assume she follows our traditions. We should know within the first few minutes."

Standing, Armond walked over to the table and grabbed his jacket off the back of the chair. Smoothing it meticulously over his arm, he turned and looked at Victoria. "I'm going to bed. I'll see you in the morning. Do you want to meet for breakfast?"

"No. I'm going to see if I can run somewhere near the hotel. Do you think we can stop at a Starbucks to grab coffee on the way to the meeting?"

"Just soaking up the different culture, aren't you? You can take the girl out of the South Side but—"

"Yeah, yeah. I know the rest. Get out. See you downstairs at eight thirty," Victoria interrupted, walking after him to bolt her door.

Wide awake and curious, Victoria walked over to her laptop, used the secure connect Renoir Productions had given her, and logged on to do a little research. The information they had received from the accountants was too vanilla. Who was she? Did she have a family? Had she been educated in the States?

After about thirty minutes of searching, Victoria gave up. She considered herself a consummate researcher, yet she'd turned up absolutely nothing about this woman. Exhausted, Victoria got into bed and turned on the English-speaking TV channel for background noise.

CHAPTER

32

ADAM STEPPED ONTO the plane, turned toward business class, and walked directly to his seat. He got the same seat every time and, unless some business deal prevented it, took the same flight. He nodded and smiled at the staff as they greeted him by name, took his coat and handed him the two pillows he always used for takeoff. He noticed some of the other business class passengers craning their necks to see who the staff was fussing over. He loved that.

"Here you go, Mr. Smith." The flight attendant smiled, handing him his preferred brand of bourbon, no ice, just as he liked.

"Thank you," he said and raised his glass in mock salute to the woman he thought of as Stew One. He never used their names and even made a point not to learn them. Instead, he used a numbering system.

Stew One was his favorite right now, but that might very well change during this flight. Stew Two appeared to have gotten new, bigger boobs, from the looks of it. *A face-to-face, or rather boob-to-boob, comparison would settle the competition,* he thought as he laughed at his joke, got comfy in his seat, and took a good long pull of his bourbon.

Thinking back over the past few days, Adam felt things couldn't be better. After Japan, he'd flown to Thailand and had spent the past four days meeting clients. He took out his private, leather-bound book and looked over his notes. He had a thriving side business that also brought significant legal business to the firm, so the time he'd spent in Asia ended up being doubly profitable, at least for him.

There is nothing wrong with having my own business, Adam thought. *Billy is heir to his family's tobacco plantation and Trever to his grandfather's ranch. They don't share information about their family businesses with me; no reason I need to tell them about mine.* It brought him a significant amount of cash—more than he had ever dreamed of having as the kid who hadn't inherited any role in his family's retail business. As the youngest, he was essentially pushed out as his older brother and father hadn't wanted to share the profits with him.

Taking another pull of his bourbon, he leaned his head back onto his pillows with a self-satisfied smile, loving that his father and brother were now foaming at the mouth over his estate in the Hamptons. He'd sent them pictures when he'd purchased it last year. *Bastards had the nerve to ask who it belonged to. Now that they understand I could buy and sell their stupid retail business ten times over, they're kissing my ass.*

"Mr. Smith, would you like a refill?" Stew Two asked.

Leering directly at her tits, Adam said, "Honey, I'd love one. And," Adam said, touching her arm and beckoning her to come closer, "five hundred bucks if you undo just a few buttons on that uniform so I can see a bit more of those new assets. They are new, aren't they?"

"Let's see the five first."

Almost salivating, Adam reached into his inside breast pocket and pulled out a wad of bills. Handing her five hundred dollar bills, he asked, "Now, the answer is?"

"Brand spanking new double *d*'s."

"Baby, congratulations. You just became Stew One."

CHAPTER
33

P ULLING BACK THE heavy curtains in his suite, Billy squinted as he looked out over the ocean. The sun was already high in the sky over Miami, and the penthouse gave him views up and down the coast. The partners always gathered somewhere warm the first week of November to lock down final estimates of funds to be received year-end and to finalize the next year's projected revenue.

Hearing the knock at his door, Billy called, "Come in. It's open."

"This is my favorite time of year. Counting our cash," Trever said as walked over to admire the view. "Where's Adam?"

"He called and said he'd be about five minutes late. He had to change his projections because of a new client he got yesterday. His staff is finishing the updates."

"Man, he's been raking it in over the past few years. The business he set up advising US clients who want to do business in Asia and vice versa has been beyond anything I would have predicted," Trever said.

"I think, Trever, we are reaching the point where he'll want a bigger piece of the pie. He's thrown a few lines into the water hinting at that."

"I've seen them. Adam is anything but subtle. As far as I'm concerned, though, that will never happen. We agreed that, no matter what happened year to year, the three of us would share the firm's profits equally. None of us wanted to leave ourselves open to the traditional law firm bullshit of partners tearing each other apart over clients and money. He was certainly happy enough when we began and he could barely reel a dead fish into our boat, let alone one that was worth eating."

"When one begins to make money, one often forgets who helped him along the way," Billy responded.

Hearing a light rap, Billy and Trever turned as the door opened. "Gentlemen, how are you on this fabulous Miami morning?" Adam greeted them with a huge smile on his face.

Billy and Trever glanced at each other, knowing where this was headed. Adam saw the exchange and couldn't have cared less. He used to dread their annual meetings. He'd arrive agitated and unhappy and stay that way until the end because his numbers had historically been much lower than theirs. Adam was forced to sit there for hours as kudos were given back and forth between Billy and Trever, the rainmakers. About three years ago, Adam's revenue began increasing significantly, and consequently, his feelings about this meeting had changed. Last year, he'd been only a few million behind Billy and only half a million behind Trever. Judging by his demeanor this morning, Billy and Trever bet his revised figures placed him in the number one spot for the current fiscal year and projections for next.

Walking over to the fully stocked bar, Adam searched until he found what he was looking for. "Ah, here we are," he said.

"A bit early for champagne, isn't it?" Trever asked, using the exaggerated drawl he saved for times when he wanted to make a point.

Pulling expertly on the cork until it loosened into his hand, Adam filled three crystal flutes. Handing one to each of his partners, he answered, "Not at all. Today is one of celebration. This is one of the best years we've had as a firm, and I'm predicting amazing things on the horizon, some of which I'll discuss with you during the planning phase."

Unable to take much more of Adam crowing, Billy suggested, "Shall we begin? Adam, you have new numbers to give us?"

Adam pulled documents from his folder and passed them out. "I had to revise my numbers and the firm's cumulative revenue this morning because two of my largest clients committed to paying their December invoices before the end of the year for tax purposes. We'll email their invoices on the thirty first, and they'll wire the funds into our account before midnight."

Adam sat back while Billy and Trever poured over his changed figures. He almost laughed watching them try to keep their eyes from popping out of their heads.

Billy made a few notations and felt a bit annoyed at losing his number one spot to Adam, but at least he was still a few million ahead of Trever. Looking over at Trever, he asked, "Ready?"

"Yup. Adam," Trever began, "congratulations. You've done a great job over the past few years and, based on these numbers, this year in particular. You helped beat our firm projections by more than three million. You've really outdone yourself."

"Thank you, Trever. I am rather proud of my numbers."

"I couldn't agree more, Adam," Billy joined in. "You've done a fantastic job of expanding into Asia, and that's been key to significant growth for our firm. When no one else thought it was going to amount to anything, you persevered and now, look what you've built."

"A few questions about next year's projections, Adam," Trever stated.

"Of course."

"You're projecting an almost 20 percent increase in your revenue stream. That's a significant increase and, coupled with Billy's and my projections, the overall firm projects an increase of more than 30 percent. While I don't for a minute doubt your ability, our projections have always been on the conservative side. I don't want to change that."

Adam knew he'd be questioned about his projections for the coming year and had been looking forward to it. "Trever, I appreciate your concern, and I don't intend to change the way we project firm revenue. This is my conservative number."

Billy's eyebrow quirked slightly, and he looked directly into Adam's eyes. "If this is your conservative projection...just for kicks, what's the number you think you'll actually bring in the door?"

Adam smiled, relishing the attention. He finally understood why his partners had always loved these meetings. It was exhilarating to discuss revenue and projections when you were at the top of the heap.

"I think the best thing I can do is to give you the number I'm comfortable with, which is the conservative one. In almost fifteen years of doing this, none of us has been off by more than 5 percent, yet we've never drilled down into each other's actual projections. Let's leave well enough alone, shall we?"

"I agree," Trever said.

"Fine," Billy acquiesced. "Will you need additional staff or attorneys to reach any of these numbers? We want to ensure you have everything you need to hit your targets."

"No. I'm good with the team I've got. If we're done with this part of the meeting, let's turn to the planning phase."

Both Billy and Trever nodded.

Adam reached into his folder and passed around a color-coded chart. "This is what I believe the firm can do over the next five years. Take a minute, digest it, and then we'll discuss."

Trever looked up first. "Adam, while I appreciate the exuberance reflected in these numbers, there is no way we can staff up quickly enough to bring in this kind of revenue."

"I have to agree," Billy joined in. "These numbers are too high, almost fantastical."

"Let me explain," Adam said, pulling out two additional documents. "This one," he said as handed it around, "shows my projections of our revenue and costs if we expand to these countries organically, meaning if we hire and train the people we need. This next one,"—he nodded at the second document—"shows our growth rate if we strategically purchase firms native to these countries and bring some of their best income-producing people on board. As you can see, the difference is striking."

Both Billy and Trever took their time looking over the documents. "How solid are these numbers?" Trever asked.

"Rock solid. The firms I've listed expressed an interest in selling. Each provided me with its financials for the past three years and projections for the coming year. The next steps, if we agree, are for the three of us to sign confidentiality agreements and arrange to meet their partners."

"How long have you been working on this?" Billy asked Adam, looking at Trever in a silent ask if he had known.

Adam caught the exchange. For years, he had put up with their shit doesn't stink attitudes. It was more than rewarding to watch them try to keep their footing when he had just walked them to the edge of the cliff.

"Over the past three years," Adam answered, pulling out a final set of papers and handing them to his partners. "We can discuss the details today, and I'll answer any questions you might have. But the prudent thing to do is to execute these documents and then arrange meetings. The managing partners are willing to fly to the US, so there should be little, if any, disruption to your schedules. In fact, I'd like to arrange the first meeting in February. That will give you enough time to review the background information I've provided and for us to have a second meeting before they arrive."

"That's fast. Why the rush?" Billy asked.

"No rush. It's opportunity knocking. If we don't walk through the door, I promise you, one of our competitors will. They've given us first opportunity, but they won't wait forever."

"Why would these two firms have come to us first?" Trever asked.

"They know and trust me. And, let's not sell ourselves short. We've built a good firm with a solid reputation. They believe, like we do, that the legal profession will continue to be dominated by mega firms that service the international corporate community." Sensing his partners' reticence, he reassured them. "Meeting with them doesn't mean we have to proceed, but not meeting them would be one of the stupidest decisions we could make."

"Here's my concern," Billy said. "Except for 10 percent, the three of us have complete and total ownership of our firm. As far as I know, there are no other firms like that. I have no intention of altering that arrangement, and I doubt Trever does either." Trever shook his head, indicating his agreement with Billy. "So, if they can't have ownership of the pie, why would they want to merge their firm with ours?"

Adam got up, grabbed the champagne, and refilled his partners' glasses. "I think I can convince the majority share-holders to sell us their firms lock, stock, and barrel. That way, we get rid of the equity partners by paying them a hefty sum to step aside, and we keep the smartest and hardest working associates and non-equity partners."

"Why in the world would they want to do that?" Trever asked. "I'm sure they've worked through the same numbers you've shown us. It would make no sense for them to walk away from a potential gold mine."

"I'm sure they'll have their reasons," Adam said as he smiled and raised his glass. "To us, to world domination, and to the future of Acker, Smith & McGowen."

Billy and Trever glanced at each other, wondering the same thing, but the amount of money they would make if Adam's deals went through would make them some of the wealthiest lawyers in the world. That was all they needed to give Adam the go-ahead. "To us," they echoed.

CHAPTER
34

I T WAS HER favorite time of day. *There's something tangible and calming about twilight,* Victoria thought as she breathed in deeply, savoring the fresh air. It was the first time she'd been outside the building where she and Armond had been locked in meetings all day. "I'm a bit embarrassed to admit this, but I actually thought the sun might not set in the West in Hong Kong."

"Really?" Armond responded with a sideways glance.

"Oh, don't give me your smarter-than-thou look. Not all of us were brought up with a silver spoon in our mouth and daddy's private jet waiting outside our kindergarten class. I've only been out of the country one other time. How would I know?"

"I don't know. You've had years of schooling," Armond answered with a dose of sarcasm. "Perhaps you'd pick it up along the way?"

Victoria gave Armond a good, strong elbow jab in his ribs.

As they walked in silence toward their hotel, Victoria felt at peace. It was the feeling she always got when she'd put in a solid, productive day's work. She'd apparently been tense earlier, nervous about adding value for Renoir Productions, because she could feel her shoulders and neck relaxing. *At least now*, she thought, *I can enjoy the sights and sounds of Hong Kong.* Looking around, Victoria understood why Hong Kong was called the Pearl of the Orient. The soaring skyscrapers, the nightly light show, and the deep blue of the harbor made it a tucked-away gem. If she had to describe the city, she would say it was alive. It felt as if every beat and pulse had a purpose. Everyone was in a rush. And if she listened, she could hear as many as five different languages being spoken at any moment. Enjoying the sense of relaxation, mixed with the heady power and beauty of the city, she linked her arm through Armond's. "I feel much better today. I think the jet lag's finally worn off."

"I'm glad to hear it. Just in time for the trip home," Armond responded, steering them through the throng of people.

"I'm assuming it's easier on the way home?" Victoria asked hopefully. When she got no response, she gave him a nudge. "Armond? Are you ignoring me?"

Armond had been watching Victoria's hair sway as she walked, thinking it had an almost ethereal quality. Shaking his head, he willed himself to stay focused on the increasingly crowded sidewalk traffic. "I'm sorry, what did you say?"

"I asked if the jet lag is easier on the way home," Victoria repeated.

"No. The trip home's a killer," Armond answered, glancing at Victoria. "It usually takes me a good five days before I feel somewhat normal and a full week before I stop nodding off in the middle of the day."

"Well, that's not what I wanted to hear," Victoria responded. "We return to the US the day after tomorrow?"

"Yes. We leave on Wednesday and because we'll cross the International Date Line, we arrive on Wednesday. The day we lost on the way out, we get back on the way home."

"Weird. But I'm glad to hear it. I have a major hearing in federal court on Friday. As soon as we land in LA and I turn back into Cinderella after stepping off your private plane,"—Victoria gave Armond another nudge with her elbow—"I'll have to catch the next flight to Chicago and prepare on the flight home. Our briefs were filed almost two months ago, and at this point, I can't remember half the issues."

"Oh," Armond said, surprised at how sad he felt at the thought of her leaving.

"Oh, what?" Victoria asked, looking up at Armond.

"I had assumed you would stay in California at least through the weekend so we could brief my parents about the trip and maybe have a few days to relax."

"I'm sorry, Armond. I had no idea you wanted me to stay after we returned."

"Can't you push the hearing?"

"No way. My opposing counsel's a dick—I mean, a real big one," Victoria said, using her hands to express just how big a dick she thought he was. "There's no way he'd agree to move the hearing. Besides, the judge let us know he set aside two hours Friday for oral argument. If we called his clerk this close to the hearing date to reschedule, I'm sure he'd blow a gasket."

"Who are you in front of?" Armond asked, not yet willing to give up.

"The chief judge. As you recall, he's known for taking a piece of your ass if you try to move anything on his schedule."

The thought of Victoria returning to Chicago made Armond realize just how much he missed working with her day-to-day. Even though he'd been her boss at the firm, they'd become so close they would often finish each other's thoughts. They'd developed a routine, meeting every Thursday after work to unload the week. He missed that.

"Let's do this," Armond suggested. "I'll have the company plane take you back to Chicago after I get dropped off in LA. That will save you at least eight hours, and you can prep for your hearing in peace and quiet. You'll get a good meal, be well taken care of, and be rested when you land." Victoria opened her mouth to object. "Nope, not done." Armond held up his hand to stop her before she could utter a word. "And, since we've finished with the investor meetings, we can discuss them over a very fancy dinner tonight and get a preliminary lineup."

Victoria continued walking and said nothing. "Well?" Armond asked.

"Oh, are you done now? May I speak?"

Armond smiled at her tone. "Yes, to both questions. Proceed."

"I don't see how I can justify costing Renoir Productions that kind of money just to make it easier for me to get back for a hearing. It's unrealistic, a waste of money, and not my style. Also, I don't want your father to think I'm taking advantage of you or your company. So, thank you for the offer, but I'll just fly commercial, if you don't mind."

"I do mind, and you're not flying commercial—end of discussion," Armond responded a bit gruffly.

Victoria stopped mid-stride. Turing to face Armond, she tilted her chin up and put her hands on her hips. "First, I don't really care if you mind. Second, don't ever, ever, ever again tell me when a discussion is over. And third, you hired me to be part of your legal team. I'm not your lackey, so this bossing around thing isn't going to fly. And, finally—"

Victoria felt herself being yanked forward into Armond's chest. As she looked up into his eyes, she thought, *This will change everything.* Then, he kissed her. It was like an out-of-body experience. Armond was like a brother to her. He had been her mentor and boss. As coherent thoughts began to return, Victoria's eyes flew wide open, her head snapped up, and her forehead smacked hard into Armond's nose.

"Jesus Christ," Armond groaned. "I think you broke my nose."

"I'm so sorry," Victoria said, "but—isn't this a violation of some sort?"

Armond grabbed his handkerchief and held it to his nose. "What the hell are you talking about?" he said as he pulled it away to reveal blood.

"I'm your lawyer and—"

"You're not my lawyer. You're Renoir Productions' lawyer."

"Yes, but in any event, isn't there some ethics rule about lawyers can't be involved with clients?"

Armond stared at her open-mouthed. Despite the throbbing in his nose, he threw back his head and laughed. He put one of his arms around Victoria's shoulder, held the other to his nose, and turned to walk into their hotel. "God, you're an idiot. It was just a kiss, and no, there's no rule that deals with our situation. And even if there was, who's going to report us—the communist on the corner?"

"Listen, Armond. I don't want to ruin what we have," Victoria said honestly as they were enveloped in the relative calmness of their hotel lobby.

"I don't want to ruin it, either, Victoria. It was a spur of the moment thing that will probably never happen again," Armond replied, watching her over his now almost fully bloodied handkerchief.

Feeling disappointed at that thought, Victoria tried to change her mood and avoid any further conversation on the topic. Grabbing his arm, she led him toward the elevator. "Let's get you upstairs to your room. I'll get some ice for your nose while you put your feet up and your head back. It should stop bleeding in a few minutes. If not, I've always wanted to see some of that Eastern medicine in action. I'm sure the hotel can recommend someone nearby."

"I'm not going to be the guinea pig for some random Eastern medicine man just to satisfy your curiosity. I'll be fine. Who knew kissing you would result in a deadly blow to the head?"

"Right? I'll have to issue a warning in the future. Do you still want to head out to dinner, or would you rather stay in?"

"It's one of our last nights in Hong Kong. There's a place I want to take you that's one of my favorites."

"Does it have food I can eat? You know, like items other than thousand-year eggs or chicken feet. God, what I wouldn't give for a cheese plate and a glass of wine. And, what's the attire?

"Trust me. You'll love this place, and the attire is five-star, all-out fancy. Let's meet in my room in an hour, shall we?"

"Works for me," Victoria said as she opened the door to Armond's suite so he could keep his head tilted. She prepared a wash cloth wrapped around ice, stuck it in his hand, and pointed at the sofa. "Now, go sit, put your head back, and don't move for fifteen minutes. If the bleeding doesn't stop, call me. We'll stay in and order room service." Victoria waved as she shut his door behind her.

As soon as she walked into her room, she dialed Kat. While the phone made clicking noises and finally began to ring, a fleeting thought crossed Victoria's mind. *Perhaps it's the middle of the night in Texas.* Looking at the time and day on her watch, she rubbed her forehead. "Okay," she said out loud, "for Texas, I subtract eight hours and add a day so it's—or is it add the hours and subtract the day? God, I have no idea." Shrugging her shoulders, Victoria felt little guilt at the thought of possibly waking her best friend. There had been plenty of times during law school when Kat had stayed out until the wee hours and then banged on their apartment door because she had forgotten her key or called Victoria in the middle of the night for a ride home from a party. Now, it was Kat's turn.

"Well, hello, my little world traveler. How are things in the East?" Kat's voice came over the line.

"Kat! I'm glad I got you. You weren't sleeping, were you? I have absolutely no idea how to do this time translation thing," Victoria said, relieved her friend had answered the phone.

"There's a little thing called the World Wide Web, not to mention your phone, both of which will convert the time for you with just the push of a button, but I have a feeling you would have called no matter the time. Am I right?"

"Need I remind you of the countless times you woke me out of a sound sleep—at least two of those before major exams—so I could retrieve your hammered ass from some party? What time is it there?" Victoria responded, ignoring her friend's sarcasm.

Kat looked at her watch. "It's a bit after six in the morning."

"Then why do you sound so perky?"

"Because I just finished boot camp," Kat said, anticipating the reaction she would get from her friend.

"You what?" Victoria exclaimed, as if on cue. "Boot camp? You've never exercised a day in your life."

"Well, now I am. I'm running too."

"When you say running, what do you mean?"

"Oh my God, Victoria. You can act so superior when it comes to running. You know, putting one foot in front of the other at a pace faster than a walk," Kat responded sarcastically.

"Now I know for sure the end of the world is near," Victoria said laughing. "Seriously, though, what happened that made you start exercising?"

"Nothing happened. I just spend so much time sitting at my desk or in meetings that I decided I had better change my behavior or my perky booty was going to cease to exist. You know what a narcissist I am. I can't walk into a room and not get noticed. I know, I know. Not very forward-thinking of me, but it's the truth and I'll deny I said it if you ever repeat it outside the confines of this phone call. But enough about me and my fab body, what about you? How's the trip? How's Hong Kong? That's one place I haven't been, and I'm dying to go."

"First, let me thank you for that unexpected admission about your narcissism. I'd go into a rant about all the things that are wrong with what you said, except right now I have more important matters to discuss than your future sagging ass," Victoria answered.

"Hmm. Well, I can't imagine what could be more important than my ass, but okay, I'm game. Shoot," Kat responded upbeat.

"Armond kissed me," Victoria blurted, cringing, her heart racing. She was holding her breath, waiting for a reaction, but instead, there was silence. Thinking they were disconnected, Victoria said, "Hello?"

"I don't think I heard you. Repeat, please," Kat ordered, needing time to absorb what she thought she heard.

"Armond kissed me. You heard me the first time, Kat," Victoria responded, this time closing her eyes as she relived the scene in her head.

"What kind of a kiss? On the cheeks as in hello? Or, on the lips as a friend? Or, perhaps it was celebratory? Describe, please," Kat demanded.

"Kat, I have no idea how this happened. We were just walking back to our hotel, he pulled me in, and we kissed. Oh my God! Every time I say that out loud I get palpitations. I'm absolutely mortified. How do I continue working with him? I don't want to lose him as my friend." Victoria's rising panic was stopped short. "What the hell is that noise you're making? Are you laughing or crying, for God's sake? This is serious, Kat."

Kat had to rummage around in her designer gym bag to find a tissue. She'd been laughing so hard through Victoria's insane dissertation over a kiss that she was crying. "Oh yes, so serious. You might be pregnant," Kat announced as she burst into another round of hysterical laughter. "You must be the only person on earth who didn't see this coming. We've all been waiting for something like this for months."

Victoria was stunned into silence.

Knowing her best friend as well as she did, Kat knew she had just delivered a shocking and—for Victoria—likely mortifying truth. "V," Kat continued in a calm voice, "I know what I just said is likely upsetting to you, but it shouldn't be. There's nothing to be upset about. Armond is—"

Victoria interrupted, "My mentor, my pal, my confidant. What do you mean you were all waiting? Who's all?"

"Your close friends: Mary, me, Jen, and even Robert recently mentioned it. Your mom has made a few comments about the possibility too."

"Oh my God. I feel like an absolute idiot. Was Armond in on the conversations too?" Victoria responded, speaking more to herself than to Kat.

"Absolutely not. I don't think either of you saw it coming," Kat responded, using her best soothing voice. "But it's no big deal. Things like this happen. Just be glad it didn't happen while he was your boss at the firm. He's a great guy. I see nothing but good here."

"That's because you're not working for him and his family's business or with him on an overseas trip to Hong Kong…and because he's not your mentor," Victoria said, getting angry that her best friend seemed to be discounting her concerns.

"I'm not saying you don't have a point. I'm just saying this isn't all bad. So what if you two do decide to date? What's the worst that can happen?"

"Kat, really?" Victoria responded with frustration. "The worst is that we come out of it hating each other and are no longer friends—that I lose one of the most important relationships of my adult life."

"Okay, you have a point. Here's what I suggest. Why don't you calmly discuss your concerns with him? All your points are good ones and come from your interest in not losing your friendship with him. Where is he now, by the way?"

"He's back in his room, trying to stop his nose from bleeding."

"I'm almost afraid to ask," Kat said.

"I headbutt him after he kissed me. See? Look what happened after only one kiss," Victoria said, now seeing a sliver of humor in the ridiculousness of it all. "Well, really two," she quickly snuck in to get the full truth out there. "Imagine the death and destruction if we have sex."

"Wait. Did you say two? This is a second kiss? When was the first, and why did I not hear about it?" Kat asked, now a bit irritated at not hearing about the first time.

"It happened a few days ago. It was nothing." Victoria tried to dismiss it, becoming worried as she heard Kat's tone change.

"Well, it doesn't change anything," Kat said, trying to back off her tone, as it wasn't the right time for a deep dive into the possibilities. Right now, all her friend needed was some perspective. "Talk to him, V. You'll find the right balance. In the meantime, I'm signing us up for the New Year's 5K run in Houston. You should worry more about how I'm going to kick your ass at that race with my family as witness to your demise."

"Keep dreaming, my friend! By the way, I'm assuming everything's fine with my cases. I haven't heard a peep from you, Jenny, or Mary."

"Jenny's doing an amazing job. She and Mary make a fabulous team. If you have enough work, you might want to consider bringing her on board full-time."

"I've thought about that. We'll see how things shake out over the next few months. Speaking of cases, how are you and Robert doing on mine? I don't want it to fall off everyone's radar."

"Far from it," Kat responded. "We think we have a plan that might lead to critical evidence. I'd rather not go into detail now. By the time you're back in the States, we'll have our thoughts worked through, so we can present a cohesive package."

"That's great news, Kat. Thanks for jumping in to help Robert. It sounds as if you've carved out a working relationship."

"We've worked a few things through. I think we're moving in the right direction." Kat smiled as she examined her freshly polished nails, thinking of her last encounter with Robert.

"I'm relieved to hear that. Okay, I gotta go. I have to get ready for dinner with Armond. He was really quite a baby over a run of the mill, bloody nose," Victoria said, feeling her bearings begin to return.

"Give Armond a hug and a *friendly* kiss for me, will you?" Kat stressed the word friendly and laughed as she hung up the phone.

"Everyone's a comedian," Victoria said as she walked toward the shower to get ready for dinner.

CHAPTER
35

"COME IN," DR. Natarajan said as she looked up from her desk when one of the firm's newest associates knocked and peeked around her door.

"Do you have a moment?"

"Of course. How can I help, Sarah?"

"Can I speak to you in confidence?"

"Yes. Please sit down," Dr. Natarajan said as she sat back in her chair and placed her pen neatly in front of her.

"I don't want this to go anywhere else, but I don't know how to handle it. I assume that, as head of HR, you would handle these situations," Sarah said, fumbling over her words.

"I won't know until you tell me. I assure you I will maintain our conversation in total confidence."

Taking a long breath to steady herself, Sarah began. "Mr. Acker called me into his office to discuss an assignment for a tech company that hired the firm to handle their efforts to go public. He said it was a great opportunity and that he wanted me on his team. Then he asked if I was interested.

Of course, I said yes." Sarah paused and looked down at her hands.

Dr. Natarajan sighed, anticipating where this was headed. "Go on, Sarah."

"As I was leaving his office, he came up behind me, shoved me against the door, and pushed up against me. He told me I was on his short list and that he always helped those on his short list get ahead, especially if they helped him."

Dr. Natarajan watched as Sarah began to cry. She went around her desk, handed her a tissue, and sat beside her, waiting for her to calm down. "Then what?"

"Nothing. I pushed him away and told him I was engaged. Now what happens?" Sarah asked.

Walking back around her desk, Dr. Natarajan was silent for a moment. "Sarah, do you like being a lawyer?"

"Of course. It's been my dream for as long as I can remember. I took on significant student loans so I could go to one of the best law schools in the country, and I worked hard to graduate at the top of my class. Why?"

"Understand that I'm here to help, so please take this in the spirit in which it's being offered. The reality is if you ever want to work as a lawyer again, you'll do nothing. You'll tell no one. You'll continue with your career as if it never happened."

"You can't be serious! How can you tell me to do nothing? Aren't you supposed to handle these situations? I came to this firm, in part, because of its reputation for promoting and bettering women. One of the named partners just assaulted me. You have to help me."

Dr. Natarajan stood, signaling the discussion was over. She'd learned long ago that the more she allowed these young women to do a deep dive into their situation, the more complex it became for the firm. "My dear, I am helping you. You have only to listen. Never speak of it again if you want to remain a viable, practicing lawyer with a career ahead of you. Now, let me pull a few strings and see where else we might find for you to work."

"What do you mean where else? You mean another firm?"

"Yes, exactly. We'll give you exceptional references and get you a good position, along with a significant parting bonus. There are a few documents you'll have to sign, of course, including nondisclosure and confidentiality agreements. Should you violate either of these, the firm will not only sue you for damages, but it will also seek return of all funds paid."

"What if I want to stay at the firm?"

"Oh, my dear, that would be a life-altering error on your part."

"Why? I can make a formal complaint, and then he'll have to account for his actions. Maybe that former associate who filed a lawsuit against the firm will be interested in my story," Sarah blurted out.

Dr. Natarajan walked over to her door, and pushed on it to make certain it was closed. She then returned to face Sarah, leaned down, and almost spat in her face. "Now you sound stupid, and I know from everything you've just told me—and from your file—that you're anything but. Do you really think you have even the slightest shot at winning against one of the most powerful firms in the country? Do you think anyone will believe you over Billy Acker? The man can have any woman he wants, yet you're going to convince a jury of your peers that he chose you?"

She walked over to her cabinet, retrieved papers and pushed them and a pen across her desk. Taking a softer tone, she said, "Sarah, I'm trying to help you. If you file a claim or discuss this with anyone, this offer will be off the table for good. This type of behavior happens. In your next position, when something like this happens again—and odds are it will—I suggest you learn to live with it. Think of a way to use the power you have in the moment to your advantage."

Sarah was shocked and felt suddenly exhausted. She hadn't expected this when she walked into HR. Standing, she said, "I need time to think this over. I'll get back to you soon."

"Sarah, the terms of the offer expire when you walk out that door. I'm offering you a significant sum of money and a new, better position at a top-tier firm, where you can do the kind of work you trained to do. Don't be stupid," Dr. Natarajan said as pushed the papers closer to Sarah.

Sarah began to cry out of frustration and as reality sunk in. She had debts to pay, and she couldn't expect her hardworking, blue-collar parents to help. Picking up the pen, she slowly signed her name on the bottom line.

CHAPTER

36

"OKAY, GIVE ME an update. What've you discovered since our last meeting?" Jack barked as he rushed into the room and sat at the head of the table.

Jason nodded at Samantha. They had agreed she would go first, and he would wrap up. They had also agreed that if Jack began one of his abusive tirades while one of them was talking, the other would try to distract him while they got him back on topic. Neither of them knew if their plan would work, but they agreed it was better than passively sitting and being screamed at, or being a witness to the screaming for God only knows how long.

Samantha could tell by the energy he had swept into the room that Jack was in a foul mood. She took a deep breath and kept a hopeful thought. *Maybe if I speak quickly, he'll hold his powder until it's Jason's turn. Not a very loyal thought,* she noted inwardly, *but it's everyone for himself when it comes to Jack.*

"What the hell are you waiting for?" Samantha jumped, as Jack's bark brought her quickly back to reality.

"We've questioned all the lawyers on the hiring committee and the personnel in the human resources department about their practices and procedures. We've also questioned the nominating committee members about the requirements for partnership and how that process is handled. So far, it all seems organized, clean, and clear."

"Jesus, what the hell does 'organized, clean, and clear' mean? Is it your time of the month? Because you sound like you have shit for brains right now," Jack snarled.

Samantha knew it was best not to take Jack on when he was in one of his moods, but she also wasn't going to cower under his bullying. "The firm's followed the accepted processes other firms use for hiring and partnership determinations, which have previously been found to be non-discriminatory and proper by the courts when they've been tested." Samantha looked at Jason, signaling his turn.

"However," Jason began, "the firm has no explanation for why we are statistically out of whack with comparably-sized firms regarding the number of female lawyers that leave."

"Oh, for Christ's sake. Now you sound like her," Jack said as he jabbed his thumb in Samantha's direction. "Maybe your hormones are on the same schedule. I've heard that happens when women work together."

Ignoring Jack, Jason pushed on. "So, the issue remains. Why is our firm well below the statistical average?"

"Why do we care?" Jack asked out loud, although he was talking to himself. He shot out of his chair and dragged the whiteboard out of the corner. Using a black marker, he wrote *WHY* and *JURY*. Jack adopted a professorial tone. "We care because the jury will want to know why, and Victoria and her lawyer will come armed with evidence to grind

194

our deficiencies into the jurors' heads." Jack walked toward the back of the room and asked, "If I were them, what would I do?"

Samantha and Jason leaned back in their chairs and knew better than to open their mouths. While Jack could be a real asshole, there was no doubt he was one of the best trial lawyers in the country. This type of ranting display was when he was at his best. Focused and fine-tuned, Jack almost always spewed gems and his two protégés were more than willing to retrieve every bobble.

"I would bring in other firms' managing partners to testify to their firms' stats on women," Jack answered himself and walked rapidly back to the board to write *managing partners*. "Of course, they'll tout their great female-to-male partner ratio and use their obligation to testify as a marketing opportunity and try to take our business. What else? What else?" Jack paced as he spoke. Taking huge strides back to his board, he wrote, *consulting firm.* Turning and pointing at Samantha and Jason, he said in a manic tone, "I would bring in a consulting firm, specializing in diversity, to testify to our sorry as shit statistical lack of female partners. I'm missing something. What is it?" Jack asked as he stepped back and stared at his board. "Of course. The most obvious thing is almost always the most elusive." His eyes seemed to glaze over and then focus again. "I would bring in the women themselves. 'Tell the jury, Ms. X, why you left the firm right before partnership after you worked for six years and put in sixty hours every week? I'm sure the jury will understand how you suddenly concluded after all that education, time, and hard work that the law was not your calling. Well, that certainly makes sense, doesn't it ladies and gentlemen of the jury?'"

Samantha and Jason had no idea where he was headed at this point. "Goddamn it," he suddenly yelled, making both Samantha and Jason jump, "we need an answer. What does the firm say when you ask why all these women left?"

Samantha looked at Jason, hoping he'd field the question but saw that his head was bowed in a deliberate effort to avoid eye contact. *Pussy*, she thought. "Jack, everyone we spoke with blamed the women. They said they all made life choices right before partnership eligibility," Samantha answered, catching Jason's eye and throwing him a withering look.

"Or," Jason jumped in, "they said the women didn't have big enough books of business, so they knew they'd never make partner and left."

Jack paused mid-thought as he walked back to his brain trust of a whiteboard and drew a line down the middle. With the information he'd already written on the left, he labeled the right side *Us/Defense,* and listed two bullet points under the new heading: *life choices* and *small book of BS.* Standing back, he looked at his creation. "Well, that looks and smells like shit. Unless we can pack the jury with middle-aged, uneducated white men who believe they've been passed over for just about every opportunity and have a bone to pick with anyone who isn't them, we're screwed. Any disagreement with that?"

Both Samantha and Jason remained quiet, understanding that this was a rhetorical question. "Well, Goddamn it. What do we need?" he shouted.

Not sure she knew what the hell he was talking about but unable to sit like a lamb waiting for the slaughter, Samantha blurted out, "Evidence?"

"Exactly. What kind of evidence?" Jack continued.

"We need former associates to be able to explain why they left the firm."

Jack nodded and headed back up to the board to write *witnesses: former associates.* "What else?" he asked, now staring at Jason. After a minute of silence, Jack screamed, "Oh, for Christ's sake. What the hell are you being paid for? You have absolutely no idea what we need."

"Documents?" Jason responded.

Samantha ducked as the marker shot by so close to her head her hair moved, narrowly missing Jason's face, and slammed into the wall. "How about expert testimony of our own? Ever think of that? Jesus Christ," Jack spat in disgust as he retrieved the marker. "There must be some expert whore somewhere who, for enough money, will testify that women do make these life choices for whatever the fuck reasons they may have and that this is not unusual.

Having almost been maimed, Jason was now fully alert. "We'll need an expert who will also opine that one woman partner is the norm, not a statistical anomaly, for a firm of our size. I highly doubt anyone is going to put himself or herself out there on that limb."

"You highly doubt," Jack responded caustically.

"Really?"

Holy shit, Samantha thought, *here we go.*

"That's what you've learned after working with me for—what is it now—six years?"

While the better course of action was for Samantha to stay quiet, she'd simply had enough of the abuse. Even when it was only peripheral, it was incredibly damaging, so she tried to change Jack's path. "Give us a few weeks to get experts lined up. There's no reason to have any further discussion based on a hypothetical."

Jack straightened his suit, shifted his tie, looked at his watch, and seemed to snap out of it. "The end of the month—that's all the time you've got—or consider your careers at the firm over." Turning, he calmly walked out the door and down the hall.

Jason waited a minute, got up, and shut the door. "I hate that man."

"Unfortunately, sharing your feelings won't help us right now. We need to find witnesses and experts. I'll take the experts and you look for witnesses," Samantha directed.

"We'd better move everything else off our plates. Asshole's given us only two weeks."

CHAPTER
37

VICTORIA KNOCKED SOFTLY on Armond's door and pulled her cashmere shawl tighter. While she waited, she mentally shook herself and tried to relax.

It was only a kiss. After all they'd been through, they should certainly be able to handle that. *Plus, he's the one who kissed me*, she thought, *so why should I feel uncomfortable?* Pushing her shoulders back, she began to feel better. Just as she threw her hair back over her shoulders in a feeling of defiance, Armond opened the door, showcasing a red nose, but otherwise looking remarkably recovered.

"Well, I see you've recovered from your mishap," Victoria said, sounding much harsher than she had intended.

"Indeed. The next time I kiss you, I'll be sure to wear protective head gear." Stepping back from the door, Armond motioned. "Come in. We need to make a quick call to my father before dinner. He's asked that we let him know our thoughts."

"Fine. But we haven't made any final decisions," Victoria answered, distracted by his reference to a next time.

"He understands. He wants our general thoughts about the trip and the Asian investor pool, as well as a timetable for when we'll deliver our recommendations." Armond speed dialed his father on speaker and set the phone on the table between them.

"Well, well. It's the world travelers. I've been waiting with bated breath for you two to call," Phillip answered.

"Victoria and I are well, thanks for asking," Armond responded.

"Don't get clever with me. You two have been gallivanting around Hong Kong now for close to a week, and this is the first I've heard from –"

"Oh, you two, ignore him," Armond's mother cut in. "His nose is out of joint because he's not there handling it himself. With the company growing, he'll need to learn to rely on you two and others to handle more and more matters. Victoria, how do you like Hong Kong? I assume Armond's at least taken you to one of their talented tailors. They'll make you a one-of-a-kind outfit to your exact measurements and specifications. Even better, once they have your measurements, you can order clothes, and they'll ship them to you."

Victoria smiled at the excitement in Angelika's voice and looked over at Armond. "Hong Kong is amazing. The number of people here from all over the world far outstrips what I imagined. The city's such a unique combination of sophistication and old world, but it all fits together somehow. It's really impressive."

"What about the tailor? Have you had the time yet?" Angelika pressed.

"Not yet," Victoria said, watching Armond signify tomorrow. "Apparently, we're going tomorrow."

"Enough about tailors—" Phillip broke into the conversation. "Tell us about the investor pool."

"In one word, impressive," Armond jumped in, knowing his father did not like chitchat when he was waiting for an opinion. "Overall, the meetings were productive and informative. We intend to rank them, taking into consideration not only their financial capability, but also our assessment of whether they can really be hands-off."

Victoria bent forward toward the speaker. "Only two of the potential investors requested cameos in the film: one for himself and the other for his mistress. We told them Renoir Productions has a zero investor participation policy."

"Good. The last thing I want to deal with is some investor's idiot mistress. Did either of them lose interest?"

"Nope," Armond answered. "In fact, we're under the impression they're all rather anxious to get their money out of their countries and into a legitimate US investment. Compared to US investors I spoke with before the trip, they were far less interested in the casting possibilities and far more concerned about how fast we can get the contract and wiring instructions to their lawyers."

"Armond and I think that the interest in getting their money invested in the US will work to Renoir Productions' advantage."

"In what way?" Phillip asked.

"Less contractual niggling. We don't think they want the legal teams to hold up their investments."

"We think some of these investors are literally ready to wire the funds tomorrow," Armond added. "They all present as liquid. There's a good chance our upcoming project can be fully funded by the end of next month, depending on the number of foreign investors you want in this project."

"That's great news," Phillip responded. "I had a feeling the investor pool over there was going to be strong. I assume you can track the legitimacy of the cash to make sure it's not coming from any illicit activities. The last thing we need is to get mixed up in some violation of money laundering laws."

"I hired a US firm that specializes in tracking foreign investors' cash origins. They're turning reports around almost as quickly as we get the information to them. So far, they've opined that the origin of our current potential investor pool's funds appears clean, although they're quick to point out that nothing is 100 percent certain and there are many ways that money can be cleaned."

"I assume we're getting their opinions on these investors in writing?"

"We are," Victoria answered.

"Great news! Finalize your opinions and send us a memo before you get on the plane. While you're traveling home, we'll look it over and make our final decisions after we've asked any questions. Victoria, you'll be our guest at the house for a few days."

Realizing it wasn't a question but rather a request, Victoria looked over at Armond for help and shook her head. "I'd love to, but I need to catch the next flight back to Chicago as soon as we land. I've left my practice for too long, and while everything is running smoothly, I need to get back to my cases. But if you need me to discuss final thoughts or answer any questions, I'm sure I'll have plenty of time for a conference call while I'm at LAX waiting for my flight."

Armond watched Victoria but said nothing, knowing his father would not take no for an answer.

"Victoria, I fully understand how important your firm is to you," his father began on cue. Armond leaned back, prepared to listen to his father work his magic. "I remember when I began this company. Angelika had to threaten me to get me to take even a few days off, so I'm right there with you. But let me suggest an alternative plan that might suit us both. Spend the night with us and leave first thing the next morning. That way we can have the face-to-face meeting we prefer, and you can get some sleep and recover a bit from jet lag before heading home. We'll have the company plane take you to cut out all the time suck of flying commercial. We should be able to get you home by midday. Does that work?"

Victoria sat back and looked across at Armond. He simply shrugged his shoulders, knowing his father would get his way.

"Thank you, Phillip. I really appreciate the offer, but I can't let you use your plane just to take me home. If it means that much to you, I'm happy to stay the night, and I'll get the first flight out in the morning."

"Great!" Phillip exclaimed, slamming his hand down on the table in front of him. "We'll see you in two days, and we'll have dinner at the house."

The line went dead, and Armond smiled at his father's abilities. He tilted his head at Victoria in a silent request for her thoughts.

"He won't let me fly home commercial, will he?" Victoria asked.

"Nope." Armond smiled. "That's what I thought."

Armond held out his hand to help her off the couch. "Shall we?"

"I'm famished. Bring your notes. I want to get agreement on our ranking of the investors."

"It's all in my head. I don't need any notes."

Victoria rolled her eyes at his ego, but she was grateful they were apparently back on track and didn't need to discuss anything but business tonight.

* * *

As they left their hotel and stepped out into the busy evening, Victoria looked around at all the people. "Even though this is our sixth night here, I can't get over how cosmopolitan this city is. I know I'm speaking from total ignorance, given that the only other country I've seen is Bermuda, but I'm consistently impressed."

"I've been here a few times, one of which was before the city reverted back to Chinese control from the Brits. While there've been changes, so far, the city's maintained its vibe," Armond said as he took Victoria's arm and steered her into an elevator in an unmarked building. "I think you'll like this place," Armond said as the elevator began its hurtling trip to the top. "It offers authentic Chinese and also American food, like burgers and fries. If you want to be adventurous, which I highly recommend since you're here, you can have a few bites of Chinese food while still getting your fix of fries."

"You know I'm not adventurous with food," Victoria answered, wrinkling her nose.

"Indeed," Armond rebuffed.

"No need to be an elitist. It's just that I have a delicate palate but you go right ahead."

As the elevator doors opened, Victoria stood stunned.

Armond smiled and took pity on her, knowing the scene playing out in front of them must be a hit to her senses. "Ladies first, or are you going to stand here and continue to gawk?"

"No. Of course," Victoria barely whispered. Her senses were immediately assaulted by a type of beauty and elegance she'd never seen. Vivid red and gold carpets strategically placed across the floors of the expansive rooms were accented by intricate scenes, created by what appeared to be gold leaf on the interior walls and elaborately carved furniture. The outer glass walls revealed a stunning view that seemed to change slightly with each passing second. Victoria's eyes darted from the view to the activity on the inside and then back to the view. "What is this place? Are we moving?" Victoria asked.

"Over the course of the meal, we should complete the circle, so we'll see 360 degree views of the city and the harbor."

"Wow."

"I can't quite recall when I've heard such an exquisite vocabulary. As to where we are, the restaurant is owned by one of the most sought-after chefs in the world. He believes in different kitchens, menus, and sections in each restaurant, so diners can have a unique experience, depending on their mood. It took me three months to get a reservation, so you can understand why I wasn't going to let a little thing like a broken nose get in the way," Armond said as he gently touched just under his nostrils to ensure there was no further bleeding.

"This is beautiful, Armond. But how did you know I'd be here three months ago?" Victoria asked as they were being led to a table by one of the windows.

"I didn't. I knew I'd be here with someone so I booked it."

"Oh, of course," Victoria responded, a bit embarrassed she had assumed it was for her.

"I'll order some wine and a plate of Chinese and American bites. That way you'll be able to try something new if you want and if not, go straight to the familiar food. Does that work?"

"Perfect, thanks."

"Okay, let's discuss the investors."

Handing Armond her list, she began. "At this point, I'm comfortable with the top three. They already have funds in the US, so we don't have to worry about them being able to get their money there."

"What about the American woman?" Armond asked. "She was one of my top three candidates. I thought she was interesting."

"She is that," Victoria responded, "but we're not looking for interesting. Even though we received verification of her net worth, there's something about her…" Victoria trailed off without finishing her thought.

"In what way? I didn't get that vibe. I thought she was smart and quite charming. She certainly appreciates how American business works, and I didn't get the impression she was lying about having no desire to be involved in the film or about her sole interest being to get a solid return on her investment."

Nodding, Victoria said, "I can't disagree with anything you said. But there's something else, underneath it all. It's just a gut feeling."

Reaching across the table, Armond took Victoria's pen out of her hand and crossed her name off the list. "That's one of the reasons I wanted you involved: your instinct. If you feel that strongly about her, then she's no longer a viable option."

"I appreciate that, Armond. I do feel strongly about her, but it's just a feeling. Perhaps we should have your father meet her before we delete her from the running. She has a number of good points. As an American, she understands the culture, so Renoir Productions won't need to handhold her during the investment process, and, since she lives overseas, she won't be in anyone's way during production."

Shaking his head, Armond handed the pen back. "No need. My father doesn't want to redo the work he's paying us to do. She's off the list. Now let's choose the top three, put them in order, and enjoy our night."

Victoria raised her glass. "Thank you for this opportunity, Armond. It's been a wonderful trip, and I hope you feel, as I do, that there's been a successful outcome for Renoir Productions."

Armond raised his glass in response, watching one of the servers approach their table over Victoria's shoulder. "I ordered a delicacy to start. I hope you'll be open-minded."

"What kind of delicacy?" Victoria asked suspiciously.

"Soup."

Victoria let out an audible breath of relief. "Oh, I love soup. What kind? Egg drop? Noodle?"

"Not quite," Armond answered as he watched Victoria's face change from delight to horror as the sterling silver top was lifted from their bowls.

"Oh my God! You must be kidding! Please tell me my soup is not staring back at me."

"Pigeon head soup. The eyes will pop in your mouth!" Armond said as he picked up his spoon while Victoria excused herself and ran to the bathroom.

CHAPTER
38

JAMES STOOD AT the door and waited for her to get out of the car. He knew how skittish she was, and he got the feeling that if he rushed her or made one wrong move, she'd be gone. While that was her problem, he had opened his business to help people. Much to his surprise, he was learning there were a slew of people who'd been subject to hacking or other nefarious activities, and he was good at helping them get out of whatever mess they'd stumbled into. He'd also discovered that if he wanted to make this his life's work, he was going to have to learn to deal with all sorts of personalities and problems. Penny, as she called herself, was the perfect place for him to begin to hone his skills.

"Good morning, James." Penny gave a forced smile as she walked through the screen door he held open for her. "I assume we're alone?"

"We are. We'll have a few hours before my parents return. If you don't mind, I'd like to see it again. I've done some research, and I have a few theories."

"That works for me. I'll have to leave here in no more than ninety minutes anyway."

"First, I'd like to call you by your real name, if you don't mind, Gretchen," James began, knowing she might bolt now that he knew who she was.

Looking into his eyes for the first time, she admitted, "I knew you'd investigate me when I left. It's human nature and, I would think for someone in your line of business, particularly hard to resist."

"I've learned it's important for me to know as much as I can about my clients in order to help them. Sometimes I play along and don't let them know I've learned their real identity. I figure if they're more comfortable with the charade, then so be it. But in your case, I have a hunch that whatever this is"—James held up the thumb drive—"it will take us working together to figure it out. I'm also hoping you're willing to tell me a bit about who you were before this...um...event. While I know what's online, I'd like you to put some meat on those bones."

Gretchen sighed and rubbed the back of her neck. Fidgeting was a habit she'd developed in college to buy time when she wasn't sure of her answer. It'd been years since she'd had to resort to that delay tactic. Before this happened, she'd been immensely confident in herself and her abilities. Now, she was one conversation away from becoming one of The Moms, and that scared the shit right out of her—more than trusting this twenty-something boy with her story. "Since I'll never be one of The Moms, you're my only choice," Gretchen said, cocking her head and holding out her hand.

"I've no idea what you're talking about, but I promise I'll do everything in my power to ensure you won't be sorry." James reached out and shook her hand. "Okay, I'm listening."

CHAPTER

39

K AT LEANED BACK in her chair and propped her bare feet on her desk. She hadn't realized how exhausted she was until she sat down to read the confidential report she'd just received via courier. Between running the Miami litigation, handling the financing on her family's developments, and working on Victoria's case, she'd been run ragged. She pushed herself up and walked over to her bar to pour herself a glass of wine. Leaning out her office door, she called out, "Emma, do you want a glass? I'm opening my Friday best."

"No thanks, Kat. I've got to get home to my kids before my husband feeds them something other than food for dinner. I'll take a rain check."

"Enjoy your weekend," Kat returned.

"I will. You need to get out of here too. How late are you staying?"

"Just a bit longer. I'm fine. Go home. Say hey to your kids and hubby for me." Kat shut her door, settled back at her desk, and began to read.

Ten minutes later, the phone rang. She was so startled by the breach of silence she almost dumped her wine.

Breathing deliberately to calm her rapidly beating heart, she glanced at the caller ID and answered the phone, "Are you reading this?"

"That's why I called. The investigator must have delivered it to each of us at the same time," Robert responded. "By the way, how are you?"

Kat smiled at his tone. "I'm good. Busy but very grateful for it. You?"

"All good in Chi-Town, thanks. Listen, I just finished reading it. Are you through?"

"About halfway, but it's—"

Robert interrupted. "Bizarre! I've seen hundreds of investigative reports in my career, but this one is different. I just wanted to let you know that this is not the norm. Call me the minute you're done," Robert ordered before he hung up.

"Okay, good chat," Kat muttered. About fifteen minutes later Kat called Robert and walked over to the bar to refill her glass.

"Well? What do you think?" Robert asked.

"I'm calling BS. I don't buy this quality-of-life excuse. It makes absolutely no sense. I mean, no one works that hard for six to seven years and then wakes up one morning with an insatiable desire to work on crafts or bake cookies or learn to sew or whatever other nonsense is in this report, and walks away from the ability to earn six or even seven figures. I'm not buying—"

"Kat," Robert interrupted, "there's more than just that. I agree that it doesn't make sense. But there's something else.

He was only able to find a rather small percentage of the women. Where are all the others? He's an investigator. Finding people is what he does. Typically, these types of reports have a line on all, or a significant percentage, of the women."

"What are you suggesting?" Kat asked.

"I don't know. He's one of my best investigators. Something's off. I need to meet with him. Do me a favor, Kat."

"Of course," Kat answered, having never heard calm and cool Robert this amped up.

"Make sure this document is locked in a safe only you can access. I'd feel better if it wasn't left in your office, not that I don't trust your staff—"

"Sure, no problem. I understand. I'll take it home and keep it in my private safe. You're kind of freaking me out. What is it you think is off?"

"I don't know, and I don't mean to sound dramatic. It may be nothing, but I'll call you as soon as I know something. I gotta run. Bye." Robert hung up and Kat was left staring at the phone, annoyed at having been hung up on two times in less than an hour.

CHAPTER
40

THEY WOULD LAND just in time for dinner with Armond's parents. Watching the California coast come into view made Victoria realize how excited she was to get back. One of the first things she wanted was her favorite coffee and scone. She didn't care if it was time for dinner. Her body clock told her it was time for breakfast. Victoria was grateful that, except for a few hours at the beginning of the flight when she and Armond had discussed the final line-up of investors they would recommend to his parents tonight, they had both spent the remainder of the trip sleeping.

"What are you smiling about?" Armond asked, looking across the aisle.

"As corny as it sounds, I'm happy to soon be back on familiar soil."

"I understand completely. I always feel that way. Although I'd bet half our company profits from our next film that what you're really excited about is being able to eat your pedestrian food."

"You would win that bet. I was actually going to ask if we could stop and grab a coffee at my favorite place, and I'm dying for a scone. The pastries over there were just not the same."

"Wouldn't you rather have champagne or wine?" Armond asked. "It will be seven in the evening by the time we touch down."

"First coffee, then I'll advance up the drink spectrum. I just woke up, and coffee comes right after I open my eyes."

"Then, of course. We want to keep our newest counsel happy. By the way, when are you going to bill us for your time?"

Victoria reached into her bag and handed Armond an invoice. "Since I bill at the end of each month, which was yesterday or today—I can't keep what day it is straight—I thought I should let you see the amount before I officially bill your company." Victoria tried not to wince as she handed the paper to Armond.

Turning on his overhead light, he looked it over, folded it and put it away.

Victoria almost jumped out of her chair waiting for a reaction. It was the largest invoice she'd ever given a client. Even when she'd been at Acker, Smith & McGowen, working almost eighteen-hour days to meet a deadline, she had never turned in a bill that large. She couldn't stand it anymore. "Well?"

"Well, what?" Armond responded.

"Is it too much?" Victoria asked. "Will your parents be upset?"

"Victoria, of course it's too much. It's a legal bill. When have you ever heard of any client who thought a legal bill was not too much? It's outrageous and hard to swallow, but it's your bill," Armond finished and turned to look out the window.

Just then, the captain walked back to let them know they'd be landing in about fifteen minutes. As soon as he was back in the front of the plane, Victoria said, "Armond, then let me revise it. I don't want your parents or you to be upset."

Armond turned back to her and laughed out loud. "V, there's nothing wrong with your bill. Last year, we used one of the top LA firms, and the bill we got was three times the amount of the one you just handed me. You're a bargain!"

"Wait, what? Three times the amount?"

"That's what I said. Stop devaluing your work. You're good at what you do, and you deserve to get paid for every hour you do it."

"Three times the amount? Well, you do know I still have to bill Renoir Productions for this stopover and for the time I worked on the flight, don't you? Perhaps my rate per hour just went up."

Armond cocked his brow. "Don't push it." They smiled at each other as the plane landed smoothly on the LA tarmac.

CHAPTER

41

WHILE ADAM HADN'T planned to return so soon, it had given him an opportunity to meet with each of his Asian clients one more time before the end of the year.

Happily, their businesses were booming which meant the firm's business would continue to boom as well. When companies did well, they hired and paid for lawyers at an almost fevered pace. The flip side was when economies slowed and companies had to tighten their belts, lawyers were one of the first expenses to get cut.

Adam had learned this lesson the hard way during the recession, so while things were good, he intended to rake in all the legal work he could get, picking every possible legal dollar from his clients' pockets. It wasn't the most officer-of-the-court way to practice law, but it worked for him.

While he waited, he watched Bangkok turn from day to night from the height of his hotel suite. As the lights along the shore of the Chao Phraya River came to life, a slight snarl crossed his face at the thought of how dirty it was. Garbage from years of restaurants, hotels, and people dumping whatever they no longer wanted floated in the brown water.

While a clean-up effort was underway, he would never understand why tourists insisted on riding in small boats through the filth to see the sights.

He felt his phone vibrate. *Finally*, he thought. Checking the caller ID and seeing it was blocked, he asked, "Where?" He rolled his eyes at the answer but decided it wasn't worth the effort to disagree. "I'll meet you in fifteen minutes."

Heading out of the hotel, he was immediately enveloped by stifling humidity and throngs of people. He walked about a mile and entered one of the better-known ping pong bars. Adam paid the entrance fee and sat at the bar next to a large man with a defensive tackle-like football player build.

"Have you seen one of these shows before?" the man asked. "I have no idea how these women can do all these things with their—"

"I'm not here to chitchat. What's the status? And, in the future, I refuse to meet you at one of these places," Adam insisted.

Having been in this business for so many years, the man well knew that many people who hired investigators felt they were of a different, better class. He could understand where their attitude came from since they were typically in positions of power and had fought their way to the top. He often wondered, though, how ignorant these people were not to consider that he likely knew things about them they wouldn't want made public—like the assignment they had hired him to do. Remembering this was his last meeting before he retired, he slapped Adam on the back just to screw with him and said, "Sure thing. Here's a copy of what I gave them."

Adam took the envelope and was about to shove it into his bag and leave when he felt the man's giant hand wrap firmly around his wrist. "What the hell are you doing?"

"It stays with me. You can look at it right here," the man responded, his affable look changing to a steely glare.

While Adam's antennae went up, he wasn't about to be bullied by some lackey he paid. "Listen," he said, shifting his tone to one of camaraderie, "I respect and understand your need to protect yourself. You can trust me. I am, after all, paying you a very hefty sum, and I'm sure you'd like me to continue to do so."

The man laughed out loud and slapped Adam on the back again. "You're threatening me. Oh, that's rich," he said, intensifying his gaze and squeezing Adam's wrist even tighter. "You little shithead, do you have any idea how many heads of state I've dealt with? CEOs and politicians? Can you imagine the secrets I hold on them? And you think I don't have information on you and your little pip-squeak partner friends?"

Adam was stunned. He searched his brain for a way to exit what should have been an easy meeting and return to the safety of his hotel. He'd worked with this man for years and had never experienced this behavior. Mustering whatever charm he had to the surface to overtake the fear, Adam said, "Let me buy you a drink as an apology. We got off on the wrong foot tonight."

A sudden smile came across the man's face, and Adam felt the pressure on his arm abate. "I knew we'd see eye to eye. Now, why don't you take a look at this document before I torch it? Then, we can discuss my additional terms."

"Additional terms?" Adam asked. "This was the end of the assignment."

His companion roared with laughter. "You are a hoot! Of course it's not the end. There's more they want and unless you want me to get it for them, there's much more I'll need from you."

"How much more?" Adam asked.

"With all I know about you and what's been going on, I'd say seven figures is fair."

Adam's mouth hung open in shock, while the woman at center stage began shooting ping pong balls from her hooha, some of which whizzed perilously close to his head.

CHAPTER
42

GRETCHEN LOOKED FORWARD to her meetings with James. He was smart, savvy, and, most importantly for her, he felt like her hero. She knew how ridiculous that sounded but it was how she felt, and it was a good feeling to have after years of being in her self-imposed solitude. He also respected her privacy and didn't push her. Over the past month, they'd met three times. Each time, she'd opened up a bit more about who she had been and sadly, who she was now. When it got too painful, they'd stop talking about her and he'd tell her his plans.

Gretchen was amazed a kid James' age was earning a significant income from clients all over the country. What had started as a lark, was a successful and profitable business. He was waiting for her at his door. Looking at his eager, smiling face, Gretchen realized James had become more than a hired gun. He was her friend. She'd forgotten how good that felt.

"It's a beautiful day. I thought perhaps we could walk and talk if that's okay with you."

"How much time do we have?" Gretchen asked, a bit nervous about a change in routine.

"All the time in the world. My parents are gone until next Monday. They drove down to southern Illinois to visit my grandparents. I have the house all to myself," he answered with a huge smile on his face.

Gretchen couldn't help but laugh out loud. "Hmm, you look like someone who's about to have his first party without his parents. When's it happening? Tonight, or have you planned a weekender?"

James stuffed his hands in his pockets and looked down before he answered. "I don't really have any friends my age. I never fit in at high school. Partying was the kind of thing all the kids wanted to do, but it never really interested me. I've always hung out with people much older than me...you know, like you." He looked over and smiled.

"Well, I can understand that. You're incredibly smart and on your way to becoming a successful business owner while most of your peers are pledging frats or sororities or getting notches on their belts." Gretchen empathized. "But you, you're someone special, and nothing can beat that. And, I'd love to go for a walk while we talk."

"Great," James said, a smile lighting up his face. "Give me a minute. I've got to get something." He turned and ran into his house.

He came bounding out with a bundle of puppy joy running beside him. Straining to the end of the leash, the puppy started to run, stumbled over its oversized paws, and threw its weight into Gretchen. Laughing and bending down to greet the new addition, she asked, "What do we have here?"

"His name's Sam. He's a shepherd mix. I got him from the humane society. He's eight weeks old, neutered, and ready to rumble. I hope you like dogs."

"I love them. We always had dogs when I was growing up," Gretchen responded, squatting while Sam cuddled between her legs and licked her face. Laughing, she sat on the ground so the pup could thoroughly check her out.

James was grateful Sam had done exactly what he'd hoped—bring a bit of unguarded joy to one of his favorite clients. While he knew he couldn't get this involved in all his clients' lives if he wanted to grow the business to its potential, Gretchen had become one of his favorites, and she'd also given him legal advice.

"Okay, let's go. He's not a great walker yet. Kind of dawdles along," James warned.

"He's perfect," she answered, scratching behind his partially-folded ears. "Absolutely perfect. Would you mind if I held his leash?"

"Not at all," James answered. As they neared the corner, he asked, "Is there a point where you'd like to start?"

Gretchen felt panic rising and her heart racing. Once she began, there'd be no going back. For more than two years, she'd kept the shame of it to herself, but she couldn't go back to being afraid of what she'd done—if she'd really done those things.

As if reading her mind, James offered, "If it's easier for you, I can ask questions and you can answer."

"That would be better."

"How long ago did this happen—the envelope under your door?"

"About two years ago. This coming August will make three," she answered, clearly remembering the day. "Do you have the envelope it was delivered in?"

"I don't. I tossed it right after I opened it. It was a plain manila with no origination marks of any kind. Other than a confidential mark, there was no handwriting or postage or return address. None of that was unusual though, as I'd often received work the same way."

"Did you watch it right away?"

"No. I thought it was work. I waited until later that night."

"Tell me a bit about your work: where you worked, how long you were there, what you specialized in," James said, wanting to step away from her having to relive watching it for the first time.

Gretchen felt surprisingly at ease as she watched Sam play with a leaf blowing in the wind. For the first time, she felt no emotional pain remembering her former life. "I'd been a lawyer for almost seven years. I worked with officers, directors, and the management of companies, helping them with corporate governance and regulations."

"Okay," James said. "Now, once again, in English, please."

Gretchen nodded in appreciation. "Now you know how I feel when you talk. There are rules and regulations that companies and management must follow. I helped them stay on track and ensured that they didn't screw the pooch, so to speak."

"Can you give me an example?"

"Sure. Let's say you own a company that wants to do business with a foreign entity. The US has certain rules and regulations that control that type of interaction, one of which is the Foreign Corrupt Practices Act. If you violate the provisions of the act, the federal government can charge you with a crime. Simply put, I would help shepherd your business toward achieving its goal without being penalized."

"Hmm. Could you have pissed someone off by, for instance, preventing a deal because you didn't like the cut of their jib?"

Gretchen thought for a moment, then shrugged. "I guess anything is possible, but that's unlikely. Typically, if I was concerned about a transaction, I'd alert the person handling it and we'd think through ways to get it done without the questionable person or money."

"What if someone had been financially hurt by your advice? Maybe they'd want you out of the picture."

Gretchen bent down to scratch the pup's belly as he rolled around in the soft grass, exposing his stomach and kicking his gangly legs into the air. Thinking for a minute, she looked up at James, squinting to keep the sun out of her eyes. "I suppose that's possible, but the decision wasn't mine to make. The company's management had to sign off on any changes."

"Yes, but you were the one who alerted them to an issue and gave the recommendation of go or not go, true?"

"All true."

"So, I think it would be important for you to make a list of companies you represented where you quashed a deal or stopped an investor from getting involved."

Nodding her head in agreement, Gretchen stood to continue their walk.

"I hate to ask this, but were you involved in any extra-curricular activities?"

Gretchen glanced at James sideways and decided to give him a bit of a hard time. "You mean like soccer or running a marathon?"

"No, no. Like…well…were you and your husband into alternative lifestyles?"

"You mean were we hippies or into Rastafarianism? No," she answered, wondering how much more painful James was going to make this for himself before he simply asked.

James glanced at Gretchen and saw she was just about to burst out laughing. "You're yanking my chain, aren't you?" he said, relieved.

"Yes. And, no. We did not, nor do we, engage in free living, alternative arrangements, or sex with more than each other. We're quite traditional."

"So it's safe to assume then, that this was not from a jilted lover or some sex psychopath?"

"Yes, very safe."

"Is there anyone you can think of who might have been jealous of you? Perhaps a coworker?" James continued.

"No one I can think of. I was well-liked as far as I knew and was on the partnership track. I would have been up for consideration by the nominating committee over the next year or two."

"Why didn't you ever go to anyone with this?"

"Two reasons. First, I was afraid I had done this, and if I had, my career and my marriage were at risk. Second, the note implied that if I went to anyone, it would be available in the public domain. I believed them."

"Okay. I think that's enough for now. But I do want you to concentrate on that list. See what you can recall. Now, let's head back to the house. I want to show you what I've found."

CHAPTER

43

"WELCOME HOME," VICTORIA stretched and said out loud as her plane landed at O'Hare. The crew had been nice enough to agree to her request to leave LA before dawn. That meant that, even with the time change, she could make it to her apartment, take a quick shower, and still get to her office by noon.

Picking up her phone, she texted Mary to give her the schedule for the day: *Noon to two, no interruptions so I can catch up on the hundreds of emails. Two to three, meet with you to address any fires. After that until five, no interruptions so I can prepare for my hearing. Finally, set calls with Jenny and Kat for a status on my cases.*

As the plane rolled to a stop, Chen thanked Victoria for allowing her to practice her makeup skills and told her the Renoir family had hired a car and driver for her to use as she needed for the remainder of the day.

Once Victoria was settled in the car, she checked her phone and saw that Robert had texted her. Dialing his number, she expected to leave a message. "Well, the world traveler has returned. Are you sure you're ready for us mere Chicago steak and potato mortals?" he joked.

"You can take the girl out of the South Side but—what's up? I saw your text and thought I'd get your voicemail. I just got off the plane and I'm on my way home to take a quick shower and then head to my office. How are you? How's my case? I feel like I've been gone forever."

"Everything is good. Kat has been a big help. I must say I didn't expect it but the spoiled little rich girl from Houston has a brain in that pretty little head of hers."

Victoria cocked her head as she listened. Robert was prim, proper, and straitlaced. His referring to Kat as a pretty little whatever was rather shocking. Victoria began cautiously, not wanting to scare him back into his proper four walls. "It sounds like the two of you got along better than you thought you would."

"She's smarter than she looks, and I'll deny I ever said that if you tell her," he said. "We'd like to do something a bit out of the ordinary for your case, and I want to discuss it with you first, of course. Do you have time to meet today?

"Well, now I'm dying to know what it is. Unfortunately, I have zero time today. I have a huge argument in federal court tomorrow, and my day is devoted to preparing and returning calls. I can meet tomorrow afternoon when I'm finished in court. Will that work?"

"Perfect. Just give me a ring when you're done and come on over to my office."

"I'll probably be done around two. Since it will feel like nighttime for me, I'd rather meet somewhere where I can have a heart-healthy Chicago steak and drink some fabulous red, if it's okay with you. Are you willing to meet me at the mansion?" Victoria asked, wondering if she sounded insane trying to go to the best steak house in Chicago in the middle of a Friday afternoon.

"The old Victoria would have bristled at the notion of imbibing in the middle of the day, and she certainly wouldn't have suggested a huge steak for lunch. Seems a bit of the lifestyle of the rich and famous has rubbed off on you."

"I'm in no mood, Robert. I'm jet-lagged and sick to death of looking at soup with eyes, and fish with eyes, all staring at me. I'm starved for real food that doesn't watch me when I'm eating it. Just meet me there."

Before he could respond, she hung up.

CHAPTER

44

"I'M IN THE middle of a very busy afternoon, doctor. What can I do for you?" Billy said, making sure his irritation at the interruption came across loud and clear.

"I think it's what I can do for you," Dr. Natarajan responded.

Billy looked up from his desk, took his reading glasses off, and sat back in his chair. "You must know by now how much I abhor that type of psychobabble. What is it?"

"You know I've worked very hard to resolve quite a few complaints over the years. So far, we've been lucky that most of the women were ready for a career change or wanted a slower pace, and so acquiesced to our suggested exit strategy. But Billy, your pursuit of the newest female associate at the firm is causing problems."

Billy sighed. "Listen, we pay you well to do your job. Part of it is to handle anything that comes up and make it go away. I don't interfere with how you do your job, and I don't want to be bothered with the details. Why are you really here?"

"Sarah came to me."

"Sarah?" Billy asked, genuinely not following the conversation.

Making every effort not to roll her eyes, she responded evenly, "Yes, Sarah. The newest associate assigned to your group. Big eyes, short hair, big tatas."

"Ah, yes. Sarah," Billy said with a satisfied look, quite pleased he had recalled one of the hundreds of associates that work at the firm. "Quite smart that one. Top of her class. She was one of the few exceptions we made about not hiring from Harvard." Then, with a confused look on his face, he asked, "Why did she visit you?"

Dr. Natarajan used all her self-control not to respond with sarcasm. "Did you have a one-on-one meeting with her in your office the other day?"

Billy thought for a while. He had so many meetings and calls during his days it was hard to remember even a few hours ago.

For a moment, Dr. Natarajan thought, *Perhaps I've been lied to. Maybe Sarah scammed me and nothing happened.*

Then, Billy quickly leaned forward, almost toppling his crystal decanter and glass set. Speaking slowly and deliberately, he asked, "She went to you because of a little grab ass?"

It is quite remarkable, Dr. Natarajan thought. *The level of entitlement and the extent of self-denial is unlike anything I've seen in all my years of clinical and research work.* "She wanted," she responded, turning to ensure the door was tightly closed, "me to help her file a claim against you and the firm to hold you accountable, and she wanted to keep her job at the firm to boot."

"That's utterly ridiculous. I barely touched her." He paused. "And goddamn if I only touched her shoulder," he said, looking absolutely bewildered.

"I was told you had a rather detailed discussion with her about what you'd like to do to her."

"Well, so the hell what? She's an adult. All she has to do is say no. I've never forced myself on any woman, and I have no intention of starting now," he spat, standing in anger. "You know what? I've had it. I want her fired!" he said as he began pacing.

Thinking she had to play this one carefully as his ego was involved, she nodded. "That's what I thought you'd say. She left the firm an hour ago. She signed a release and—"

"I hope you had her sign a nondisclosure agreement as well."

"Yes, of course. She was also escorted out of the building by the security team," Dr. Natarajan finished. She decided not to tell Billy about the amount the firm had agreed to pay her to get her to sign the release. He'd see that soon enough. "Good work. I don't want anyone in the firm who needs to be coddled. If she can't withstand a bit of harmless attention, she certainly wouldn't have been able to handle high-stakes negotiations. Good God, can you imagine the problems she would have caused if one of our clients gave her a few compliments?" Shaking his head as if agreeing with himself, he picked up his glasses to return to work. "It always works out for the best."

"I'm glad you're pleased," the doctor responded, working to hide her disbelief at how utterly clueless he was at the impropriety of his conduct. Of course, she had no empathy for these simpering, spoiled American girls. *While I began my childhood begging for food and money in the streets of Mumbai, they grew up with every opportunity and now whined about a few unwanted advances*, she thought, recalling where she had come from.

"Is there something else?" Billy asked, surprised she hadn't made any move to leave.

The doctor mentally shrugged back to the present and silently reminded herself to be grateful. "Actually, there is."

"Well, what is it?"

"When you, Trever, and Adam hired me, it was to develop a cradle-to-grave system to ensure the three of you always kept control of the firm. That system had to keep highly motivated and talented people at the firm without becoming frustrated they weren't becoming partners. I think the product I developed has been quite successful."

"Without question. You know how highly we value you and your service to the firm." Billy gave her a half-salute. "In fact, on your way out, talk to my assistant. The two of you can organize a celebratory dinner of sorts for the four of us. It's certainly overdue." Billy pushed the intercom, signaling Sherrie to come into his office.

Undaunted, the doctor continued, "You did not, however, hire me to run around behind you to pick up after your sexual indiscretions."

When his assistant walked in, he kept his eyes glued to the doctor's and snarled at Sherrie, "Get out!" Billy stood, poured himself some of the room temperature water he insisted be kept on his desk, and walked over to sit next to the doctor. Working to regain control of his temper, he used his best calming voice and asked, "What is it you want?"

"I want to be a shareholder in the firm. I'm as much a part of this firm as the three of you. I've been here from the beginning, and but for me handling your indiscretions, you would be hanging from the highest me-too tree in the land by now."

Billy was not surprised by her request. He'd expected it years ago. He was, however, concerned about her implied threat.

"I had no idea you felt such motherly concern for the women of the firm."

Understanding that Billy was chumming the waters of her past trying to get her to bite, she sat in silence. She'd long ago psychoanalyzed the three of them and knew how to push their respective buttons. It was almost comical that Billy thought he could out-do her expertise. Billy's weakness was his constant need of adoration, particularly from women. When he didn't get it, he'd react inappropriately by lashing out with rash comments or wild decisions.

"Fine, but—" he began, after about thirty seconds of silence.

"Fine," she interrupted. "Ten percent should do the trick."

Billy jumped up out of his chair and threw the glass across the room. Within seconds of it smashing against the wall, his office door flew open, and his assistant appeared again. "Are you okay? I thought—"

Billy screamed, "Don't think. Get out!" Turning to the doctor with a beet-red face, he leaned over her, placing one hand on his desk and the other on the arm of her chair. "You must have lost your mind. That amount would disrupt the firm and the current order. I'll give you 2 percent of the firm's profit, but you can never be a shareholder of the firm. That's out of the question."

"That won't work. I'll start at 5 percent and work up to ten over the next five years. And, I'll agree not to be a share-holder, as long as I receive the dollar equivalent to the percent we've agreed to. Take it or leave it."

Billy knew he was in a hard spot. "Fine. But, there are conditions. You will never ask for more money or a larger share. If you do, your discharge will be immediate, and you'll need to repay your profit share. You'll also have to sign a nondisclosure and confidentiality agreement. I assume we have a deal." Billy was not asking.

"We have a deal," Dr. Natarajan said, leaning forward with an outstretched hand.

Ignoring her hand, Billy walked back around his desk, put his glasses on, turned back to his work, and without looking, ordered, "Now, get out of my office. Oh, and one more thing," Billy said, pausing. Looking into her eyes, he continued, "Don't ever lecture me about my conduct again. I promise, you won't like the response."

Annoyed with his attitude and that she would not be a shareholder, but satisfied that she would be incredibly rich, Dr. Natarajan turned to leave, without a care in the world for the women who would walk into this office and be helplessly molested at his hands.

CHAPTER
45

"**V**ICTORIA!" ROBERT GREETED her with a hug. "How was the trip? How'd your argument go? Wow, I hate to say it, but you look like death warmed over."

"Well, thank you, Robert. I feel much better now that you've confirmed I look the way I feel. What a charmer you are. Do you use that same honesty with all the women you date? I bet it really seals the deal in the bedroom," Victoria quipped. As they waited to be seated, Victoria glanced at her reflection in the restaurant mirror. "Oh. My. God! I knew I didn't look great this morning, but I certainly did not have these two giant bags under my eyes. They're big enough to hold groceries!"

Robert enjoyed watching her turn her head from side to side in the mirror. "What, may I ask, are you doing?"

Without taking her eyes off the mirror, she retorted, "I am trying to see if I really look this bad or if it's just a weird angle."

"I'm not touching that one," Robert said under his breath, leaving Victoria to wrestle with her insecurities while he used his family connections with the staff to get them seated in the sought-after fireplace room. "Come on. Move away from the mirror for your own safety," he joked as he turned her to follow the host to their table.

"This is perfect," Victoria sighed, feeling the warmth from the fire begin to seep into her bones. "Thank you."

Robert looked at her with affection. "You're more than welcome. But did I have a choice?"

"No, of course not. But I appreciate that you capitulated," she said, giving his arm an affectionate pat. "I really am thankful to you and Kat for putting so much effort into my case. I hope you know Sophia and I consider you family. If there is ever anything you need, you have only to ask."

"I know, and I feel the same. While I wasn't sure what to think when you two first walked into my office, it was one of the best things that could have happened to me. So-phia's connections alone have brought in a ton of new clients. She really is a wonder."

Victoria smiled fondly. "I have no idea what I'd do without her. Cheers to Sophia," Victoria said as she and Robert clinked water glasses. Picking up her menu, Victoria glanced longingly at its contents. "There's something almost blasphemous about toasting with water. I'm done working for the day and intend to head home to sleep as soon as we're finished, so I'm ordering wine to go along with the Kat-inspired giant steak I intend to eat." Using every last ounce of her dwindling ability to concentrate, Victoria focused on Robert and asked, "What did you want to discuss?"

"I'm way ahead of you," Robert said, nodding apprecia-tively at the waiter stepping up to their table to showcase the wine Robert had prearranged. Robert took a sip, nodded to the waiter, and watched while Victoria took a sip.

"Perfect," Victoria sighed with appreciation.

"I'm glad you approve," Robert said with some amusement, knowing Victoria's wine palate was totally unrefined. He could have ordered the cheapest of wines and her response would have been the same. Taking a piece of paper out of his breast pocket, Robert unfolded it while he spoke. "We received the investigator's report while you were gone."

"And?"

"And it's not as robust as I'd expect."

Victoria put her wine down, figuring she should try a bit of restraint judging by how jet-lagged she felt, or she'd be sloshed at half a glass. At the very least, she wanted to make it through the steak she'd been craving since about her third day in Hong Kong. "What does that mean? Why not, and what did you expect?"

"Take a look." Robert handed the report across the table. Watching Victoria open it, he explained. "Typically, I'd get a rundown on at least 90 percent of the subjects."

"Wait. What?" Victoria shook her head. "I'm sorry. It's been awhile since I've been involved in the details of my case. What was he looking for?"

"It's amazing what a few trips on a private plane can do to a once-brilliant mind," Robert said jokingly. "Witnesses, Victoria. We need them for your case. I want to get as many women as possible to testify about their experiences at the firm. I'm betting that if we talk with these women, we'll find a significant number were asked to leave or were given offers they couldn't refuse."

"Right. So, why's the list so short?"

"Exactly the point. This is an anomaly. I've never gotten this kind of response in the past."

"I assume you spoke with the investigator?" Victoria asked, handing it back.

Nodding, Robert replied, "He said the assignment has been difficult because of the firm's lack of information about the women."

"Shouldn't he be able to track their social security or social media or something to come up with information. I'm no expert, but it seems to me that investigators should, well, investigate. The lack of forwarding information should be the beginning of his job, not the end, shouldn't it?" Victoria asked.

"I've used this guy for years, and he's always been spot on. I didn't grill him because I trust his methods and he promised to continue looking. We were supposed to have a follow-up call, but he's been nonresponsive, which isn't at all like him. However, Kat and I have an idea we want to run by you. If it works, we won't need an investigator. I'd like to ask that you find your one ounce of patience and summon it forward while I explain."

Victoria looked quizzically at Robert. "Shoot."

"Here," Robert handed a folded paper across the table.

Victoria unfolded the document, disappeared behind it for a minute, then folded it up and handed it back. "No," she said as she picked up the menu again. "Now, I'm absolutely famished. Let's at least get our appetizer orders in while we decide what we want for dinner, or whatever meal it is here. How does fried calamari sound? After that, I intend to continue with the Chicago heart-healthy plan of a ginormous steak, sautéed mushrooms, and a double baked potato with absolutely everything on it."

"Victoria, at least let me give you our reasons." Robert ignored her plea for food. "Stop rolling your eyes and sighing. We've put our hearts and souls into thinking about this, so stop acting like a spoiled child and let me finish."

"Well, when you frame it so nicely, how can I do anything other than listen?" Victoria responded, recognizing that she sounded like an ungrateful brat, but unable to stop herself.

"We want to run this as an online announcement with the three most popular news sources in the country. We expect doing so will draw national attention to the lawsuit and to Acker, Smith & McGowen and force them to the table to discuss settlement so the bad publicity will stop. Many of the companies they represent insist on diversity within their vendors, and that includes the lawyers they hire. They'll get calls from some major clients demanding they fix the situation, or they'll find another firm to handle their work. As you pointed out at our meeting a while ago, knocking them off their game is a good thing, and this will do that. Finally, it's the best shot we've got to find witnesses."

"Robert, I really appreciate the thought you and Kat put into this, and, more importantly, I recognize how out of the box even suggesting something like this is for you. But..." pausing for a moment, Victoria began to reconsider Robert's idea. After all, she was the one who suggested they interject a third rail into this case rather than languish on the three-year trial track. "Okay. I'm thinking. Where are you planning to run this?"

Robert's smile did a wicked dance as he handed her a list. "The largest news sources in New York, Chicago, and LA," he spoke quietly as if he'd just revealed a national secret. "I see I've stunned you into silence. Never seen you at a loss for words before. I bet you wish you'd thought of it yourself," he finished, beaming.

Sitting back in her chair, Victoria took a long sip of wine and sighed. Not only was she exhausted and jet-lagged, but she'd had a difficult time in court. She and her opposing counsel had been randomly chosen to play along with the judge's personal game of Tag, You're Screwed. The rules were simple. Out of nowhere, the judge would start to screw with his chosen prey. The goal then, for the unlucky lawyer, was to divert the judge's attention to his or her opponent, or to someone else in the courtroom (hard to do but well worth it if you could swing it). Kind of like a game of tag, except it wasn't fun and your reputation and livelihood might be negatively affected. There were a number of legendary tales about the game. One that had always scared Victoria was that the judge had arrested one of his chosen prey for contempt of court for shouting in the courtroom even though the judge had repeatedly told the lawyer to speak up. Nothing was off limits, or so the legend warned.

Luckily, Victoria had been just tired enough and in no mood to take shit from anyone that she'd had no problem throwing her opposing counsel under the bus, and the judge's focus remained on him for the rest of their argument.

"What are you thinking?" Robert asked, concerned by her uncharacteristic silence.

"I'm thinking about how lucky I was in court."

Robert began laughing. "Ah, it was your turn today. Tell me," he said, looking forward to a good story as he grabbed doughy, warm bread from the basket, slathered it with butter, and handed it to her so she wouldn't pass out.

Victoria recanted her experience and ended with, "Honestly, I'd heard about it but never seen it. One minute you're arguing before a lucid, brilliant judge, and the next, you're in a fight for your professional life."

240

After a pause, Victoria said, "Robert, to be completely transparent, I'm not sure how I feel about my personal situation being thrust onto the national stage. I just want to get it done and make a change so others don't have to go through what I did."

"I understand, but think about it realistically. How are you going to make a change if no one knows about it? It's kind of like the philosophical thought 'if a tree falls in the forest and no one's there, does it make a sound?' If you make a change and no one knows about it, how does that help anyone? Almost always in these cases, the plaintiff receives a settlement offer that is conditional on her signing a confidentiality and nondisclosure agreement. Of course, the bad actor suffers no repercussion, and the improper conduct continues unchecked. In a sense, it's almost as if the bad actor is emboldened since he's gotten away with it and is free to continue on his merry way."

Victoria sighed again, rubbing her eyes as her exhaustion began to amplify. "I understand your point and it's a valid one. I need some time to think it over. I'm too tired to decide now."

"Fair enough," Robert answered. "Now, let's get that steak before you pass out."

CHAPTER

46

S HE SAT IN her car and waited, watching the dark grey clouds move in ominously from the west. Huge, billowing puffs of power marched across the sky, hungrily devouring the blue that had been there throughout the day.

Gretchen had lived in the same town her whole life and could always tell when a storm was coming well before the sky revealed the slightest hint. When she was a child, she used to look up at the sky, tilt her head back, and announce to her family on the bluest of blue, sunny days that a storm was coming. Everyone would laugh at how cute she was, predicting the weather. But by the fifth or sixth dead-on forecast, while they thought it odd, her family shrugged their collective mental shoulders and thereafter relied on her for all things weather.

A fist suddenly slammed against her driver's side window. "Goddamn it!" she yelped and turned to glare at the perpetrator as the coffee she'd been holding dribbled down the front of her formerly crisp white blouse. James mouthed sorry as he walked around the front of her car. Gretchen unlocked the passenger-side door and growled, "Really? You can't just walk up to my car like a normal human? You've got to pound your fist against the glass?"

"I'm so sorry," James said. "I had no idea you didn't see me. You were looking right at me. That must have been one heck of a daydream."

"Hand me your water bottle, and hold what's left of my coffee while I try to salvage my shirt." Taking a piece of crumpled-up paper towel from the glove compartment, she soaked it with water and began swiping. "Great. Now it's evenly spread across the front of my shirt rather than in one spot." Giving up, Gretchen turned to James with a sigh. "Okay, what's so important you dragged me out when we're about to get our first major winter storm?"

"What are you talking about?" James responded, looking at the sky. "There are only a few clouds, and it's way above freezing."

"Trust me. It's a gift. Now, what's up?"

James grinned. "I have some good news. I think I've identified some of the people in the room with you, and I think I know how they did it."

"What do you mean how they did it? You mean how they made me do those things? I'm assuming I was drugged," Gretchen answered, no longer embarrassed to discuss the video with James. At this point, he knew almost all there was to know about her. Literally and figuratively.

"I don't think you did those things. I think they were created."

Gretchen stared at James, not fully understanding but feeling a spark of hope in her chest. "Explain."

"There's new technology that can recreate someone's face and expressions and use them so it appears the person is doing whatever the creator wants them to do."

"That's not new. People have been taking head shots and putting them on different bodies for years."

James shook his head. "No, it's not that. This technology essentially clones the person. It analyzes and memorizes every part of a person's face, expressions, mannerisms, and body. It then takes that information and runs with it. Meaning it essentially becomes that person. It can predict the way that person would react in any situation, even creating expressions the subject has never made." James pulled a document out of his folder. "Here. Read this. It will explain it better than I can."

Gretchen's eyes flew over the article, and she handed it back.

"Hey, it's important you read it," James objected. "It's critical you understand so we can piece together who might have had the desire and talent to do this to you."

"How can you be certain that's what happened? Maybe someone just drugged my drink or food? And I did read it and memorized it too."

James smirked. "What are you, some kind of speed-reader?"

"Yup. And I have an eidetic memory."

"Wait, you have a photographic memory?"

"I do. Now, let's focus. How does this work?"

"It appears it examines hundreds of photos or videos of the subject, then takes all that information and recreates the subject. It's quite amazing," James finished, obviously in awe of the technology.

"How do you know that's what happened with me?"

"Because I finally figured out how to reverse engineer it. As I began to pull your video apart, so to speak, things started to fall apart. Some of the frames become almost like... well...a stutter."

"You're absolutely certain it's not me in that video?"

Gretchen looked at James, grinning from ear to ear.

James burst out laughing, happy for her happiness. "I am absolutely certain that whatever that is in the video is not you."

Gretchen grabbed James by the shoulders, hugged him, and began to cry. "Do you know what this means? I don't have to be one of The Moms," she sobbed on his shoulder.

Uncomfortable, James patted her on the back with an awkward tapping motion. "Okay, let's talk about next steps," he said as he pushed her gently back to her side of the car.

"Sorry," Gretchen hiccup-sobbed as she tried to control herself. "All this time I thought I had cheated on my husband and was a horrible person." Straightening her coffee-covered shirt and dabbing at her tear-stained face, she began to laugh.

James gave her a look like a dog side-eyeing his human. "Maybe it'd be best if we discussed next steps next time we meet. I don't want to overwhelm you."

"James, relax," Gretchen ordered, pulling herself together and putting on her tough exterior once again. "I just needed to let out a bit of emotion. Now, what's next?"

"The list. I want you to add anyone who might have wanted to hurt you and why. Also, who might have had the expertise to use this technology. It's still new today. Whoever did this was way ahead of the curve. Use that memory of yours. Pull up situations you were in before this happened. The slightest odd comment or expression might lead to something. Don't discount anything, and write it down, even if some of it seems unimportant to you," James said as he got out of the car.

"Will do," Gretchen said, giddy she wasn't the person she had believed herself to be for the past two years.

Resting his forearms on the open passenger-side window, James fixed a smiled on his face so his next thought wouldn't scare his client and force her back into that weird self-exile place she'd been in when he first met her. "Listen, I don't want to upset you, but it may be time to involve the police."

"No. This is my fight." Looking directly at James, she reached across to grasp his hands. "Promise me you will not tell anyone. Remember, you signed an agreement. That still stands."

"I would never do that to you. You must at least know that about me by now. Trust me, Gretchen," he reassured her, squeezing her hands.

"I do trust you. But understand, I didn't involve them two years ago, and I'm not about to now. The last thing I want is this film in more hands."

James nodded. "I understand. Just keep that option in the back of your mind. There may come a time when we'll need help. Anyway,"—James stood to head back into his house—"I'm happy that you're happy." He rapped on the hood of her car. "We'll meet in a week. By that time, you'll have notes, and I'll have finished my work. We'll work through what comes next then."

As she headed home, Gretchen glanced in her rearview mirror and saw James standing on the curb, waving and smiling. For the first time in a very long time, she felt comforted.

CHAPTER
47

WILLOW GRABBED TWO pillows and pulled them over her head. *Jesus*, she thought, *nothing blocks the soul-sucking screams from the new girl.* It had been going on for almost a month. Willow couldn't remember another time when such disruption had been allowed in the house.

She heard the sharp rap on her door as it flew open and slammed against the wall. "You're looking a bit worse for wear," Madame said, pushing the pillows off Willow with the point of her shoe as if poking at a bug one is not sure is dead. "I received a complaint about you this morning," she continued as she walked around the room, opening the armoire to search it. Sometimes clients became involved with her talent and gave them gifts, like jewels or money. Of course, all gifts belonged to her and she encouraged her girls to voluntarily turn them over, but, more often than not, they tried to hide them. She always found them.

"Is there a reason you're here?" Willow heard herself say, surprised at her tone.

"Be careful, Willow. You may be one of my favorites, but that's because you're a hard worker and know your place.

Don't mistake my appreciation of your work ethic for any sort of emotional attachment." Madame handed Willow one of her handkerchiefs. "Here, wipe the spittle from the corner of your mouth. Unfortunately, I heard that you haven't been your energetic self. A few of your clients have been disappointed and if they're disappointed, then I'm disappointed. I suggest you improve your performance before I decide to let you spend a week in one of my ping pong bars. That class of clientele is decidedly lower than what you're used to here at the house. Quite frankly, I doubt even the quantity of drugs you pour into your system will be able to block that experience."

Usually, Willow had no reaction to Madame's comments. She'd heard these same types of critiques from time to time over the course of—what was it—two or three years now. But over the past month, since all the screaming had started, she'd begun to feel. While she'd always been indifferent to the suffering in the house, she was feeling what she thought might be anger. *Or was it sorrow?* She could no longer tell the difference. But Willow was lucid enough for the moment to know her place. "It's hard to concentrate with all the screaming. Why haven't you gotten rid of her?"

Madame's eyebrows raised. "Willow, I had no idea you were still so lucid. I thought by now all that would be left of that once-brilliant mind would be putty. To answer your question, she has the ability to be one of my higher-priced assets, just like you." After a pause, Madame continued, "I have a job for you. I want you to train her."

"What? Why would I do that? I have no idea how to train her."

"You do, actually. You're both cut from the same cloth, smart and beautiful, but each of you took a wrong turn in life and ended up here. I want you to make sure she understands there are no more choices in her life, except, of course, to please me. Explain to her that the consequences of failing to fulfill her single duty are very disturbing."

Willow simply stared in response. Maybe she was too drugged up and she was hallucinating. It wouldn't have been the first time.

"Willow, I'm not asking you. I'm telling you. You'll begin tomorrow," Madame said as she turned and walked out of the room.

CHAPTER
48

VICTORIA WOKE TO a beautifully sunny, yet crisply cold Saturday morning. While she had slept, decidedly cooler weather had set in, and it had that permanent winter feel.

Sitting up, Victoria forced her feet out of bed and to the ground. She felt like she'd been beaten over the head with a bat. "Coffee," she called out, as if it would come at her command. Shuffling into her kitchen, she was annoyed she'd neglected to make it before she'd gone to sleep. "Well, shit," she added. "Hmm, I see my vocabulary needs a bit of work," she said while she bumbled through the routine of making coffee. When she had just finished clicking the on button of her cheap, from-law-school coffee maker, her buzzer sounded. "Who the hell can that be?" Victoria checked the time and was surprised to see it was past nine. She never slept past six, and even sleeping until then was rare.

"Victoria, I'm coming in," Sophia's cherry voice rang out as she unlocked the door with her key. "Hi, my love," she greeted, wrapping Victoria in a warm hug. Holding her at arm's length, she looked her daughter up and down. "You look wonderful! Are you just getting up? You never sleep this late. Is something wrong?"

"Mom, you look amazing, too, and no, nothing's wrong. Apparently today is the day I'm feeling the full impact of jet lag. I felt fine until, well, this morning. It also could be the effect of the disgustingly large steak I consumed yesterday."

"I'm sure it's jet lag, and of course you ate like that. I'm sure you were hungry after your long flight back."

"It wasn't the flight. I spent almost every meal trying to steer clear of eating odd creature parts."

"Really? That sounds fascinating. I would love to go there someday."

Victoria crossed her legs on her sofa and sipped her coffee. "How is it that you're the adventurous one and I got all the paranoia?" she asked affectionately.

Sophia smiled. "No idea. You've always been a bit of a pain when it comes to food, and I say that with love. What did Armond have to say about your finickiness?"

"Plenty. I don't need to hear more from my own mother."

"Fair enough. Now, tell me all about it."

"I have a better idea. I need to get off my ass and go for a run and then catch up a bit on work. Why don't you come back for dinner, and I'll treat you to our favorite Italian restaurant. We can chat while we eat some great food, which apparently is my new favorite pastime and all I think about."

"Perfect," Sophia said as she kissed her daughter on the cheek. "I have a ton of things to get done today. We didn't all just fly in from Hong Kong on a private jet," she teased. "I'm so happy to have you home. I'll see you in a few hours. Oh, one more thing, and it's rather serious."

Victoria looked worriedly at her mother. "What is it?"

"You smell funny. And it's not a good funny. Take a shower and for heaven's sake, wash your hair," Sophia ordered, slamming the door behind her just in time to avoid the pillow hurtling into it.

CHAPTER
49

THE WEEK HAD been exhilarating. Jenny finally felt like she was getting her legal legs back. She'd taken two depositions for Mona in one of her divorce cases and she'd nailed them. She'd forgotten how much she loved preparing for trial. She liked everything about it, including the discovery phase, but her favorite part was interacting with witnesses.

Jenny stepped out onto her deck and looked at the intense blues and greens of the ocean. There was no morning gloom today. The large seafaring boats miles away were clearly visible. Inhaling the salt air appreciatively, she called her two dogs, who came running, yapping and jumping around excitedly at her feet. They knew the routine. Jenny reached down, leashed them, and walked down to the beach. It was too early for the general public, so with the exception of a few of her neighbors already in the water, she had the beach to herself.

Finding a spot on the sand, she wrapped the leashes around a small bush and laid out her towels. One for the boys and the other for her. "Be good boys," she commanded but then laughed, as they were already busy digging holes in the sand and terrorizing whatever crab scurried by. She'd only have time for half her morning swim because Victoria had scheduled a call to catch up on the cases Jenny had handled.

Jenny walked to the water's edge and gingerly allowed a few toes to touch the waves. As always, it was freezing. Steeling herself, she walked into the swirling water until she was up to her buttocks, stood for a minute to acclimate, then dove under an incoming wave. The first few seconds were frigid, but as she took her beginning strokes, her body either got used to it or got so cold her nerves simply stopped transmitting the warning of cold water to her brain. *Either way, it works*, she thought happily, while her arms pulled against the incoming waves.

A little more than half an hour after she began, Jenny came out of the water and heard her phone ringing. "Victoria, hi! How are you, and how was your trip?"

"Jenny, it's good to hear your voice. You sound great. Is this a good time?"

"It's perfect. I just finished my swim and I'm sitting on the beach with my dog children enjoying the sun."

Victoria couldn't help but snort. "Well, I just finished a run along the lake. But unlike you, I'm inside with a blanket wrapped around me because we're starting to shift into winter, and the wind was brutally cold. I'll be taking a hot shower as soon as we're finished."

Jenny shrugged her shoulders as someone who had given up on convincing a friend to stop a bad habit. "I keep telling you and Kat that you're more than welcome anytime at my home. It has amazing views of the ocean and, after about a few hundred steps, puts you right at the beach. It's magical."

"Yes, well, the freezing-ass wind coming down from Canada is magical as well," Victoria responded.

"Why don't you come out around Christmas? We can make it a reunion of sorts. A celebration of the time we all met in Houston. Well, you were there in spirit. Armond doesn't live too far away, and he and Robert can join us. What do you think?"

Without even thinking about it, Victoria said, "I can't, Jenny, but it's a great offer."

Jenny refused to let it go that easily. "Why can't you? We can make it into a long weekend so everyone doesn't have to clear their schedules. You have your own firm. You don't have to report to anyone. Why not enjoy that?"

"Because—" Victoria stopped herself. In the past, she never would have considered such a frivolous trip. Work first had been her motto. If she had any time and energy left, she could play. She liked it like that, and it had worked for her. "Here's the thing—" *Maybe there is no thing*, she thought and stopped again mid-sentence. *After all, my way of doing things got me fired from my first job. Perhaps it was time to rejigger a bit.*

"Listen, you really don't have a good reason not to—"

"Screw it," Victoria interrupted, without even realizing Jenny was talking. "I tried all work and no play and look what happened. You know what? I'm in. You work on Mona and Kat, and I'll work on Armond and Robert."

"Really?" Jenny said surprised, never having expected Victoria to agree to come.

"Really."

"Wow. Okay, then. Let's pick two weekends to give everyone an option and then whichever one works will be the one."

"Done. I'm looking forward to it. Now, let's chat about the cases you handled while I was gone. I prefer problems first."

"You'll be happy to hear there really weren't any problems that couldn't be handled. The only thing I've been dreading telling you is one of your clients asked if I can be her main contact lawyer rather than you," Jenny finished, scrunching her face tightly as if to prevent the words from leaving her mouth.

There was silence. "Victoria, I want you to know I am one of the most loyal people you'll ever meet. I would never try to steal one of your clients. I have no idea what happened. One day we were chatting about her case, and she just blurted it out. Say something. Please."

Victoria stood and speed-paced around her tiny apartment. "Hell yes!" she yelled.

Jenny was not sure whether she had heard her correctly, so she tried again. "It was not my intent to have any client leave you and—"

"Stop!" Victoria interrupted. "I heard you the first time, and I know you would never do that. Listen, I've been thinking about changing a few things. I know this is rather sudden, and I don't expect an answer from you right now, but I'd love to have you come on board." Victoria realized she was a bit short of breath and that her heart was pounding. "I couldn't pay you a lot—not yet—nothing like what you'd get from an established firm, but you'll be able to try cases and develop work. What do you think?" Victoria finished in a rush.

"I think—"

"Wait, wait," Victoria insisted. "I said you didn't have to answer now, so I don't want you to answer now. We can talk in a few weeks and then if you're interested, we can chat about the specifics."

"Victoria, I want the job!" Jenny shouted gleefully into the phone, trying to get a word in over Victoria's rambling.

"Geez, do you always go on and on when you offer someone a job?" Jenny laughed.

"Don't know," Victoria answered. "I've never offered another attorney a job before. Apparently, I need to work on my delivery. But, Jenny, I really have no idea how much I can afford to pay you. I need to think about it, so I want you to understand that when I figure it out and if it's not what you want, I'll certainly understand if you change your mind. I won't be offended, we'll still be friends, and I'll still come to your beach house."

"Okay, that's fair. But here are my two conditions. First, I don't want to move to Chicago. Are you okay with that?"

"I'm more than okay with that. In fact, I'm thinking you'll give me a perfect reason to open a California office. Renoir Productions wants me to continue working on the next phase of their investor raise. I have a feeling I'm going to be spending more time out there, as they want me on the ground for critical meetings."

"Congratulations, Victoria! You deserve it. I was going to ask about the trip and how you liked Hong Kong, but it obviously went well."

"Thanks. It did go well. Armond and I worked together for so many years that we easily found our ebb and flow again." Victoria winced as the words came out of her mouth, thinking about their *interactions*, as she'd begun mentally referring to them. "And Hong Kong was eye-opening," Victoria answered, smiling at her wit. "Before we get off track, what's your second condition?"

"I want to focus on gender issue cases as much as possible. How do you feel about that?"

"I feel just fine about that. In fact, I think it may lead to a ton of work. But, until you can build that practice and we can get things under control, I'll need you to commit to work on the matters currently in the firm. Are you okay with that?" Victoria asked.

"Absolutely. I have no issue handling any and all matters you want me to handle. I'm so excited!" Jenny got up off her towel, grabbed her dogs' leashes, and began to walk down the beach. "You know, there's no reason I can't work out of my home until we need an office. I mean, it's not like clients are dying to go to their lawyer's office anymore. That would save you a ton of money, and I won't have to fight traffic to get to an office for no reason."

"Good point. Let me think about it a bit more, and I'll get back to you before the end of this week. Okay?"

"Okay," Jenny answered.

"Now, I need to get off the phone. I have an obscene number of emails waiting for me."

"Enjoy dinner tonight, and thank you for the opportunity."

"You're more than welcome. You deserve every bit of it. Talk soon."

"Well, boys," she said out loud to her two dogs, "I'm back!"

CHAPTER
50

HER MOBILE PHONE vibrated: *Need to speak with you asap.*

Kat read the text and glanced at the diamond-encrusted watch her father had given her for her last birthday. She couldn't help but smile every time she checked the time. While it was truly a thing of beauty, it was also a reminder of how privileged she was to hold a VP title at one of the fastest-growing development companies in the country. She was also keenly aware that people often whispered behind her back, sometimes not so quietly, that but for her being the founder's daughter, she'd never have gotten the job. Because Kat recognized the truth in that sentiment, she was consistently hell-bent on proving, to herself and others, she deserved her position.

She picked up her phone and texted: *Give me a few minutes. On a call w my attys. A lot of blathering.*

"Okay, gentlemen. I've had enough. It's almost noon here. I'm hungry, and I know you're an hour later on the East Coast," Kat interrupted. "Let's break and reconvene in three hours. I want to make it clear that by the end of our call today, I expect a definitive plan outlining the road to trial within the next six months."

As she expected, the eruption from the other end was loud and uncensored. "Kat, that's not feasible," she heard before she hung up.

Kat stood and stepped out of her heels and into her tennis shoes. "Just wait until you hear the next agenda item. You think you're upset now...." Kat said with a slightly evil look on her face. Picking up her phone, she buzzed Emma, then sat back down to jot a few notes. She wanted to ensure she had all the relevant statistics. Kat saw no reason why lawyers, like every other business person, should be exempt from showing some substantive accomplishments to get paid.

"Done so soon?" Emma came in and sat down.

"I couldn't take it anymore. They take hours to say what could be said in in less than one. And Robert asked me to call him, so I had a legitimate reason to end the pain. We're reconvening in three hours, so I need a few things from you before then."

"Shoot."

"First, do me a favor and ensure everyone's on the line before you connect me. I don't want to waste more time than I have to."

"Of course. Next?"

"I need some information about this firm: the total number of hours they've billed over the life of our company's case, the average hours billed per month, and the average lawyer's billable dollars per hour."

"Will do. Have you told them yet?"

"Nope. I thought it would be the perfect end-of-day announcement. If I tell them now, their Ivy-League heads will get twisted and anything substantive they have to say will take a back seat. I want to wring any and all ideas out of them before I say a word. I have another favor to ask."

"Okay."

"Can you stay late tonight in case the call goes longer than expected? I want you to interrupt and get me off the call as soon as they get their balls in an uproar."

Emma nodded. "I wouldn't miss it for the world. Any particular excuse you'd like me to use?"

"Nope. Just come into my office around two hours after the call begins. That way, you'll be in the room when I make the announcement and I can nod at you when I've had enough."

"Done."

Kat's phone began to ring. "It's Robert again. He's never this impatient. I'm going to get it. Thanks, and let me see that billing information as soon as you have it."

"You got it," Emma said, closing the door on her way out.

"Robert, I was just about to call you back. Can you give me a minute? I'm heading outside to walk a bit before my afternoon schedule kicks in, and I don't want to talk in the elevator."

"Sure," he said and hung up.

As soon as Kat stepped out into the always-humid Houston air, she called him back. "I appreciate that you're Chicagoan born and bred, but next time, a little small talk before you hang up would be nice," Kat teased.

"I don't want to raise your expectations," Robert said. "Otherwise, you'll be crushed later."

"You know, I think you might be developing a sense of humor. What's up?"

"Well, we need to connect about Victoria's case. You've been MIA, and I've needed your help."

"I'm sorry and you're right. I'm trying to move our company's case against Highline to trial, and my team of

261

high-priced lawyers seems to spend their time—and my family's money—playing with themselves rather than moving the ball. It's been frustrating, but things are about to change."

"Thanks for the visual. If anyone can ruin a man's private time, my money's on you."

"Oh, very good! Another bit of humor from the Midwest," Kat responded fondly.

"In any event, if you want my input on anything, you know I'm here for you."

"I appreciate that."

"Anytime. After all, I think we're past the friend zone, don't you?" Robert fished, annoyed that he sounded a bit desperate.

Kat had no idea how to respond. While they'd thoroughly enjoyed each other the last time she'd been in Chicago, it had been nothing more than a few embraces. She didn't want that bit of interaction to create a problem between them. "Would you mind if we passed on that topic for the moment? I have a lot on my plate, and I'm assuming you do, too, or you wouldn't have urgently texted and called me."

Robert was disappointed but not surprised she'd punted his overture down the field. He knew Kat fancied herself a man's lady. She'd often talked about how she never intended to get married and wanted to enjoy men the same way men enjoyed women.

"Sure. No problem," Robert replied, tamping down any emotion he felt. "I had lunch with V last Friday and—"

"How is she?" Kat interrupted. "I've been so busy I haven't even had a chance to talk with her."

"She's great. Tired, as you'd expect from the trip, but, other than that, great. Apparently, the trip was a success, and

Renoir Productions has already asked her to stay involved in the next phase of the project."

"I'm glad and not surprised."

"But we have a problem. I presented our idea about the announcement, and had she not been so exhausted, I guarantee she would have had a fit. The best I could do was to get her to promise she would think about it. So, I thought it would be a good idea for you to weigh in with her before she makes up her mind and we can't get her to budge."

"Did you tell her our thoughts on the matter, or did you simply hand it to her?" Kat criticized.

"Listen, Kat. I don't appreciate the backseat driving," Robert growled.

"God, Robert, I'm sorry. I didn't mean to sound like that. I was simply trying to get to the bottom line before I have to reconvene with my lawyers."

Robert sighed. "Understood. Victoria's concerns are she'll become national news and gain a reputation that she's a problem and no one will want to work with her for fear she'll file suit against them if they look at her crossways."

"I assume she understands we don't have the witnesses we need."

"She knows. She reminded me she already had to start her own firm after she was fired. She's concerned that if we take this path, her clients or potential clients will stay far away from her, out of concern that either she's a trouble maker or the focus will be on her in any matter she handles for them."

"She has a point, Robert. I can't blame her. It took guts for her to file suit against the firm in the first place. She essentially put her hard-earned reputation against that of one of the largest firms in the world. And let's not forget what that son of a bitch, Billy, threatened to do to his own mother before our court hearing. I wouldn't put it past them to run a counter article, ripping her to shreds."

"If they did that, we'd be in court filing a defamation suit," Robert responded.

"But the damage would be done. What company is going to hire a lawyer that's in the national news in a negative way? Maybe she's right and we simply have to think of another way."

"I've handled these cases for almost twenty years now, and without a doubt, the biggest asset the abusers have is their accusers' fear their accusations will become public knowledge. Victoria can be one of the rocks that begins to break the dam of fear. If she goes public, then others will."

"I completely agree with you. But again, what happens to the women, like V, who step ahead of the curve? Do they need to give up their careers? That can't be the answer. Let me think about it. I'll call you back." Kat hung up and walked through the park to her favorite bench. Watching the kids run through the fountain and listening to their happy squeals, she let her mind drift. Sitting quietly, she felt the breeze and watched the water shoot up into the sunny sky until the drops morphed into glittering crystals. Then, she smiled, stood, and walked quickly back to her office.

* * *

Emma poked her head into Kat's office. "They're all on the line."

"Thanks. Don't forget to get me off the call a few minutes after I announce their new fee arrangement."

"No worries, I've got my alarm set for two hours from now. If you need me any sooner, just send a text."

"Okay. Oh, one more thing, and it's critically important. I just sent you an email with a list and a few instructions. Work on getting as much of that information as you can to me by the end of the day. Then, call Armond and my father and find out if they, or anyone they know, have connections to the decision-makers at those companies. Tell them I'll fill them in later tonight."

"Will do. Have fun!"

"Actually, I think I will," Kat responded, deciding it was about time she exerted control over the litigation. She was intimately familiar with the concept of return on investment from all her years working in her family's real estate development company, and the ROI on this investment was in the shitter. "Time for a rude awakening, boys," she said before she picked up her line and connected to the call.

CHAPTER
51

I T HAD BEEN two weeks since Victoria had returned from Hong Kong. Blessedly, she'd finally slept through the night and not experienced what had become a routine and unwelcome midnight shot of adrenaline.

I'm finally beginning to feel normal again. Well, at least like myself, if not normal, she thought and laughed at her wit. "Maybe I should have been a comedienne," she said out loud as she doodled on her legal pad and waited.

"Um, let me disabuse you of that thought," Robert said as he rushed into his conference room and shut the door. "There is nothing even remotely funny about you," he finished sarcastically.

"You know, I do have some amusing thoughts. I just don't share them with others." Victoria cocked her head back a bit recognizing she sounded like a recalcitrant child.

"If you say so." Robert smiled and sat down. "Ready?"

"Always."

Robert connected the call. "Hey, Kat, sorry to keep you waiting."

"Hi guys. Listen, I hate to rush this along, but I have an unexpected change in my schedule. I have only about thirty minutes, so no time for chitchat," Kat answered as she put her end of the call on speaker.

"No worries," Victoria responded.

"Okay, the purpose of the call is to discuss ways to obtain evidence to support Victoria's case," Robert began. "Just to recap, they're refusing to turn over personnel files and we've received scant information about the women that left the firm. As you both know, but for a few names, my investigator came up empty-handed and has now apparently gone out of business. So that traditional investigative avenue is closed for now. We've already spoken to the women he found and each of them claims she left voluntarily, all for various reasons, and that she had no bad experiences with the firm. At this point, we're left with Victoria's word against that of the firm and these women."

"Don't forget about Armond," Victoria interjected. "He'll testify to what happened to me."

"He will," Robert agreed. "But he'll only be able to testify to what he knows. Unfortunately, he has no information about what the Troika was doing, or planning to do, about you or other women behind the scenes. So we need to show a pattern and practice of conduct toward women to prove our case."

"Yes, but he can testify to the quality of my work and that I was not the one who created the apparent secret process that resulted in slow paying claims, can't he?" Victoria insisted.

"Of course, and he will. But let's be realistic about his testimony. On the positive side, he'll certainly say you were given a yeoman's assignment of launching a new insurance company. We'll have him describe all the work you did in order to turn what was just a twinkle in the investors' eyes into a full-fledged, profitable company. He'll then go into meticulous detail about your creation of the claim review process. Unfortunately, he'll also have to testify that something went wrong with that process and claims weren't being paid, but stalled. None of us can say how or why that happened yet. Because you were in charge of it and it went to hell in a handbag supports the firm's decision to fire you."

"This is ridiculous!" Victoria fumed. "You mean to tell me that, after a year of litigation, the only evidence we have is a group of women who loved the firm and chose to leave of their own accord and one of my best friends who will testify that I was in charge of the process that ended up screwing thousands of people?"

"Not quite. We have at least one witness who works at the insurance company who will testify that the process you put into place is not the one executed and that the claims department received countervailing directions."

"Who is the witness? Michelle?"

Robert nodded. "She'd been trying to get in touch with Kat and me, and she was smart enough to retain a lawyer to help protect her from any potential retaliation by the insurance company. She's fully on board to testify."

"Well, that's good news. She's rock solid and smart, and we had communications back and forth while she was getting those emails. She tipped Armond and me off. I just wasn't smart enough to see that I was going to be blamed."

"Unfortunately," Robert continued, "we haven't been able to trace the origin of the emails. But Kat is working on getting that information in her lawsuit as well, and she can tell you about her progress in a minute. My overriding concern is that, in order to prove the firm chose you as a scapegoat because you're a female who dared ask for early partnership and an increase in pay, we'll need other women to come forward and testify they were also treated unfairly."

"Well, we don't have that, so now what?" Victoria said, sounding dejected. "I'm beginning to feel like this was all a huge waste of time."

"Kat has a plan for the announcement I showed you a few weeks ago we think has a good shot of working. We'd like you to open your mind and be patient as we explain it. Then, you can comment, if that's okay with you," Robert suggested calmly.

"Oh my God. That again? I thought I put that to bed by ignoring it," Victoria responded, clearly frustrated.

Knowing she had a short fuse when it came to rehashing old ideas—what she would call spinning—Kat jumped in. "We completely understand you don't want this lawsuit and the fact that you were fired from the firm to be in the news any more than it's already been."

"Okay, great. Then we can stop talking about this. I'm trying to build my practice, not destroy my career. You know very well that women who speak out on these issues might be lauded for a moment, but where do they go from there? We all know the answer. That's not what I want. I want a career in the law. Period."

"V, listen. You know you're like a sister to me. Believe me when I tell you I would not suggest what I'm going to say next if I didn't believe it would work and that you'll come out of it with your legal coffers full. Will you give me just five minutes to explain and then promise me you'll think about it?"

Victoria sighed and nodded. "I've come this far. The allegations of my suit are already public, and, of course, I trust both of you completely. I'll listen and then give you my final answer by this evening. But, I want both of you to promise that if I don't agree, we'll reconvene to consider next steps, one of which may be to drop the litigation."

"We promise," Robert responded. "But I'm going to fight you like hell about dropping this suit."

"Robert, will you hand the list of companies to V?"

Thirty minutes later, Victoria left Robert's office with a lot to think about.

CHAPTER

52

GRETCHEN HAD SPENT the past few weeks thinking hard about who might have wanted to hurt her and why. Unfortunately, she'd had a difficult time coming up with names. Instead, she'd decided to develop a list of people she'd spent most of her time with during the year before the event. There were now twenty people on that list, but none of them stood out. Grabbing the list and her purse, she looked at the sitter. "I'll be back in about two hours." Then, she crouched down to kiss her daughter. "You missy, need to be a good girl. If you are, Naomi will text me, and I'll bring you a present."

"Okay, bye momma. Bye-bye," her daughter squealed happily as she gave Gretchen a perfunctory hug and gently pushed her out the door so she could play with Naomi.

Gretchen looked over her daughter's head and smiled at Naomi, who said sheepishly, "I'm sure she'll miss you once you're gone."

Gretchen laughed, appreciating that her daughter didn't cling and scream when she left like some of The Moms' kids.

"You and I both know that's BS, but I love that she loves you. See you later, and thanks."

Once in her car, she put the address into her phone's GPS and noted it would take about thirty minutes to arrive. While apprehensive, she was willing to take this next step to see what, if anything, the hypnotist might help her remember. James had suggested it, and over the past few months, she'd grown to trust he had her best interest at heart.

* * *

The room was dimly lit and sparsely decorated, and there was some sort of softly falling water-like sound in the background. Feeling confused yet rested, Gretchen was surprised to see the woman sitting across from her. "You did well," she said as she stood and handed Gretchen a glass of water. "I'm going to step out for a few minutes so you can regain a bit of yourself before you leave. Would you like a cool towel?"

"No. I'm fine, thank you." It was coming back now. "Did it work?"

"Remember I asked you to note the time in your journal before we began? Check it and then look at the time on the clock." The woman nodded toward the wall. "I think you'll have your answer."

"Did I say anything?"

"You did, of course. However, I suggested during the session that you write down anything that was important to you. As I explained at the beginning, I never look at my patient's notes. Why don't you take a minute to look at your notes? When you feel composed, I'll be right outside."

Gretchen was surprised how refreshed she felt, almost as if she'd taken a nap—one of those good naps, the kind that leaves you feeling energized, not the kind that makes you feel groggy and like you need to sleep another eight hours.

Looking at her journal, she noted that the pen was stuck in the middle of the pages. She opened it and stared. She had circled and heavily underlined, as if she'd gone back and forth with her pen, time and time again, one of the names on her list. Two other names had also been circled. Next to the heavily underlined name, she'd written a number of descriptive words. Shocked that she had apparently remembered something under hypnosis she hadn't on her own, she opened the door and saw the woman sitting at her desk.

"Any questions?"

"Yes, did I tell you anything about what I wrote in the book?"

"You did not. You just began writing."

"I don't recall. Shouldn't I recall why I wrote it and what the meaning is?" Gretchen asked, dismayed.

"Not necessarily. Sometimes, your subconscious gives you only what you can sustain. Other times, you'll remember everything in a few hours or even days. Let your mind rest. Don't overthink it. It will come to you if it's meant to."

* * *

Getting into her car, Gretchen laid her head back against the seat. She wasn't tired, but she was tired. It was the weirdest feeling and one she really didn't want to visit again. Picking up her phone, she texted James: N*eed to meet. Finished session. Got information. Don't know what it means.*

As she got ready to leave, she got a return text. It was a smiley face emoji, his favorite and the only one he ever sent to her, probably because he'd learned she hated it. *Stupid little face*, she thought as she smiled and began her drive home.

CHAPTER

53

"KAT, ARE YOU certain your backup plan will hold?"

"I am, V. I wouldn't have told you about it otherwise. Everyone in my family and some of my parents' closest friends, including Armond's family, pulled strings and called in favors so I could have a one-on-one with each of the people on that list. I explained the situation and what we are trying to do. To a person, they're on board."

"Why would they have an interest in doing something like this? It could drag their companies into a mess that might cut against them."

"None of them believes that. In fact, a number of them already had the wheels in motion to do something along these lines anyway. They just hadn't pulled the trigger yet. This gives them an opportunity to market the fact that they support those who act as whistleblowers. They've all signed on to give your firm legal work once you go public with the announcement. So, instead of losing business, you've gained guarantees of new business from these companies."

"Kat, I can't thank you and everyone else enough for all you've done. I'm forever indebted to you all," Victoria said.

"Oh, for heaven's sake, V, stop. You and your mother are family. After all, Sophia took care of me the three years I spent in Chicago for law school. My parents are more than happy to be able to give just a little bit back."

"You don't think this can backfire?"

"V, anything is possible, so I can't promise it won't. You know that. But you weren't meant to be a bit player in life, and I think you've known that all along. You've always said your goal was to have power. Well, here you are, my friend, about to step into your future."

"Okay, I'm in!" Victoria said, suddenly feeling determined, excited, and anxious all at once. "I'll need you and Robert by my side. When are you flying in?"

"I'll be in next week before it goes live. I'll call Robert and tell him to show you the final mock-up. I've seen it and I wouldn't change a thing, but you need to approve it. You might also want to warn Armond and Sophia."

"God, this feels good! I'm so tired of walking this tightrope, feeling both shame and pride for having brought this lawsuit."

"I need to go. I've got a ton to do before I leave for Chicago. Look for the final draft within the next twenty-four hours. I'll see you next week. If you need me before then, just let me know."

"I will. Now, go call Robert before I change my mind."

CHAPTER

54

"**D**AMN," JAMES SAID in awe of his talent, as he leaned back in his chair and stretched his arms above his head. For the past twenty hours he'd stopped only to eat, pee, and communicate with his virtual tech guru group. Each of them had told him no one had yet figured out a way to back into the software to track the user's origin. "But I did!" he said with a smile, trying to stretch even further. He couldn't wait to brag about it. He would gain incredible notoriety in the tech world, and as news of his breakthrough spread, he expected a significant increase in clients. Maybe he'd even be able to grow the business enough to convince his parents that college was a waste of time and their money.

Smelling something foul, James took a quick sniff around until he leaned in toward one of his raised arms. "Whoa," he gasped as his head snapped back. Standing for the first time in hours, James limp-walked over to the mirror and made a face. "Okay, I look as bad as I smell." Leaving the tiny room in his parents' home that served as his bedroom and office, James headed toward the kitchen. "Coffee, then call, then shower," he mumbled as he poured the last of the now overheated coffee his parents hadn't finished before they'd left for work. "Great. I smell and talk to myself, two of the top qualities people look for when hiring a consultant. I'm sure I'll have no problem attracting clients." Deciding he'd had enough conversations with himself, he picked up his phone.

"Did you find anything?"

"Well, good morning. How are you?" James teased.

"How am I? I'm ready to get my life back and every minute we chitchat about bullshit is a minute I've lost."

"Wow! You can be a tad intimidating. I'm afraid to see what you're like once we've figured this out and you're back to full throttle."

Gretchen placed her phone between her shoulder and ear as she finished washing the morning dishes. "You have no idea. Now, what did you find?"

"Everyone said it couldn't be done but I did it. None of them could figure it out. I've just solidified my name in the annals of tech history," James said, feeling happy and energized.

Gretchen got very still and used her most measured and calm voice. "What do you mean 'everyone said'? Who have you told? We have a nondisclosure agreement."

Realizing he was being too loose with his words and remembering that he was dealing with a serious situation, and essentially her life, James reassured her. "No one knows what I'm working on or about you or anything about your case. What I meant was, I'm part of a virtual group. We discuss all the new technology and this identity cloning technology has made a name for itself as being untraceable. I needed any inroads my peers had made into cracking its code."

"And?" Gretchen said, relieved but annoyed he had yet to tell her anything of substance. "James, for the third and last time before I put the phone down and drive over to your house to beat it out of you, what did you find?"

"The identity marker. About thirty minutes ago."

Gretchen was afraid to find out the identity of the person who had done this to her, but she knew she had to know. *What if it was a relative or someone I'd considered a friend?* She feared. "Who is it?"

"What? Oh, I don't know yet," James answered as he took a sip of the lukewarm, foul-tasting coffee.

Gretchen felt like she was going to explode. James had been her only confidant and her sole source of support regarding her secret. They had worked well together, and for the first time, she wondered if she'd misjudged him. He sounded like an idiot. "What do you mean you don't know? You just told me you found the marker."

"I'm sorry. I'm speaking tech. I said I found the identity marker, which is a step to finding the source, but it's not the source. It's more like a fingerprint. Well, not quite that specific but close. The next step is to find out who it belongs to. But it shouldn't be that difficult."

"So, this is a good thing and a big step?" Gretchen asked.

"Yes, it's a very good thing. Had I not found it, we would have had no way to find who did this. I called to let you know the good news and arrange a time to get your list. It may give me insight regarding anyone who might have been involved."

"I can meet you this afternoon at three."

"Perfect. Meet at my house. Oh, one other thing. Anything you can add to the list about the people on it will be helpful."

"Like what?"

"Like email, home and work addresses, the companies they worked for at the time this happened, what they do for a living—that kind of thing."

"All that is already on the list, but why does that matter?" Gretchen asked.

"It might not, but it may be the critical link." Turning to put his empty cup in the kitchen sink, James got a second whiff of himself. "Listen, I need to go before I knock myself out from my own stench. I'm getting in the shower. See you this afternoon."

Gretchen left the last of the dishes in the sink and walked into what had been her office to again review the list. While she'd never believed in the mumbo jumbo universe shall provide nonsense, she couldn't deny she felt as if something had shifted. She was close to getting her life back, and she intended to do everything in her power to make that happen.

CHAPTER

55

A S SOON AS she landed, Kat jumped in a cab and headed to Robert's office. She'd agreed to be there by six to listen to the publicist's suggested responses to questions the press likely would ask Victoria if everything went as planned and it went viral.

Kat and Robert had decided Victoria would stay with Kat and Sophia at a hotel for the next two days in case the press or someone who might not like what she had to say became aggressive. Kat had already reserved a suite in her company's name and ordered a late-night spread of food, guessing they'd be exhausted, hungry, and unable to go out to dinner once it was over.

As the cab pulled up to Robert's building, Kat texted Victoria. *I'm here. On my way up now.*

She received a one-word response. *Terrified.*

Kat frowned, knowing Victoria's confidence was critical to this working. She needed to come off as the leader she was, the woman Kat had always known her to be: strong, smart, determined, unflinching. But from the moment Victoria had been escorted out of her old firm, something almost imperceptible had changed. It was as if some genetic string to her strength had been chewed on, leaving a weakened chord. Kat sighed. While she completely understood Victoria's fear, as there was nothing and everything to lose, Kat's job at the moment was to build her up to a healthy, ball-busting state of mind. Then, she could confidently shoot the video to be linked to the online announcement and respond to the press.

When the elevator opened, the receptionist immediately signaled to Kat. "We're glad you're here," she said as she began to walk her down the hallway. "They're in the large conference room. Robert asked that I bring you back right away. Is there anything you need?"

"I'm good. Thank you," Kat answered as she plastered a smile on her face and opened the door. There were lights and cameras set up around the room and crisscrossing electrical cords snaked across the floor. A giant screen had been set up to display whatever was picked up by the camera. Everyone in the room was quiet and standing still as the publicist and Victoria worked through a mock interview. Robert saw Kat and held up his hand to signal her to wait while he quietly walked over so as not to disturb Victoria.

"I'm glad you're here," he whispered, giving her a warm hug.

"Me too. How's she doing?"

"Under the circumstances, really quite well. She's nervous, though, and it shows. I think now that you're here, we may be able to knock that last bit of uncertainty out of her. Your timing's perfect. We're just about done with the first run-through. Come sit over here and see what you think," Robert said, walking her behind the cameras while Victoria finished the final practice question.

After the camera lights were off, Kat waited until Victoria finished with the publicist and then walked over. Wrapping her in one of her signature hugs, she said, "Well, it looks like you're about to become national news. How do you feel?"

"Nauseous. Like a deer in the headlights. Like a turtle on its back. Scared shitless." Victoria answered. "I'm hoping this will go forward without much fanfare and we'll get what we need without it becoming newsworthy."

"That might very well happen," Kat said, cautious not to say anything that would add to her friend's already-nervous state. "But if it does get national attention, you're ready. Either way it's all good. Let's knock the crap out of that last bit of nerves, shall we? What's the worst that could happen?"

"Well, people will judge me. They'll think I deserved to be fired and that this is just sour grapes. I'll be known throughout the country as that girl who was fired from one of the largest international firms for accusing the founders of wrongdoing when they are known for diversity and helping women. I'll lose all my clients and never be hired again, destroying my dream of being a lawyer. Do you want more?"

"Is there more?" Kat asked with a smile.

Victoria smiled back. "No, not really. I think that about covers it."

"Okay. Let's look at those things. First, instead of losing clients the moment this goes public, you're gaining some heavy hitters. Second, you don't need to be hired by anyone again because you opened your own firm, which is doing very well. And in less than a year, you'll be opening a second office in California—"

Victoria put her hand on Kat's arm to stop her. "Wait. How do you know about that?"

"Jenny told me. Is that a problem?"

"Of course not. I'm happy she told you. I would have told you, only it just happened, and we've both been so busy we haven't had time to connect. I just wanted to be certain it wasn't public knowledge."

"Well, it will be."

"What do you mean?"

"Have you spoken with Armond? Does he know about your new office plan?" Kat asked.

"Of course. I called him as soon as I finished speaking with Jenny."

"And?" Kat pushed.

"And he was ecstatic. Obviously, one of the reasons I even considered opening a West Coast office is because Renoir Productions committed to use my legal services on all its investment and transaction matters."

"Then, this is the perfect opportunity to turn questions about you and your former firm into small-town girl takes on global firm and wins-type publicity. Announce your new West Coast office tonight, and tell the world that your firm works for the movie industry. There are few shinier baubles that attract the attention and adoration of the masses than Hollywood. My bet is that by the time you're through talking, the world will wonder why those idiots got rid of you and you'll get a shit-ton of new business."

Victoria felt her stress begin to ease, and rather than feeling conflicted over what was about to happen, she felt, for the first time, like it was the absolute right path. "How much time do I have before it hits the Internet?"

"A little less than an hour," Kat answered. "Why?"

"I need to get on the phone with Armond to see if Renoir Productions is okay with me making that announcement." Victoria looked around the room to find Robert in what now looked like a sea of people. "Robert!" she called excitedly. Looking over, he motioned that he would be right there. "He's rather sweet in a nerdy kind of way, don't you think?" Kat said.

"I'm sorry?" Victoria responded, not sure she'd heard her best friend correctly. But before she could pepper her with questions, Robert was by their side.

"Kat, would you explain what we've discussed? I'm going to call Armond and see if they're on board. If they are, my publicist and his will need to speak and draft talking points in enough time that I can practice them."

"Whatever you said to her seems to have done the trick. She seems absolutely ecstatic."

"Here's our thought," Kat answered as she explained their plan.

"I love it! Small town girl takes on big firm and wins! Everyone likes a David versus Goliath story." Robert smiled as he looked over at Victoria and saw her nod her head. "All right, it's a go. Kat, stay by Victoria and keep her in this good frame of mind. I'll connect the two publicists, and we'll have a statement to her in less than ten minutes."

"I've got this. Go do your thing."

* * *

At precisely 8:00 p.m., the top national news sources carried Victoria's announcement as part of their online content, along with a link to her video. Each of the papers ran with different titles, everything from "Lawyer Hunts for Witnesses" to "International Firm at Center of Gender Storm." Irrespective of the title, Robert and the publicist made sure her statement read the same:

After many years as a lawyer at Acker, Smith & McGowen, I was fired because I asked to become the first female partner and for a pay increase. To hide the real reasons, the firm blamed me for something I did not do. They threatened to ruin my career if I did not sign a confidentiality agreement, forbidding me from discussing the facts. They endangered my career, livelihood, and self-esteem.

I'm grateful to those who stood with me and helped me put one foot in front of the other in the first hours, days, and months. I now have my own firm and I'm thriving.

About a year ago, I filed a lawsuit against the firm to change this culture. Today, I'm taking this unusual step to ask other women who left the firm to contact my lawyers because I believe what happened to me happened to others. I believe we can help each other. I know it's time.

Thank you, Victoria Rodessa

The room erupted in applause as those who had worked on the case and announcement finished reading and watching her video.

"Okay, everyone, okay," Robert moved his arms in a downward motion as a signal to calm down. "Hopefully, our work is just beginning. Let's monitor social media and the phones. Let's see if we get any interest."

The room was silent as everyone waited. After five minutes, Kat looked at Robert out of the corner of her eye, signaling her concern that perhaps it wouldn't get picked up the way they had hoped. But just as she was about to say something to Victoria to keep her spirits up, she heard one of Robert's assistants shout to the room, "Our website just got a slew of registrations. Almost all of the comments indicate they have information."

Less than a minute later, another announced, "I've got two stations on the phone asking for an interview. They'd like to book her for their remaining late-night shows tonight. Are we good?" He turned and looked over at Victoria.

Kat touched Victoria's shoulder. "Well?" she asked. "Let's kick some ass!" Victoria responded.

"That we'll do!" the publicist added, getting caught up in the excitement. "Okay, Victoria, just as we discussed, my team will hook you up to the equipment. You'll be able to do the interviews from here. We'll use the backdrop with your law firm's name and logo. Makeup will play with you a bit to make sure you're ready for television," she said, her team moving in to work on Victoria's face and hair.

"Victoria, you have a phone call." Kat walked over and handed her phone to her friend. "It's Armond."

"What did you think?" Victoria asked excitedly as the glam squad relentlessly fussed with her face like it was a field in need of tending.

"I think you're fabulous and it's an amazing move. My parents told me to tell you, and I quote, 'The Renoirs are very proud of you and stand with you 100 percent,'" Armond relayed.

"Give them my deep thanks. But do not use the *c* word or it will be bad juju. Let's wait until after my television appearances and see how it's received," Victoria cautioned.

"The *c* word? I've never used that word in my life. Are you daft?" Armond responded, offended.

"No, no, no. Not that *c* word. Why in the world would you say that?" Victoria asked, exasperated.

"Well, my pet. I have absolutely no idea. But, may I remind you you're the one who suggested I was going to say it?"

"I meant the word people say for good job, well done… you know. It begins with a *c* but isn't the *c* word."

Armond began to hear a bit of hysteria in Victoria's voice so he knew to respond calmly. "Okay, I get it. I won't say it until you give me the all clear. Can I speak with Kat again?"

"No, you can't. And don't use that Victoria is starting to lose it tone of voice with me. I'm not a child. I've got this."

"Okay, well, good because—" Armond pulled the phone away from his ear, looked at the blank screen, and started to laugh. The little pain in the ass had hung up on him.

CHAPTER

56

HE SIGHED AS she caught a glimpse of her face in the mirror. She was aging. *Not getting old yet*, she thought, *but definitely aging.* There were a few more crow's feet around her eyes, and a couple of those horrid lines that run up from old peoples' lips. She made a mental note to call her plastic surgeon in the morning. An aging madame was not a good look.

Sitting at her ornate desk, she unlocked the top drawer and pulled out one of her most prized possessions. The well-used journal was leather-bound with small remnants of gold that formed the outline of an unidentified family crest, quite possibly from one of China's long-perished royal families—at least that was the theory of the shopkeeper from whom she'd purchased it on one of her first trips to China. She recalled with a satisfied smile that, before the owner had sold it to her, he insisted it remain in its glass case to protect its value as a Chinese antiquity. Not one to follow directions, the first thing she'd done after completing the transaction was borrow the shopkeeper's hammer and smash the glass.

Ignoring his overly dramatic shrieks, she'd carefully plucked the journal from the glass shards and left. Once outside, she'd reverently opened the journal and had been pleased to see her gut was correct. The pages were blank, waiting for her.

Madame turned on her desk light, flipped through the journal, and found the letter she'd jammed between its pages in a rare show of temper. She'd long ago learned that bad decisions were made in moments of anger or passion. It had been almost a month since she'd read the letter—enough time, she thought, for her to re-read it without feeling rejection and isolation. She unfolded the letter, read the first few paragraphs, and slammed it onto her desk disgusted. She was still emotionally attached to the outcome.

Sitting in stillness to gain clarity, she knew it was time to move forward with the next phase of her life. She had always been attuned to the universe and its signs. Her changing appearance, coupled with her reaction to the letter, told her to proceed on the path she'd been considering for the past few months even though she recognized she might not be allowed entry into proper society. She shook her head to banish her negative thoughts. They never helped.

She scanned the letter and drafted an email to her lawyer. There was no good reason she'd been rejected. Her portfolio was solid. There were fewer than fifty people in the world with more assets. She wanted in on that deal, and she was not about to let one letter stand in her way. Just as she finished sending the email, she received a news alert. Reading the headline, she rolled her eyes in disgust but forced herself to follow the link. *After all*, she thought, *if I'm going to reenter society, I'll need to get up to speed on current issues.*

After reading the story and watching the video a second time, she sat stunned at the power of the universe, letting all that had happened over the past hour sink in. She then picked up her pen, made a few quick notes in her journal, and knew exactly what she needed to do next.

CHAPTER
57

"DID YOU MAKE the deal, boys?" Big Bill asked.

"We did, exactly as we discussed," Jeremy answered as he shut his office door.

"So, I'm in the clear?"

Jeremy picked up the phone and called his partner. They had a pact that neither would speak to Big Bill alone about anything—ever. They didn't trust him. Shuffling papers on his desk, Jeremy said, "Let's wait for Scott. I want him to be able to add details I might miss so you have the full picture."

"Fine. While we're waiting, ask that fine piece of ass of a receptionist you have out there to bring me a glass of whisky neat. What's her name?" Big Bill demanded as he walked around Jeremy's office picking up different knickknacks, looking them over, and then setting them down.

Jeremy knew it was futile to correct his client about how he referred to the receptionist, so he didn't bother. "You can't have anything to drink. Your deposition in the civil case is this afternoon, and it would be totally inappropriate for you to give sworn testimony under the influence."

"Who's gonna tell 'em? I'm not," Big Bill belted out a laugh.

Before Jeremy could respond, there was a light rap on his door and Scott entered the room. "Bill, good to see you again," he said as they shook hands.

"I'm sure it is. Every time you boys talk to me it costs me a fortune," Big Bill said, making himself at home in one of the oversized chairs.

"Okay, here's where we are," Jeremy began. "The feds want all the information and evidence you have about your insurance company's slow pay of the claims. In exchange, they'll grant you immunity. It's a sweet deal, Bill."

"Come on, boys. I didn't do anything in the first place. They would never have made anything stick and they know it," Big Bill insisted.

Jeremy and Scott resisted looking at each other, knowing their facial expressions would convey their disdain at the utter ridiculousness of their client's unrestrained cockiness. Jeremy continued advising Big Bill as if he hadn't said a word. "The lawyers taking the deposition will want the same information the feds understand you will provide, so it's important that what you put on the record today is the same as what you tell the feds. I'd like to do one more run-through of your testimony to ensure you have it down pat. There is no room for error," Jeremy finished.

Big Bill lit one of his cigars. "Whatever you want to do as long as when I walk out of that deposition this afternoon that chapter of my life is closed and I can move on."

CHAPTER
58

"TO VICTORIA!" ROBERT nodded at his friend. "Congratulations! You're the darling of the media and a new role model for women across the country. I'm proud to have you as a client, but I'm prouder to call you my friend. And to all of you," he gestured, his arm sweeping across the room as he turned his attention to the assembled group of technicians, publicists, and marketing gurus, all of whom had worked on the announcement. "We couldn't have done it without you. Thank you for your expertise, time, and attention to detail, all of which made this a huge success!" Polite clapping built to hooting and hollering, as Robert opened the first bottle of champagne. "Victoria, would you like to say a few words?" Robert asked as he walked around the room filling glasses.

Victoria stood and smiled. She was bone-tired from the media blitz that had gone on for the past twenty-four hours, and she would much rather be at home, lying on her sofa. But she knew the effort their team had put into making their strategy a success and she would not have missed this celebration for the world. "I would. Thank you, Robert. First, I can't thank you and Kat enough for your combined efforts to bring me to the table on your crazy idea in the first place. And to all of the people in this room who worked tirelessly to get me ready for prime time,"—there was a smattering of laughter—"and to those who coordinated all the moving parts so it went off without a hitch, I'm forever in your debt. This is a breakthrough moment and you were all instrumental in making it happen. I'm so proud and thankful I had the honor of working with each and every one of you! Cheers!" Victoria, Robert and Kat raised their glasses in salute to the assembled group. "But, perhaps even more important is that when all this is all said and done, Robert promised to treat us all to a fabulous celebratory dinner." She laughed as she raised her glass in Robert's direction as the room went wild.

Robert played along and winced. "Yes, thank you, Victoria. I think that's enough from you!" he said to laughter. "But in all seriousness, folks, I understand the response has been overwhelming. It would not have happened without the talent in this room. Thank you, again. Now please, enjoy the food and champagne. Let's celebrate!"

* * *

Two hours later, Robert, Kat, and Victoria sat alone, alongside empty bottles and half-eaten plates of food, reviewing the lists of contacts and comments they'd received. "These responses are amazing. Now what?" Kat asked.

"My in-house team will handle initial contacts to determine which of these are legitimate. Once they've finished, they'll give the vetted list to me. From there, Jenny and I...

By the way, I thought this would be a perfect project for Jenny, if both of you are okay with that. She'd mentioned to me that she's used to dealing with potential witnesses and knows what to look for and how to whittle a list down."

"That's right up her alley. There's no one I'd trust more. Our California office won't be up and running for a while, so she has a bit of time. But not much," Victoria said, pleased at the sound of a West Coast office.

"Great. Then Jenny or I will contact those that appear to have critical information, and my associates will follow up with the others."

"I'm happy to help," Kat said.

"I was hoping you would say that." Robert smiled at Kat.

Victoria thought she saw an odd look pass between them but decided it was neither the time nor place to dig deeper. She was overtired, and she could have imagined it. "What do you want me to do?"

"Nothing. I think you're going to be hounded by the press for a few more days. And unless you feel otherwise, I'd like you to go silent for a bit as we sort through what we have," Robert answered.

"That works for me. I want to get back to my normal life."

"Oh, V," Kat began, "I don't think things will ever be the way they were before your little media event, but I think that's a good thing. I assume you've noticed that on the first page of the list are two people who don't have any information about your lawsuit. They just want to hire you. They said in their comments that they want to show their support by giving you work."

"I saw that. If they're legit, then that's great. But what do I do if I get contacted by the press?"

"Just send them to me," Kat said. "I'll be working with the publicist to tamp down further interviews unless, of course, you decide you want to do them."

"No, I'm done," Victoria stated adamantly.

"One more thing," Robert began. "Yesterday, I got a call from a New York lawyer. Apparently, one of his clients has information he believes will substantially impact our case. They want an in-person meeting and they're adamant it has to happen by Monday. His only other condition is that Victoria must be present. I've checked him out and he's legit. He refuses to tell me anything further until I tell him if we're interested."

"What do you think?" Kat asked.

"I don't see what we have to lose, although I'm not sure it's necessary for Victoria to be present," Robert answered.

"Why wouldn't I be present?"

"I don't really have an answer for that, except I don't like the idea of having you at a meeting when the identity of one of the participants is unknown."

"It's a risk we'll have to take. If he and his client want me at the meeting, I'll be there. Set it and let's see what they have to say," Victoria responded.

"Kat, if you can swing it with your other work, I'd like you at the meeting as well," Robert suggested.

"There's no way I'd let that take place without me," Kat replied.

"Great," Robert said, glancing at his watch. "It's late. Why don't we finish the last of our planning over dinner?"

"Guys, I'm beat." Victoria stood and shoved the papers she'd been reviewing into her bag. "I'm heading home. Kat, are you ready? We can grab dinner and take it back to my place, just like old times."

"If you don't mind, V, I'm kind of wired. I feel like going out for dinner. Is that okay with you?" Kat asked.

Victoria smiled, relieved she could lie on the couch and not talk to anyone.

CHAPTER
59

J ACK KNEW HE was heading into a difficult meeting. Ever since the story aired, the firm had been inundated with calls from clients around the world and reporters had been parked outside the firm's headquarters as well as the homes of Billy, Trever, and Adam. After a perfunctory knock, Jack entered Billy's office. Before he'd even taken two steps inside, Adam attacked. "Well, what the hell are you doing to control the situation, Jack, and how the hell did you let this case get so out of control?"

"Calm down, Adam. Blaming one another isn't going to get us anywhere. Sit down, Jack," Billy ordered calmly. "The situation is beyond serious. Our largest clients are threatening to pull their work if we don't get this straightened out by Monday. They can't afford to be associated with a firm that's been nationally accused of discriminating against women."

Trever leaned forward. "The senator called. His instructions were clear. We need to pull out all the stops and fix this immediately. Some of his largest donors are some of the biggest corporations and they are threatening to pull their financial support."

Jack nodded and kept quiet. One of the most valuable lessons he'd learned from his years litigating, was to stay quiet and let the client vent. He continued to nod and act as if he was empathetic to their turmoil, and he waited. Billy, Trever, and Adam eventually finished and asked for his counsel.

"I'm ready to move with our kill shot once you approve. While I know it doesn't feel like it at the moment, Victoria's conduct has actually given us the upper hand. Let me explain. I recommend we file this immediately and release it to the press." Jack stood and passed out copies of a document. "As you can see, it's a counterclaim against Victoria. I'll summarize to save time, but once you have a chance to review the detailed allegations, you'll see that we are going to hit her particularly hard. We're alleging defamation and interference in the firm's contractual relationships with our clients. We are seeking both compensatory and punitive damages. I also recommend we file an ethics complaint with the State Bar Association and seek to have her license to practice pulled. Then, we'll launch a full court media response, hitting her right where it will hurt most: her reputation. Billy, I'll need you to attest to her sexually aggressive behavior while she worked for you."

"I like all but the last bit," Billy said. "She never came on to me."

"No one gives a damn," Adam responded. "You were with her all the time. It's he said, she said. Who's going to believe her over you? We need to take her down a peg, and I like the story line that Jack's created. She's trying to ruin our reputation and all we did was fire her. A million people get fired every day and go about their business. We get the one pain in the ass who feels it's worth her while to fight us. This is getting out of hand. It's time we put it to bed, and the only one in a position to attest to her conduct is you."

"For once I agree with Adam," Trever drawled. "It gives us the perfect answer to why she was let go and why she is trying to turn this around on the firm—she's the aggressor, the one that has the issue. She never received the attention she wanted from her boss and hell hath no fury like a woman scorned. It's a plotline everyone can relate to."

"Sorry, boys. There's no way I'm putting my neck on the line with a flat out lie. What I am willing to do is make a statement that provides just enough innuendo so everyone one who reads it will understand exactly what I'm saying," Billy responded, warming to the idea. "I'll need to work with you, Jack, on an air tight statement. Something the press can't poke holes in no matter how hard they dig."

"Of course. We'll get that ready over the next few hours. Gentlemen, if I have your approval, I would like to get the counterclaim on file with the court Monday morning and then provide it, the press release, and our ethics complaint to Victoria's team by messenger. I'd like to ensure we're in full offensive mode by Monday morning."

"Go," Trever said. "Keep us advised at all times."

CHAPTER
60

E VERYTHING HAD FALLEN into place. He had left the States for Thailand right after the meeting with Jack. He had been looking forward to this little private party and weekend getaway for the past month, and he saw no reason to change his plans over a blip in that little bitch's litigation. His businesses were booming, providing him with more money than he'd ever imagined possible, and perhaps more importantly, he was respected by his numerous business partners around the world. Adam picked up his pace as he thought about the celebration he had planned for tonight. It was his reward to himself for a job well done.

As he turned the last corner, he stopped mid-stride. The scene was surreal. At least half the street was cordoned off and all traffic had been diverted. Police and medical personnel swarmed the area. Adam couldn't see what was happening from his angle, so he crossed the street to join the growing crowd. "What happened?" Adam asked the man next to him.

"Don't know. You just missed it though. A few minutes ago the police rammed open the door to that house."

Adam followed the man's pointed finger and stared in disbelief. Just then, the doors opened wide and someone in the crowd gasped, "Oh my God!" One after the other, scantily clad young women, some of whom appeared to be extremely young, were carried out on stretchers or in the arms of police officers and rushed into waiting ambulances.

"What the hell?" Adam wondered out loud. He watched another few minutes, then turned and walked quickly away.

CHAPTER
61

"**H**OLY SHIT! I'M at a loss for words, which, I might add, has never happened before," Kat confessed as soon as the meeting ended and the last of their quests left the room.

"I need to call Armond. I can't have his family's name getting dragged into this," Victoria said as she stood to step out of the room and make the call.

"There are a few other calls we need to make as well to ensure everyone is protected," Robert added as he walked over and leaned out of his office. "Sandy, can you come in? I need a few things before you leave for the evening."

Walking into Robert's office, Sandy announced, "I've been with you long enough to know that something significant is happening. I've already told my husband I may be late, so I'm good to stay if you need me."

Robert nodded. "We need you and we will be late."

"Before you tell me what you need, I think you should see this," Sandy said as she handed Robert and Kat each a stack of documents. "It was just delivered. I made a copy for each of you. I've read through it and I think you'll want to go through it right away."

Sandy sat and waited as Robert and Kat tried to speedread through the papers. "There is so much here. Have you gone through it?" Kat asked.

"I'm happy to summarize," Sandy said.

"Please," Robert responded.

"They've counterclaimed against Victoria, seeking punitive damages alleging she interfered with their clients; they filed an ethics complaint with the State Bar, requesting suspension of her law license; and they intend to issue a press release claiming—get this—that she was the sexual predator and made repeated advances toward Billy."

"Oh my God. She's going to lose her mind," Kat said, standing as she looked toward the doorway to see if Victoria had overheard. "I've got to tell her before she hears this from anyone else."

As Kat began to walk out of the room, Robert stopped her. "Kat, I have an idea. Tell her we have a plan, not to worry, and to come back in so we can discuss it." Kat nodded and left the room.

"Sandy, here's a list of contacts. I need the senior-most person you can find in this subject matter area, and I need someone who will take a call on this immediately," Robert said as he handed her his handwritten notes.

Sandy read over his notes and snapped her head up. "Robert, is everything okay? Are we in some sort of danger?"

"Everything is fine. Trust me. If you have any problems getting through to the right people, interrupt me and I'll get involved. Your part of this is critical."

"Got it. I'll be back as soon as I have the information."

"Oh, and Sandy, once you're through with that, will you order dinner for the four of us? It's going to be a late night."

CHAPTER

62

I T WAS CLOSE to midnight as Jack walked into Billy's office. As a litigator, he was used to these hours. Over the course of his career, he'd probably pulled more than a hundred all-nighters to prepare for trial. Time was of the essence in responding to Victoria's last maneuver against the firm, and since the three founders had their asses on the line, he thought they would understand the need for a midnight meeting.

Jack gave a cursory knock and walked into Billy's office. He headed straight to the bar and poured himself a scotch neat. "Billy, Trever, any interest?" Jack asked as he raised his glass.

"I'm in," Trever answered. "There's little in this world that can't be cured with a glass of scotch."

"None for me." Billy walked over to sit on his couch just as Adam rushed through the door.

"Okay, I'm here," Adam said as he shut the door behind him and shook the snow off his coat. "It's freezing out there. Couldn't this have waited a few days? I just returned from Asia and I'm beat."

"Well, sure, but by then we might have lost over half our clients and most of our revenue. How would that have worked for you?" Billy answered acidly.

"My clients don't give a rat's ass about this bullshit. They're not going anywhere," Adam answered.

"Let me remind you," Trever interjected, as he could see Adam was riding Billy's last nerve and the last thing they needed was more conflict, "that we all share in the firm equally. If the firm is found liable for any wrongdoing, each of our profits takes a nosedive, and that includes you, Adam. May I suggest you sit down and let's hear what Jack has to say?"

"Well, gentlemen," Jack jumped in before the tension could get worse, "as much as I hate to break this up, I have good news! I just finished a long call with Victoria's lawyer. They would like to discuss settlement."

"Settlement?" Adam exploded. "We're not paying that bitch. At this point, she should pay us."

Ignoring Adam, Jack continued. "Actually, he said they'd like to resolve the case in a way that is fair and amicable. He thinks he's convinced his client to resolve the matter without any payment from us."

"What's the catch? Why the sudden change?" Billy asked.

"He told me, off the record, that his client never really had the stomach for the fight, her mother pushed her to take us on from the beginning, and she doesn't want to take a chance she'll lose her law license."

"Well, maybe we don't want to settle, now," Adam snapped.

"Will you shut up?" Billy yelled at Adam. Turning back to Jack, he asked, "If they don't want cash, what do they want?"

"He wouldn't give me specifics, as he was still in discussions with his client, but he intimated perhaps some sort of a mutually beneficial joint statement and a program that benefits women and minority lawyers. They want a meeting tomorrow at eleven at his office to discuss it."

"Okay, have the meeting," Trever said.

"In order to wrap this up as fast as possible, he insisted that all parties be present: the three of you and Victoria. I agree. Otherwise, we'll spend days shuttling offers back and forth. Based on what you indicated our clients threatened, coupled with the media frenzy, we don't have that kind of time to waste," Jack finished.

Billy looked at his partners, each of whom nodded their assent. "Okay, we'll be there. Eleven tomorrow morning. Jack, I want this done and over and Victoria off our backs by the time we walk out of that room. No exceptions."

"No worries. It will all be over by the end of the day tomorrow."

CHAPTER

63

VICTORIA WOKE AT four in the morning, after only three hours of sleep since they hadn't finished their meeting until one. Even though they were as ready as they could be, she was nervous. Resolving this lawsuit had been a long time coming. She had hoped to achieve justice for herself and a change for the better for others. She needed to move on with her life. It was time to let it go. While they were hopeful they had a shot at reaching a positive resolution today, it was a crapshoot. Settlement negotiations were sticky wickets. One fly in the ointment; one emotional, illogical, or angry person; or even one lawyer off his or her game could bring negotiations to an abrupt end.

Throwing on her cold-weather workout clothes, she shuffled out to the kitchen to grab coffee and a few bites of something to eat. Waiting for the coffee to brew, she hovered over the fruit bowl, trying to convince herself to have a banana instead of her usual choice. "Screw it." She pulled a blueberry scone out of her pastry-treat drawer and began to break it into bite-size pieces.

"Are you still pretending you're trying to break your morning scone addiction?" Kat slurred from sleep deprivation as she crawled onto one of the island stools. "Let me make a prediction. It will never happen. There, all done. You no longer have to suffer through these morning mind-fucks you put yourself through. You can thank me by handing me a cup of the blackest coffee in this apartment."

"Here's what I think about your prediction," Victoria shot back as she raised her middle finger.

"Apparently, neither having your own law firm nor international travel experience has improved your level of sophistication. In fact, it seems you may have sunk even further into the gutter," Kat responded haughtily. Receiving no response, she shrugged. "Hey, V, since you're right by the cooktop, how about making your like-a-sister best friend some eggs? My preference is scrambled, but I'm open to chef's choice."

"Um, sure. I'll get started on that right away. Why don't you wait right there and let me know if you like what you get?" Victoria said as she sat on the ground to tie her running shoes.

"Don't tell me you're going for a run. It is pitch dark and utterly freezing."

"No. Of course not. I'm busy on those eggs you're waiting for," Victoria responded as she stood and pulled her winter windbreaker over her head. "Now, you just sit tight and think about what's coming to you," Victoria smirked.

"Hey," Kat said as Victoria turned the doorknob to head outside. "I know you're anxious about today, V. I am too. But we've all done our best and that's got to be good enough."

"Kat, I appreciate, more than I can say, all the work you, Robert, and the rest of the team have put into my case. You've all done more than I can ever repay you for and I have no complaints. But the outcome of this case rests on my shoulders, and as far as I'm concerned, good enough is never enough. Now, I've got to run to shake this out of my system. While I'm gone, enjoy your eggs, and for God's sake, get your ass in the shower so you're ready on time. I'm leaving at seven with or without you."

"God complex," Kat mumbled as Victoria slipped outside and firmly shut the door behind her.

CHAPTER
64

"ROBERT, YOU CALLED the meeting so why don't you begin," Jack said as soon as everyone had settled into their chairs, each side on opposite ends of the table.

Kat glanced at Victoria and was incredibly proud of how calm she looked. There wasn't a nervous vibe emanating from her body. If the stiletto was on the other foot, Kat thought, she wasn't sure she would have been able to pull it off with the same level of cool Victoria displayed. It was, after all, the first time Victoria had been in the same room with Jack since he threatened her and had her almost forcibly thrown out of Acker, Smith & McGowen's headquarters. And she'd only seen Billy, Adam, and Trever that one time they were in court on their motions to admit Kat and Jenny as lawyers, and that hadn't been without its own drama.

"Okay, gentlemen. We received your counterclaim, your ethics complaint to the bar, and the press release you intend to disseminate today. As far as my client and I are concerned, none of this is going in the right direction," Robert began.

"Yes, well, we intend to kick your ass and nail hers to the wall," Adam spat as he glared at Victoria.

"Jack, I'd like to have this meeting move forward without these kinds of threats. Is that possible?" Robert responded, ignoring Adam and speaking directly to Jack.

"There's a lot at stake and quite a bit of damage has been done to our firm by your client's baseless allegations. It's understandable that there will be a bit of venting, but let's get right to it, shall we? Based on our conversation last night, we expect a significant offer from your client to resolve the matter today. Part of that offer will need to include a complete statement about her conduct and it will, of course, also need to exonerate our firm."

"Victoria." Robert nodded. "Would you like to tell them your offer?"

"Thank you, Robert." Victoria paused and looked around the table, mentally reviewing what she was about to say and hoping they had all their ducks in a row. She glanced at Kat, who nodded slightly. "Gentlemen," she began as she took in a breath, knowing that once she began there was no going back, "prepare to be screwed. First, and no later than by the close of business today, I will become the new managing partner of Acker, Smith & McGowen. Second, you will execute all necessary documents to transfer all of your shares in the firm to me for the sum of one dollar. Third, you will express regret for your conduct and vow to make up for it with the work you do for the remainder of your practicing careers. If you do these three things, I will not proceed against you personally for monetary damages and we will not ask that you be disbarred. We will, instead, suggest you be allowed to perform certain charitable legal work that we choose for you, and if you perform well, we will author appropriate letters attesting to your good deeds to the various courts in charge of your criminal cases."

"What the hell is this, Robert?" Trever drawled as he leaned forward and pointed at Victoria. "You're screwing with the wrong people you sanctimonious little twit. I'll have the Senate launch an investigation into you and your pitiful excuse for a firm faster than you can say, 'I fucked up.'" Turning to look at Robert, he continued, "This little bitch is insane. Robert, if you allow this to continue, we'll report your ass to the bar and add you to our counterclaim." Adam jumped up, grabbed his coat, and got ready to leave. "I'm a busy man. The rest of you can sit here and play house with this little slut, but I have no intention of wasting any more of my time."

Billy did not say a word. He felt a rush of heat course through his body. Something was wrong. He'd worked with Victoria for years and knew her better than his partners. She did not bluff, and she was stone-cold calm and resolute. He knew they had to get out of there and regroup. "Robert, I'll give you one minute to explain why you dragged us over here to hear this bullshit. These demands are ridiculous and insulting and really should give you a window into why we fired her," he said, lifting his chin in Victoria's direction.

"Happy to, Billy." Turning to Kat, he said, "Can you bring in our first guest?"

"Absolutely," she said with a giddyap in her voice as she almost pranced out of the room. "Gentlemen, meet Ms. Caroline Carson. Ms. Carson has recently relocated to the US from abroad." Adam's inhale was loud enough to draw attention. "I believe Ms. Carson and Mr. Smith may be acquainted. Isn't that right, Ms. Carson? Perhaps you can explain."

The room grew eerily still, like the air before a prolific storm. One of the things Caroline had always known how to do was command a room. She waited until just the right amount of tension was in the air, and then began. "I'd be happy to help. Hello, Adam," she said, nodding in his direction. "It's nice to see you again."

Adam sat back down with his mouth open, visibly stunned. "When Ms. Rodessa's announcement appeared on the internet, I was still residing in Bangkok," Ms. Carson began, nodding at Victoria. "I don't typically pay much attention to disputes between parties, particularly those in the US; however, two things happened. One, I was considering returning to America to live so I felt it necessary to become reacquainted with the social and political goings-on here; and two, I recognized the woman in the video. While not pertinent to this conversation, I had met Ms. Rodessa during a business meeting, the outcome of which I hope to have reconsidered after we dispense with the business at hand," she said, looking pointedly at Victoria. "But I digress. I looked a bit further into whom she was suing, and much to my surprise, I recognized one of the founding partners of the law firm. To close the circle for those in the room, Adam was a frequent patron at my establishment. Oh, I've neglected to mention that until its recent sale, I ran one of the best escort services in Bangkok." Pausing to look at Adam, Caroline smiled and said, "I do thank you for your patronage."

Billy stood. "I've had enough. This meeting is over. Whatever my partner's predilections are is irrelevant to the matter with Victoria."

"Oh, I'd sit down if I were you, Billy," Victoria said calmly. "Trust me when I tell you, you won't like what's on the other side of that door."

Billy slowly sat back down. Victoria had always meant what she'd said. That was one of the things he'd liked about her. *God, what have we gotten ourselves into?* he thought.

"Go on, Ms. Carson," Robert prodded.

"My girls came from many different sources, most of which were never known to me. In any event, I looked at the website Victoria referred to in her announcement that listed the names and photos of women who could not be located and who used to work at the firm. And much to my surprise, one of my recent additions had worked at the firm."

"I don't believe it," Billy protested.

Robert again nodded at Kat, and within a minute, she was escorting into the room two women who were clearly underweight. Their bones protruded from their shoulders, large bags outlined their eyes, and their faces resembled skeleton heads rather than young, vibrant women. They each searched the faces in the room and at almost the same time, their eyes bored into one man.

"Hello, Adam," Willow said. "Remember me?"

"This is a colossal waste of time," Trever protested. "This woman never worked at the firm. I have no idea who she is," he finished, looking at Billy who nodded in agreement.

"Well, I certainly did," Serena said as she stepped in front of Willow and stared at Adam. "I knew I recognized the accent, but I was so drugged I couldn't connect it." Her eyes grew wider as she remembered more. "You let that man slam my head against the wall, and then you kicked me like I was a piece of meat. You piece of shit. I flew all over the world for you on your deals and made you millions, and that's how you repay me? You know how tenacious I am, so if there's anything you take away from this little reunion today, let it be this: I will devote the rest of my life to ensuring the pain I felt that day and the days of hell that followed will pale in comparison to the pain you're going to feel for the rest of your life in prison."

Robert signaled for Caroline to continue. "You see, gentlemen," she said, looking at Billy and Trever, "it seems that your partner here," she said nodding at Adam, "ran a lucrative side business of exporting, importing, and auctioning women to the highest bidders—something that allowed him access to some of the wealthiest men around the world."

Robert interrupted when Kat walked into the room with their next guests. "While there's significantly more to this story, we're up against a deadline, so we'll need to move on. Gretchen, why don't you and James tell your story?"

Before she could begin, Trever jumped out of his seat, took three strides to reach Adam, plucked him out of his chair, and began pummeling his face. Billy dragged Trever off and held Adam by his bloodied collar. "Adam, what the hell did you do?"

"Fuck you both," Adam gasped, as he tried to stem the gush of blood coming from his nose. "Both of you left them to me to handle. Where did you think they went? Thin air? Neither of you gave a shit how I handled it then. Don't act holier-than-thou now."

Robert interjected. "Gentlemen, I'm afraid there's more. Please sit. Gretchen, you have the floor."

Gretchen began to tell her tale of working her way up the firm's ladder only to receive a threatening and degrading video of her acting out explicit, disgusting sexual acts. The note that came with the video forced her into exile or face humiliation and ruin. Turning to look at Trever, she said, "I can't believe you did that to me. I was one of your staunchest supporters. I worked like an animal to make your department profitable."

"I have no idea what you're talking about," Trever said as he glared at Adam. "I did nothing of the kind, and if you acted on some sexual predilections that you chose to practice, don't blame me."

Gretchen took steps toward Trever, but James stopped her. "Listen, you sanctimonious piece of shit, she did nothing of the kind. You created a video that made it look like she did those things. The electronic origination leads right to you."

"Who the hell are you?" Billy asked.

"I'm the one who cracked the code and has all the evidence the authorities will need to go after you and your firm," James answered.

"Trever?" Billy asked.

Trever shook his head back and forth, denying his involvement, while he stared at Adam with murder in his eyes. "As fascinating as it is watching you gentlemen learn new morsels about one another, we have a lot of ground to cover. Kat," he said, gesturing in her direction. "You're on."

"Thank you, Robert. It appears, gentlemen," she began, as she walked around the table and handed a document to Billy, Adam, and Trever, "that one of you was the brains behind Highline Insurance Company's refusal to pay millions of dollars in hurricane claims to its policyholders. According to the testimony of one of the board members"—Kat flipped through the document she'd just passed out—"specifically your father, Billy, Trever here was the brains behind the scheme to defraud thousands of hurricane victims. Isn't that right Trever?"

"Why, you little bitch," Trever spat. "My grandfather will shove an investigation of you and your family so far up your asses that none of you will ever be able to walk normally again."

"Oh my," Kat answered calmly. "I'm afraid that's not very chivalrous of you and rather threatening. I see you need some help remembering your manners." She walked across the room and opened the door. "Gentlemen, they're all yours."

In walked federal agents, all flashing their badges. They grabbed Trever and Adam, cuffed them, read them their rights, and led them out of the room. "I knew nothing about any of this," Jack whined, looking stunned. "I was not involved."

Victoria looked at Jack. "Sit down and shut up, Jack. We're well aware that you're too insipid to know what's been going on." The room became quiet as all eyes turned to Billy. "Well, Billy, you're the last of the Troika. The sole remaining member. But as it turns out that's a good thing," Victoria said, glancing over her shoulder at her team, "because as the managing member, you have the authority to bind the firm. And that's just what you're going to do." Victoria slid a one-page document and a pen across the table. "By all means, take your time and read it. I want you to fully understand what you're about to do, which is agree to sign over to me all of your shares in the firm and any outstanding shares on behalf of your partners. Oh, and you'll be issuing a press release about the transfer of ownership by the end of the day, which we've taken the liberty to prepare on your behalf."

"You must be insane. I'll never sign over my shares. I worked my ass off to get the firm where it is and I have no intention of being held responsible for the conduct of my two idiot partners."

"I had a feeling you might resist." Turning to smile at her best friend, she said, "Kat, would you mind ushering in our final guests?"

"Happy to," Kat exclaimed as she almost skipped out of the room.

"Mother, what are you doing here?" Billy almost wailed.

"I'm here to help you do the right thing. From all we've seen so far, you were not involved in the sale of women or the genesis of the insurance fraud. But you were, according to Dr. Natarajan,"—she looked over at the woman who followed her into the room and whom she'd been interviewing for the past day—"involved in the firm's practice to prevent women from becoming partners. And apparently, much to my profound disappointment, you also took sexual advantage of young women at the firm."

Looking at the doctor, Billy asked, shocked, "What's in this for you? You're hurting your own financial interest."

"To the contrary," she answered. "I was only a foot soldier. Remember, Billy? I was never good enough to have shares in the firm. As I recall, I repeatedly tried to get you to change your ways and bring women into partnership roles and to stop your harassment. You refused and,"—she shrugged—"here we are."

Victoria interjected. "Here's the deal, Billy. You have one minute to execute the document transferring your firm to me and to agree to admit to your firm's discrimination or you can join your friends in the arms of the FBI for sexually abusing women across many state lines. Your choice."

"I can't believe you would turn on your own son." Billy ignored Victoria and looked at his mother.

"To the contrary, Billy. I haven't turned on you. I intend to work with you and help rehabilitate you. If I'd have turned on you, you would never see me again."

"Forty seconds, Billy," Victoria ticked off.

Billy looked around the room. If there was one thing he'd learned from his father, it was how to survive. Picking up the pen, he signed the document.

CHAPTER
65

VICTORIA LOOKED OUT over the water and had to squint to shield her eyes from the shimmering sunlight that reflected off the waves. Over the past few days, she'd learned there was a particular glare to the sun's reflection that signaled the beginning of the incredibly beautiful performance of the sun setting on the West Coast. She was surprised at how quickly she'd come to love this ocean. Now that a good amount of her time would be spent in California overseeing Renoir Productions' work and also as a jumping off point to visit many of the international offices she'd inherited, she'd decided to fully embrace the lifestyle. Over the past week, Jenny had led her in daily runs on the beach followed by freezing-ass ocean swims. *It had been pure heaven*, Victoria thought as she scribbled some final notes to discuss with her broker.

"Have you made a decision?" Jenny asked as she came out of her house carrying a bottle of champagne, followed by Armond and Mona with the glasses.

"I have. I'm putting an offer in on that home on the cliffs. It'll be the best of all worlds. I'll be your neighbor, so I'll get to enjoy all of this fabulousness and still be close enough to get to our office and my favorite client whenever he needs me," she said, smiling at Armond and brushing his hair to the side of his forehead.

"Hey guys, perfect timing," Victoria greeted Kat and Robert as they came up the stairs from the beach.

"My God! It's beautiful here. I'm Texan born and bred but it's hard to deny the pull of the ocean and the beauty of these cliffs," Kat said happily.

"What do you think, Robert?" Victoria asked.

"I love it here, but I'm a sweet home Chicago man," he said, putting his arm around Kat.

"We'll see about that," Kat responded with a ridiculous smile.

Armond raised his glass. "I'm glad Jenny convinced you all come to California for the holidays. I propose we make this a yearly tradition."

As everyone clinked glasses in agreement and settled in to enjoy the sunset, Armond asked, "Can we wrap up a few loose ends?"

"Of course," Victoria answered.

"Willow. How does she fit in? As I understand it, she never worked at the firm."

"Jenny, why don't you take this one?" Victoria nodded. "Happy to. It's fascinating, really. A number of years ago, Willow was a plaintiff in a sexual harassment lawsuit against a large corporation. As that suit was heating up, she suddenly disappeared, leaving behind a husband and young son. When Ms. Carson was backing into her connections to find out how Serena got to her, she found a common factor in a number of her other girls. That factor was Adam."

"I'm still not connecting how Adam knew Willow," Armond continued.

"It appears Adam developed an intricate and extensive network, as well as a solid reputation as someone who could discreetly resolve pesky issues for the right amount of money. He didn't confine his work to females at the firm. Willow was one of his first forays into expanding his reach. He was also adept at providing carefully crafted cover stories, if needed, so family and friends would eventually give up their search. Bizarrely, I had heard about Willow's story from some of my former colleagues, but until Ms. Carson connected the dots to Adam, I hadn't known her name."

"Then, what was Gretchen's connection?" Armond asked.

"Apparently, Adam used a variety of means to silence problem women," Robert began. "He realized he couldn't simply ship them all by the boatload out of the country. In Gretchen's situation, because her husband is a former marine and still well-connected to those with high-level clearance in the military, he decided to blackmail her instead. She only recently discovered the connection to the firm, about the same time Victoria made her announcement."

"Fascinating," Armond said.

"Indeed. We're still tying up loose ends, but I think we've gotten to the core of it at this point," Robert responded. "Okay," Victoria interrupted, "let's move out of the past and into the positive. I want to wrap up a few loose ends of my own. Jenny, can you give us a status on the victims' fund we set up? How is it doing, and have we located the other women?"

"We've raised $1.5 million in the first two weeks and money continues to pour in. As you requested, I'm in the process of finalizing the not-for-profit status, and I've sent you a list of my suggestions for board members to oversee the organization and its funds."

"That's an amazing amount of money. Jenny, I'd like you to be the chair of the board and CEO of the company once its charitable status is approved. Are you willing?"

Jenny's face lit up and her eyes got a bit teary. "Yes, of course. We can do a lot of good with that amount of money and the drive we'll have from the people I've suggested for the board. Thank you, Victoria. I am so honored."

"You're more than welcome. As far as I'm concerned, there's no one better to run that foundation than you. Now, as to the women?"

"Serena, Gretchen, and Willow are doing remarkably well. Serena and Gretchen have decided to return to the firm, and each accepted your offer to run the departments where they had worked. Willow has asked me to convey that she is more than excited to run PR at the firm, and if we're comfortable with her starting in two months, then she's on board. She continues to detox and is doing remarkably well after all the drugs she was given. And, of course, after being away from her family for so long, she wants more time with her son and husband before she jumps back into the fray."

"Please tell her I'm more than fine with two months and that we're looking forward to meeting her family once she's ready," Victoria said.

"As far as the other women caught in Adam's web," Jenny continued, "we've found all but two. Our investigators are working with my friends at the FBI and the DOJ and I'm told they have solid leads and are hopeful. By the way, Ms. Carson has been a huge help with identifying people who might have some solid information about their disappearance."

Victoria looked at Armond. "Speaking of Ms. Carson, what does Renoir Productions plan to do? She still wants to invest, and without her, it's doubtful we would have reached the resolution we did or that the women would have been found. Granted, she has her own culpability in the situation, although she insists her escort work was allowed by the Thai government. You know my very strong opinion on the subject, but it's Renoir's decision."

"My father and I are adamant that we don't want funds that have any connection, either directly or indirectly, with her businesses or conduct. We have no intention of allowing her to invest in any part of our business. However, her personal story is extraordinary, so we've asked one of our top screenwriters to meet with her to determine if it's the right fit for a documentary. We've already decided that if it's a go, all profits will go to your fund."

Victoria reached over and squeezed his hand. "I'm so pleased to hear that. But, I would ask one condition."

"What's that?"

"There is to be no mention of my name or even a reference to me in any film that might be produced about Caroline. Agreed?"

"We'll see, my pet. You know we never agree to anything until our lawyer has looked at the contract," Armond said, smiling at Victoria.

Robert interjected, "Jenny, how is Billy doing?"

"Well, I have to admit, and I know I'm biased, but I really think he's coming along quite nicely. He's been doing pro bono work for abused women and children. I think he's getting the picture. He's also agreed to fully cooperate with the authorities in exchange for immunity, although he insists he had no knowledge of what his partners were doing. He's a work in progress but so far, so good."

"Well, now that we've tied up the loose ends, I have a little something I'd like your help with. Are you in?" Victoria smiled and raised her glass. She watched in amusement as her friends groaned and looked at one another with the understanding that it was too late to change their respective life's course. Then, they raised their glasses, acknowledging that for better or worse, they stood as a united force.